# Baby Baller

# A

# Novel

# By

# Caleb Alexander

It was the niggaz versus the White boys, or at least, that was the reality of it. That was how we saw it, and pretty much how everyone else in the stadium saw it. Hell, it was just about how everyone else across the country saw it. But the media, they had to be politically correct with the situation. They billed the match as the Clash of the Titans. At least the halfway decent media outlets did. Most of the commentators called our match up David versus Goliath, and trust me, we weren't the giants. We were the poor niggaz from the poorest part of Houston, Texas. We were the ghetto's babies, as one newspaper called it. We were ghetto babies.

It was said that we weren't supposed to be here, and the commentators and everyone else loved to keep reminding of us of that. We were supposed to have lost to the rich White boys in Katy. Then we were supposed to have lost to some more White boys in The Woodlands, another rich ass neighborhood on the northern outskirts of Houston. After that, we had to play some more really rich White boys from Austin Westlake. And now, we were playing against the last great White hope. A bunch of super rich White boys from Southlake, Texas. The job had fallen to them, to crush the upstart niggaz, from one of the poorest high schools in Texas. They were supposed to put us in our place. To show the world that discipline, and teamwork, and great coaching, could always overcome natural speed and athleticism. All of us came from single income, single parent homes. They lived in mansions. Most of us had to work after football practice, or right after school. They went to expensive gyms and fitness centers and got in extra reps. They had the best equipment, trainers, facilities, and supplements that money could buy. We were happy if we had a helmet that fit right. The differences were stark, and they were real. They were sponsored by Under Armour, Academy Sports, Eastbay, and Wilson Athletics, while we were sponsored by Big Willie's Towing, and Williams Funeral Home on 8th and Westheimer.

We were Booker T. Washington High School, one of the oldest high schools in the state. It was a high school that was create to serve colored children from the rural areas of Southeast Houston. It was the school that served my neighborhood, Acres Homes. And if you know anything about Houston, or about the projects period, then you knew that mine were some of the roughest in the nation. The nickname for Acres Homes was Shady Acres. If it sounded like a cemetery, it's because it pretty much was. We were the walking dead, the poorest of the poor, the people who were just bidding their time until we died in a hail of bullets from a drive by, or were scooped up in a drug raid that would put us away for the better part of our lives. That was who we were. And I used the term 'were', because something had changed in my neighborhood. At least for now, that is. You see, Booker T. Washington High School had rallied the community.

Our football team had brought unity and pride back to our neighborhood. And for the first time in thirty years, niggaz in the hood weren't killing each other at the clubs on Friday nights. Instead, they were now in a crowded football stadium, cheering on the best thing to ever come out of the neighborhood. Our team had given our community something that it hadn't had in a long time. We had given them *something* to cheer about. We had given them hope.

The White boyz who were supposed to whip our ass, were down forty eight to zero at the half. We had put a point up, for every time one of them had called us a nigga on the field. We had put up points for every time we saw a sportscaster on the news predict how bad we were going to lose. We had put up a point for every cop who ever harassed one of us, for every homeboy Shady Acres had lost to a fucked up jury, believing a trumped up charge,

and some bullshit ass testimony. We did it for them calling us
Katrina refugees, we took our frustrations out on the football field,
and we made them pay for every closed door, every hungry night,
and every God damned crooked ass peckerwood we ever met. We
were putting our dick up in 'em, and we were showboating the
entire time we were doing it.

"Wheeeeew!" Augustine shouted. "Wheeeeeew!"

It was our war yell! Augustine had just scored another
touchdown, making the score fifty six to zero. He ran off the field,
and leaped into the air. I leaped also, and we shoulder bumped. It
was the way we always celebrated whenever one of us scored. We
would leap into the air, knock one another around, high five, and let
out our battle screech. It was a ritual we had been performing for
the last twelve years. Yes, *twelve years*. I had known Augustine
since we were five. We met on a football field back in New Orleans
some twelve years before, and we hadn't left one another's side
since. He was my boy, my ace, my best friend. And since I was an
only child, and he had lost his only sibling during the flooding after
the levy broke, we were the only brother that either of us had left.

Augustine Fortier had lived in the lower Ninth Ward just
down the street from me. His family was from Haiti, and since my
father was Haitian as well, our families bonded, and Augustine and
I became best friends. We did everything together. From riding our

bikes, to playing football, to hooping at the neighborhood park, to swimming, to playing marbles, to playing cowboys and Indians together. We grew up, shared clothing, smashed some of the same females, and even shared the same dream. We both wanted to get out of the hood, and we both loved football. We were both really good at football. And so we decided to use our love of football, to get our families out of the hood. Our dream, was to both go to Texas Christian University and play football, and then go pro together. They were typical hood dreams, but for us, we were close to making those dreams a reality. We were the number one and number two running backs in the nation. And we were both only juniors in high school.

That Augustine and I ended up in the same hood in Houston after the hurricane was more than just fate or coincidence. He was spending the night at my house in the NOLA, the night before the Hurricane hit. My mother was a nurse. She told my father that she was going to stay behind and help out at the hospital. She told him to take me and Augustine to Houston to check on her mother, and to make sure that Big Momma made it through the storm okay. My Daddy didn't want to leave, but my Momma reassured him that she would be okay inside of the massive concrete and steel hospital she worked at. And so, we headed to H-Town, making it out only hours before the storm hit.

Augustine's parents made it through the storm, but they lost their house and Augustine's baby brother to a collapsed tree. We found them a week later at the Superdome, and my Daddy brought them back to Houston with us. They stayed with me and Big Momma for a few months, until they were able to get a place on their own, just down the street from us. My Daddy, well, after he dropped us off, he went back to New Orleans to search for my mother. The night before he left, was the last time I was able to really talk to him. We got the news of my mother's death from a Red Cross worker two weeks later. I went back to New Orleans with Augustine and his parents to search for my father, but it was too late. There was nothing left. Nothing left of my home, but a concrete slab, and nothing left of my father, but an empty shell. The last time I saw him close up, he was sitting on the slab where our house used to be, staring at a picture of my mother, and crying like a baby. We tried to bring him back, we tried to get him help, but nothing worked. Mentally, he had checked out of life.

My life went on. Big Momma, and Augustine, were the only family that I had left. She was somewhere in the crowded stadium cheering her heart out, and Augustine was standing next to me. My mother, I carried her in my heart, and in the her wedding ring that I wore on a necklace around my neck. It was one of the few things that the Red Cross had been able to return to us. Big

Momma gave it to me, and I put it on a chain so that a piece of her would always be close to my heart. It made me feel close to her, and it brought me luck. It made it feel like she was watching over me.

"Baptiste!" Coach Beckwith shouted. "Our ball, get in there!"

I peered at the field, and sure enough, we had stopped them again. I stared at the scoreboard, and the score was now Fifty five to zero. It was the State Championship game, and Coach Beckwith apparently wanted to run up the score. He knew what this game meant to the community, and he knew what we had gone through all season. All of the naysayers, the doubt, the ribbing that we always took from other teams. Despite the fact that he was White, he was pissed at the other team's racial slurs toward us. And so, he was allowing us to get even, and to take out our frustrations on the scoreboard.

"Yo, let me get in!" Augustine said smiling, and pushing me back.

"Naw, fool!" I objected. "Coach told me to go."

"Look!" Augustine said, motioning toward the scoreboard. "You already have four touchdowns! I only have three! Let me get one more before coach puts in the second team!"

Augustine was my boy, and I knew he would do it for me. I

nodded giving him permission to take my place.

"Get in there!" Coach shouted.

Augustine smiled, pulled on his helmet, and ran out onto the field. Again I peered up at the scoreboard. Augustine ran a 4.24 in his forty. They had nothing on their team that could catch him. I knew that we were about to score again. The score was about to be sixty four to zero, which was ridiculous for a state championship game.

On the field, the ref blew the whistle and backed up. I watched as our quarterback called the snap count, and then our center snapped the ball. I recognized the play instantly, it was Black Smoke, a play we ran regularly. The quarterback dropped back, faked a pass, and then handed the ball to Augustine who cut to his right. He shook the other team's corner back so bad, that he made him fall.

"Go, Augustine!" I yelled. Our entire sideline cheered, as did our side of the stadium.

Augustine shook the middle line backer who had been playing us deep. He spun, causing him to fall down as well. Single handedly, Augustine was making their entire team look bad. He made another cut, but this time, he ran into virtual brick wall. The other team's safety came downhill on Augustine full steam, and at full strength. His shoulder pads struck Augustine at the top of his helmet. The hit was so hard, the entire stadium cringed at the loud crack that the pad to helmet contact made. Augustine was stopped instantly. He crumpled to the ground like a rag doll.

"Augustine!" I shouted. I knew it was bad. He laid on the ground motionless. "Augustine!"

I ran out onto the football field, and quickly made my way toward him. I was the first one to reach Augustine. I dropped down to my knees beside him.

"Augustine, are you okay?" I asked.

We were quickly surrounded by coaches, trainers, and other staff.

Augustine smiled at me.

"Don't take off his helmet!" the head trainer shouted. He too dropped down to his knees beside my friend. He lifted Augustine's hands. "Squeeze my fingers."

Augustine did nothing. His eyes focused on me. "I can't feel my legs. I can't feel anything."

"Oh shit!" Coach Beckwith said quietly. He stood nearby, frantically chewing his tobacco.

"Get a cart!" Coach Gaines shouted. "And get a stretcher! And a neck brace!"

"No!" the head trainer shouted. "Call EMS! We need an ambulance!"

Augustine swallowed hard. Second by second, his breathing was slowly becoming more labored.

"I can't feel anything!" Augustine cried out. A tear fell from the corner of his eye.

When I saw my friend crying, I knew that things were really bad. In twelve years, I had *never* seen Augustine cry. Not when he fell off his bicycle, not when his Mother whipped him, not even when he heard the news about his baby sister. *Never.* And watching him lay motionless on that field, I felt helpless.

Augustine shifted his eyes toward me again. "Take my hand."

I lifted his other hand, and clasped it.

"Promise me," Augustine started off. "Promise me that you'll keep playing."

"We gonna both keep playing, fool!" I said smiling, trying to lighten the situation.

"Promise me," Augustine said, crying heavily again. "That you'll keep going."

"*We* gonna keep going!" I said, growing angry. "Don't be talking no stupid shit!"

"Promise me you're gonna go to TCU for both of us!"

"Man, Augustine," I said, shaking my head.

"Promise me!" he said more forcefully. He started

coughing.

"Okay, okay, I promise."

"Promise me that you're going to make it," he said crying even more.

"I promise you."

"You do it for the both of us," he said. "You live for the both of us. You bring home the dream for both of us."

I could hear the sirens from the ambulance growing closer.

"Okay, man, just stop!" I told him. He was starting to scare me. His chest was now heaving up and down visibly. He was having trouble breathing.

"TCU," he said weakly.

"TCU, baby!" I said, smiling nervously. "You gonna be there! We gonna be wrecking shop together!"

He didn't respond.

"Keep talking to him," the trainer told me.

"Augustine," I said, calling his name. The flashing red lights from the ambulance, which was being led onto the field, were clearly visible. "Hey, we gonna be chilling at Big Momma's house for Christmas. She says she's gone make her famous turkey dressing, with some giblet gravy. Boy, you know it's gone be on!"

Augustine smiled at me. He closed his eyes, and he died.

Baby Baller                                Caleb Alexander

# **Chapter Two**

### **Eight Months Later**

I laid in bed, not wanting to get up and not wanting to go to school. It would be the first time in my life that Augustine and I wouldn't be starting a school year together. It would be the first time in my life that he wouldn't be banging on my window, or sitting at the breakfast table eating my cereal, waiting for me to get up and get dressed. It was a new world to me. And I wasn't sure if it was a world that I still wanted to be a part of.

I finished up the school year after Augustine's death. But I didn't participate in spring ball, or summer work outs, or even summer practice. I hadn't been on a football field since that night in December, when my best friend took his last breath, with his hand in mine. Things weren't the same. *Nothing*, was the same.

Everyone tried to convince me that it wasn't my fault. That Augustine wanted to go out onto the field. Big Momma told me that God had a plan for each of us, and no one, and nothing, could stop that plan. She said this, after I fell into her arms in tears, telling her how the coach had told me to go in, and I had let Augustine go in instead. I had replayed that conversation, and that night in my head, over and over again, everyday for the last eight months. What if I would have gone in, I continuously asked myself? Would I have cut left, instead of right? Would then Augustine and I both still be alive? What if Augustine had cut left? What if he had gotten tackled by that line backer that he shook? What if that line backer had grabbed him, and made him hesitate for just a split second? What if? What if? *What if?* I had gone through at least a thousand *what ifs* since that night. But I still kept coming back to the ultimate *what if.* What if I would have just done what the coach said, and took my ass in the game? Nothing could change the fact that Augustine went in, when I was supposed to have gone in. Nothing could change the fact that I let him go in. And nothing could change the fact that he was now dead, *because* he went in. Those were the facts. Those were the demons that I had been living with for the last eight months. I not only wanted to stay in bed, I wanted to bury my head beneath the covers, and live inside of my dark, damp room. I wanted to be able to do like my father did, and just lived within my own mind, my own world, and that way, I wouldn't have to face the world of reminders that laid outside the four walls of my house. I could see Augustine everywhere. Every street, every corner, every curb had a memory. And I was desperate to forget.

"St. Clair," Big Momma said calling out to me, as she pushed open the door to my bedroom. "Baby, you up?"

I didn't answer. I thought about closing my eyes and pretending to be asleep, but it wouldn't do any good. She would only continue to call me, and if that didn't work, she would shake me until I woke.

"It's time for school, baby," she said. Big Momma turned on my bedroom light. "You up?"

"Yes, ma'am," I said.

"I got some breakfast in here on the table," she said. "You better… hurry."

Big Momma's last words stumbled out. She must have realized what she was about to say, because she quickly closed my door after she finished her sentence. She was about to tell me to hurry up, because she knew that Augustine was going to be over soon. But he wouldn't be coming over to eat up all the breakfast. Not now. Not ever again. I could feel the tears welling up in my eyes.

I laid in bed thinking about my next steps. Big Momma would be coming back into my room in a few minutes to see if I had actually climbed out of bed. And if I hadn't she would come back again and again until I did. School was in my future, that much was sure. Big Momma wasn't playing that. But just because I had to go back to school, and just because I had to walk those halls again, that didn't mean that I had to play football. I *definitely* wasn't ready for that. I couldn't bear the thought of walking into that locker room without Augustine. I couldn't bear the thought of him not suiting up next to me, talking shit about how many touchdowns he was going to score, about how he was going to do the other team's linebackers, and then about how he was going to do the other team's cheerleaders after the game. Augustine walking through the locker room butt ass naked with nothing but a football helmet on, was damn near a tradition. I could almost hear Coach yelling at him to put some fucking clothes on. He was the team clown. He was the team's fire. He was my get-up-and-go partner. He got me hyped and motivated to make things happen. He was always the one to not only say that something could be done when others doubted it could, but he was always the one to actually go out and do it. I was now lying in bed, facing a life without having that spark in it anymore.

"St. Claire," my grandmother called out to me again. "You

don't want to be late on your first day, baby."

"I'm up, Big Momma," I said, acting like I was half yawning. The truth was, I knew that this day was coming, and I had slept little the night before. Summer had been my hiding place. I used the summer vacation to hide from the world. And now that my hiding time was over, I dreaded facing the world once again.

I climbed out of bed, rolled down the hall to the bathroom and brushed my teeth. I could smell the sweet tangy smell of maple sausages wafting through the air. And being that this was the first day of school, I knew that Big Momma had hooked things up. I made a quick job of my teeth, splashed some water on my face, and then hit the toilet where I took a long piss. I had been needing to pee since four o'clock that morning, but climbing out of bed was something that I had desperately wanted to avoid.

I finished up in the bathroom, and headed down the hall to the kitchen. Big Momma was sitting at the table reading her Bible. Some things, never changed. Big Momma and her Bible. She loved that book. She carried it with her everywhere she went, and even slept with it on her nightstand. She had to have known each and every single word in it by heart.

My Big Momma lived in the church. She had played the piano for the same church for the last forty five years. She had sang in the church choir for the last sixty, let her tell it. She started when she was a little girl, and had been singing for The Lord ever since. Big Momma's stories about faith, and about walking to church even during snowstorms and hurricanes were legendary. She always had a story to tell about something. And it was always the right story, to fit the occasion. That's what made her stories a little suspect. She couldn't have gone through all the things she said she went through in her lifetime. If she had, she needed to be on a postage stamp.

What wasn't suspect about my Big Momma though, was her faith, and the way she practiced it. Big Momma wasn't one of those go to church on Sundays and go to choir rehearsal on Thursday night type of Christians. She stayed in church, and she was always doing stuff for the church, or with the church. She was down at the jailhouse ministering to the prisoners, she was always under the bridge feeding the homeless, or over at the soup kitchen, or the homeless shelter, or the battered womens' center, or the women and childrens' shelter, or volunteering at Goodwill. She *lived* her faith. And she tried hard to give me a little piece of it. Especially after Augustine's death. But I wasn't trying to hear it, and I wasn't trying to have none of it. I questioned God like no other.

Why would God take Augustine away, I asked? He hadn't killed anyone. He wasn't a murderer, or anything like that. There were plenty of people in this world who were a lot worse, so why take away my friend's life? Why not one of them niggas on Death

Row?  Why not one of them muthafucka's out there beating up on their wives and abusing their kids and shit?  Why not one of them?  Why not an old muthafucka, somebody who's already lived a long life?  Somebody in their eighties, or nineties, or somebody who got to live to be a hundred?  Why my partner?  Was it something that I did, I wondered?  Was this a personal beef, between me and God, I asked?  He took my mother, and then he took my best friend.  So, I know it was personal on my part.  Once I lost Augustine, the church lost me.  And my Big Momma had been caught in the middle.

"I put your plate in the oven, baby!" Big Momma said, peering up from her Bible.

I walked to the stove and pulled my plate from the warm oven.  Big Momma had hooked me up with some maple sausages, some grits, some cheese eggs, and some toasts.  My plate was on swole, and smelling like a million bucks.  I hurried to the table and sat it down.  Big Momma had a pitcher of orange juice sitting on the table.  I poured myself a glass.

"You excited about school?" Big Momma started.  It was a conversation I didn't want to have.  "It's your senior year.  I'm so excited for you, baby.  You got senior prom coming up this year, and then graduation."

I nodded, and focused on my breakfast.  I really didn't want to talk about the upcoming year.  I didn't want to talk about a graduation that I dreaded. Sure, my girl would be walking the stage with me, but my ace boon wouldn't be. His mother wouldn't get to send out pictures of him in a cap and gown, or hang his diploma on her wall. All she had now were memories, where two children should be. Life was some bullshit, and it was definitely unfair.

"You gonna win another state championship this year?" Big Momma asked with a smile.

I closed my eyes. She was my Big Momma. I loved the ground this woman walked on. But I wanted to shout *no*. I had never even thought about raising my voice at my Big Momma, and even now, it wouldn't have been at her, but just at the thought of playing football, of winning, or doing it without my nig. That was impossible. Unthinkable. Our dream was a two man dream. That dream died with him on the football field that day.

"St. Claire, do you hear me talking to you?" Big Momma asked forcefully.

"Yes, ma'am," I said softly, stuffing my face with toast.

"Then act like it!" she said. "I'm sitting here asking you about school, and you acting like you never ate before."

"Yes, ma'am."

"I was asking you if you thought y'all were gonna win another championship," Big Momma said smiling again. She leaned in. "I'll bet you those scouts will really be beating down our door then."

"Yes, ma'am," I said softly. I didn't know what else to say. It was a conversation that I really didn't want to have that day. And if I told her that I wasn't going to play, it would turn into a long, drawn out discussion. Probably even a prayer session. And me and The Lord weren't actually on good terms at the moment.

"You excited?" Big Momma asked, rising from her chair. She sat her Bible down on the table. I focused on it. How could she still believe that God was so wonderful, I thought.

Big Momma walked into the living room, and then returned with a bag in her hand. She sat it down on the kitchen table. "I got you a little something."

She dug inside of the bag and pulled out a shoe box. She sat the shoe box on the table, pulled off the lid, and then held up the cleanest pair of cleats I had ever laid eyes on. They were Reebok Adizeros. Blue ones at that. They matched our school's football uniform perfectly.

"I thought you could use these," Big Momma said smiling.

I had been stunned into silence. They were beyond beautiful. They were my dream cleats.

"Well, aren't you going to say something?" Big Momma asked. "Or are you just going to sit there like a bump on a log?"

"Dang, those are... tight," I stuttered.

"Well?"

"Thank you," I told her.

"Well, go on and try 'em on for me!" Big Momma told me. She handed me the shoes. "The man at the store said that these was the best. He said that all the pros are wearing these. They supposed to be the lightest ones out there. They supposed to make you faster."

I held the shoes in my hand in disbelief. I had dreamed about having a pair since they first came out. Me and Augustine both had talked about how we could come up on a couple a pair.

"Well, put 'em on!" Big Momma said smiling. She was happy. Happier than I had seen her in a long time.

"Big Momma, we can't afford these," I told her.

"Boy hush!" Big Momma said, waving me off.

"Big Momma, you know you can't afford these!" I said shaking my head. I rose, and placed them back in the box.

"St. Claire!" Big Momma snapped. "You do *not* run my pocket book! Do you hear me?"

"I know Big Momma, but still!" I protested. "Man, we can't afford these. This could pay a bill or something."

"St. Claire, you are my grandson, do you understand me? I will worry about what we can and can't afford, not you! Have you ever heard me complaining about my bills?"

I wanted to say yes. Big Momma was on social security retirement, and a pension from the school district, where she retired from working in the cafeteria after forty years. She didn't have money to splurge on shoes, especially football cleats.

"The Lord will provide for me!" Big Momma continued. "He gives me everything that I need! Now you take these shoes, you hear me?"

I exhaled. Now I had to tell her.

"Big Momma, I wasn't even sure if I was gonna play anymore."

"Excuse me?" Big Momma said, leaning in.

I shook my head and peered down at the table. "I don't know if I want to play anymore."

"St. Clair, what in the hell are you talking about?" she snapped. Big Momma was a church going woman, but she could get gangster with it. She worked in a ghetto cafeteria for forty years, dealing with some disrespectful hood cats, so she could carry her own and give and good as she got.

I sat back down and leaned back in the chair. "I don't know. I'm just not feeling it anymore."

Now it was her turn to exhale. "Does this have anything to do with Augustine?"

I nodded slowly.

"What does this have to do with Augustine?" she asked.

I shrugged. "I mean, I'm just not feeling it anymore."

"You love football?" she asked.

I thought about it for a minute, even though I really didn't have to. I nodded.

"Did Augustine love football?" she asked.

"Yes, ma'am."

"And the two of you played it together," she continued. "And both of you not only loved football, but you loved one another. Augustine was like your brother. And I know that boy loved you with all of his heart. You know that don't you?"

Again, I nodded. "Yes ma'am."

"Do you think Augustine would want you to be miserable? Do you think that he would want you to stop playing a sport that both he and you loved? Do you really believe that?"

No, ma'am."

"Then why the bullshit?" Big Momma asked. "St. Clair, you gotta stop feeling sorry for yourself. You have to get out there, and you have to *live*. If you stop doing things, then not only have you let yourself down, but you've let your team down, you've let Augustine down, and you've let your mother down."

I quickly shifted my gaze to her.

"Your mother would want you to follow your dreams, St.

Claire. And so would Augustine. You have to go on, and you have to live life for the *both* of you. You have to go on to college, and make your mother proud. You are her only child. You are her legacy. And when people look at you, and what you have become, they will judge her. My child, was a great mother. She loved you with everything that she had. And I'll be damned if you make her seem like a failure. Is that what you want?"

I shook my head.

"Go on, and live your life, St. Claire. Do you hear me?"

"Yes, ma'am."

Big Momma dug into her shopping back once again. This time, she pulled out a pair of Adizero gloves that matched the cleats, and tossed them to me.

"Big Momma!" I bolted up from my seat as I caught the gloves. They were super tight.

"I need for my grandbaby to be looking sharp on that field when he scoring those touchdowns!" she said smiling. "Go get 'em, Running Back Baby!"

# **<u>Chapter Three</u>**

I strolled into the athletics locker room with my gym bag draped over my shoulder. The first person I saw was Big Deebo, our guard. He was 6'8, three hundred and twenty one pounds. He was a legitimate FBS prospect, with a couple of offers on the table. Alabama wanted him. Texas wanted him. Texas A&M wanted him. LSU wanted him. Nebraska wanted him. Florida wanted him. Those were the ones that were still left in the race. He had ruled out the other twenty seven teams that had been pursuing him.

"Running Back Baby!" Deebo shouted, upon seeing me. We slapped hands. "What's up, Baby Boy? Why you didn't come to summer session?"

I shook my head and looked down. He knew what I meant.

"Hurry up and get dressed, fool," he told me. "Good to have you back!" He slapped me on the back, and headed out of the locker room.

Running Back Baby was my nickname. It was giving to me by Augustine years ago. He hated calling me St.Claire, because he said it was lame. He called it a girl's name. I agreed. The only person in the world that still called me St. Claire was my grandmother. Everyone else called me Running Back Baby, or CB, which was short for Claire Baptiste. Even Big Momma called me CB sometimes. My mother used to call me CB, accept when she was angry. When she was pissed, I was St. Claire Christophe Henri Baptiste. She used a nigga's full name whenever I got into trouble. The St. Claire part came from my Haitian grandfather, whose name was also St. Claire. The Christophe Henri part came from the famous Haitian patriot and former president who fought with Toussaint, and helped to liberate Haiti. My father was one of those proud black, pro Haitians. He claimed to be a descendant of Henri Christophe, and in his eyes, Haiti was the most wonderful place in the world. The news always showed otherwise. I wasn't ready to find out for myself just yet. Maybe one day, but not anytime soon. The closest I wanted to get to Haiti for right now, was bumping Wyclef Jean, and some old Fugees albums.

"What's up, my nigga!" Big Matt, said, strolling into the locker room. He was followed by his boys, Dirty Curt and Savawn. Big Matt was our defensive end. He was a cool cat. Another D-1 prospect. At 6'2 two hundred and seventy five pounds, he was the ideal size for an end. Plus he had good lateral motion to go along with his size. He was going somewhere big for sure. But he had his heart set on LSU.

Savawn was another New Orleans transplant. Like the rest of us, he also lived in Acres Homes. He was our safety, and he was Texas A&M bound. He was six four, two hundred and forty pounds, and was a beast down field. You throw in his direction, just consider it an interception. The ball was going the other way. He was our lockdown man back deep.

"Running Back Baby!" Savawn shouted. We shook hands. He reminded me so much of Augustine that it wasn't funny. He was always cracking jokes, and playing the dozens, talking about people, and making everybody laugh. Back in the NOLA he was one of those Calliope cats. If not for Katrina, we probably would have been enemies.

"Running Back Baby!" Dirty Curt shouted. We slapped hands. Dirty Curt was our slot receiver. He was only six foot, a hundred and seventy pounds, but he had decent hands, and was quick as lightening. The kid could cut on a dime. He was only a sophomore, and he was already getting looks.

What's shaking, baby?" Savawn asked.

I shrugged . "Aint nothing."

"You ready to repeat?" Big Matt asked.

"State Champs, baby!" Dirty Curt shouted, slapping hands with Savawn. He turned toward me. "You ready to take us there?"

Normally, my answer would have been *hell yeah*. But these weren't normal times, and these weren't normal circumstances. I though about his question. I knew that I had to give him an answer, even though I wasn't sure of the answer that I had to give. The silence in the room was growing awkward.

"Hell yeah," I said, lying. I even gave them a fake smile, and extended my hand. Savawn slapped my hand.

"That's what I'm talking about, my nigga!" Savawn shouted. "State Champs, baby!"

"It's going down!" Dirty Curt shouted, in his deep Texas accent. He had a Southern accent that was deeper than most Southern accents. He pulled out his wave brush and started brushing his hair.

"Look at this ol pretty ass nigga!" Big Matt said smiling, and flashing his gold teeth. Big Matt wore his hair in dreadlocks, like a large number of people on the team. He was tatted up, and grilled out, like the rest of us.

"Aw, shut up, ol black ass, nigga!" Dirty Curt shot back. "Just 'cuz a nigga ain't got no funky ass dreads in his hair."

"Bitch, my hair ain't funky!" Big Matt told him. " Besides,

your momma told me that she like 'em."

"Aww, fat ass nigga," Dirty Curt told him.

"Both of y'all shut the fuck up!" Savawn told them. "Y'all act like y'all fucking!"

"Nigga, we'll see you outside," Dirty Curt said, slapping hands with me.

"Alright, fool!" I told them.

"Alright!" Savawn said, slapping hands with me.

"Alright, Running Back Baby!" Big Matt shouted. He slapped hands with me twice, and then snapped his fingers. "See you outside, fool."

They left me to continue suiting up for practice. The conversation hit me. I had so many people looking toward me now. I had not only my team, but my entire community looking toward me to carry the load. Last year I had Augustine with me. And together, we shared the load. Despite the fact that either of us could have carried the load alone, we had fun doing it together. But now, I had been left alone to carry the load, and the fun was now gone. Was I ready to step in and carry the hopes and dreams of an entire community? That was the question that weighed heavily on me, and it was the question that scared the shit out of me. Could I, under normal circumstances? Yeah. But now?

It wasn't so much that I couldn't physically, my questions

were more of the mental and emotional variety. For the first time in my life, football had lost its magic. For the first time in my life, I wasn't playing the game for me, but for everyone else. It was now a *job*, whereas before, it had been a dream. I didn't know what else to do, but keep walking. And that's exactly what it felt like I was doing. I was sleepwalking. I was just going through the motions. Going through the motion of living, and going through the motions of playing football.

"Dang, I was hoping to see you naked."

I turned in the direction from which the voice had came. It was my girl, Adanna. A smile shot across my face, and I rose. She hurried into my arms.

"What the hell are you going in here?" I asked.

"What?" she leaned back and smiled. "That's the first thing you asked me, after not seeing me all summer? No welcome back? No, I missed you with all my heart?"

I kissed her.

The best way to describe my relationship with Adanna is to say that she was my air. If Augustine was my fire inside, Adanna was the air that I breathed. She was the *only* girl I ever loved.

Adanna was the product of Nigeria. She was beautiful beyond words. She was a daughter of Africa, and it showed in her skin, her mannerisms, and all that she did. She had skin that resembled dark brown satin, while her hair, which she wore natural, was like jet black cotton. Her lips were full, her cheek bones pronounced, and her nose full. If she wasn't a descendant of some ancient Ghanian, or Nubian dynasty, I'll be damned. She had a regality about her. When she glided into a room, it was as if you were in the presence of nobility, and you wanted to sit up straight and watch your words. She made you act right, and she made you want to be better. She made *me* better.

Adanna was the product of Nigerian parents who immigrated to England just after she was born, and her accent was distinctly British. Her parent's divorce was the reason for her relocation to America. She fled the messy proceedings, and came to the States to live with her brothers. Little did her parents know the type of shit her brothers were into though. They were some of the biggest financial scammers in Houston. From fake credit cards, to Ponzi schemes, to illegal currency trading, you name it, they were into it. If it had to do with money, and finance, and it was illegal, they had their hands in it. Adanna was desperate to get away from them as well. She too had a dream. She wanted to go to SMU, while I went to TCU just across town in the Metroplex. Together we would make it.

"When did you get back into town?" I asked.

"Last night," she said with a smile. She had gone to stay

with her aunt in Dallas for the summer, to help out with her restaurant. Her aunt wanted her to move up there permanently, but she refused to leave me. She was going to move to Dallas, once I got into TCU, and she got into SMU. We were all supposed to do it together. Me, her, Augustine, and Augustine's girl, Victoria. I hadn't seen or spoken to Victoria in almost eight months.

"Why didn't you call me?" I asked.

"I wanted to surprise you," she said.

I wrapped my arms around her and kissed her again. We both heard a whistle blowing outside of the locker room. It was time for practice.

"You're going to be late," she smiled.

I nodded toward the door. "C'mon, I'll walk you out."

We stepped out of the locker room, and we didn't get very far before we ran into a couple of the biggest assholes I had ever met. Two of her brothers.

"What the hell are you doing?" Wilson asked, in his thick Nigerian accent. Wilson was the middle brother. He was six foot three inches, and as solid as a rock. He looked as if he had just leaped off the pages of a muscle magazine. He was *that* big, *that* swole, and *that* cut up.

"We been looking all over for you!" Nelson added. He was the oldest of the brothers. At six foot five he was also the tallest.

He too looked the part of a professional body builder. And to think, these guys were all into finance and banking and telemarketing and insurance scams, and yet, looked like they were Incredible Hulk stand ins. In my mind, I definitely had trouble reconciling the images of poor, starving, Africans, whenever I saw these assholes.

"What the hell are you doing with this cockroach?" Wilson asked Adanna. "I thought we told you to stay away from him?"

"You don't control me!" Adanna snapped.

"As long as you living under *my* roof, you obey *my* rules!" Nelson told her.

Wilson jabbed his finger into my chest. "Hey, cockroach, I thought I told you to stay away from my sister!"

I slapped his hand away.

They loved to call me cockroach. It was a derisive name for Haitians. To them, we were the lowest of the low, because we were from the poorest country in the Western Hemisphere, and competing to be the poorest country in the world.

"Leave him alone!" Adanna shouted.

"Go to the car!" Wilson shouted, pointing across the football field to his Black Lexus LS.

"Stay away from my sister, cockroach!" Nelson said, giving me the evil eye. "I catch you with her again, you know what it is!"

Wilson went further. He shoved me against the brick wall.

Hard.

"Stay away, cockroach!" he said, lifting his shirt, and showing me the handle of his Glock. "Find another cockroach, refugee."

Him, calling me a refugee, was like the pot calling the kettle black. His parents had fled the violence in Nigeria and sought sanctuary in Great Britain. According to Adanna, her father had worked for one of her country's corrupt presidents, and had to flee to London in the middle of the night with nothing more than a suitcase, and the numbers to his foreign accounts. And yet, I was the low life?

I stared at Adanna scurrying across the field in tears. I hated her brothers just as much as they hated me. They felt as though I wasn't good enough for their sister. Sometimes I questioned myself, wondering if they were right. Should I let her go, I sometimes wondered? Would she be better off without me? I loved Adanna. I had loved her from the moment I first laid eyes on her. There was just something magical about her. Something that wouldn't allow me to let go. Like I said, she was my air.

I turned back to her brothers. They could beat me, threaten me, shoot me, and do whatever they wanted to do, but I wasn't going anywhere. The even better thing was, Adanna wasn't going anywhere either. We were in love, and we had a plan. And her brothers' money, guns, and massive muscles weren't going to stop us. We were going to get out the hood *together*. We were determined to make it…*together*.

Baby Baller                    Caleb Alexander

# **<u>Chapter Four</u>**

I went back to school the next day. The previous evening's football practice had been bullshit. It was a walk through. I already knew all the plays, and I knew everything that I needed to know about my position. I basically stood there and listened to the coaches talk about simple shit to the Junior Varsity players that had been moved up to replace last year's seniors. I even had a new partner at the running back position. Because he was replacing Augustine, I automatically didn't like him. He was the first person I saw when I arrived at school the next morning.

"You ready to win in all again?" Desmond asked.

I pulled my lock off of my locker and opened my locker door. The light sent several roaches scurrying out of my locker and into the ventilation slats of the next locker. Roaches, spiders, and rats were a common occurrence at Booker T. High. Did I forget to mention how old and how poor my school was?

"We gonna be that one two punch, my nigga!" Desmond said excitedly.

I stared at him without saying anything. He was our starting JV running back last year. He helped to lead our Junior Varsity team to an unblemished district championship. He wasn't a bad dude, in fact, under any other circumstance we probably would have been cool. We were cool last year. We were even cool right up until I found out that he would be the other running back on our squad. That he was *supposedly* taking my nigga's spot, was what made us un-cool.

"What's up, my dude?" he said, lifting his hand in the air. "You ain't gonna leave me hanging, are you?"

I extended my hand, and he slapped it.

"That's what I'm talking about, my nigga!" he said animated. "You gotta get hype, baby! Get hyped!"

I wanted to curse his ass out. He was not a part of what *we* accomplished. He was not a part of the team that won state last year. *We* would not be repeating. *I* and some of the *others* would be repeating. But not him. And by him saying that, I felt like he was pushing Augustine's memory aside. It wasn't a fill in the blank position. One couldn't just be replaced in life, like a missing chess piece. Augustine was so much more than that. His life had been so much more than that.  Something was telling me, that I was gonna end up whipping this fool, behind some dumb shit that he was going to eventually say.

"Running Back Baby!"

I turned.

Savawn, and Dirty Curt were heading my way.

"Running Back Baby!" Savawn said, throwing his hands up in the air. "What's happening, baby?"

"What up, my nigga?" I said.  We shook hands and hugged. I shook Dirty Curt's hand, and embraced him as well.

"What's shaking, baby?" Savawn asked.

I grabbed my history book and closed my locker. "Shit, nothing.  'Bout to head to class."

"C'mon, we headed that way," Dirty Curt said, nodding down the hall.

The three of us headed down the crowded, graffiti filled halls of Booker T. High.  My school wasn't just ghetto, it was *dangerously* ghetto.  I wasn't just graffiti filled, and rat infested, it was also gang infested and hood rat infested as well.  One in ten of the girls at the school were pregnant at any given time.  Hood cats posted up in the hall during all hours of the day blowing kill, and kicking their iPod systems with the latest chopped and screwed re-mixes.  The metal detectors damn sure didn't work, 'cause I knew several of the homies who were always packing heat. And the overwhelming majority of the teachers just didn't give a fuck. Most just wanted a paycheck, and the fact that they had to report to Booker T. High to get it, spoke volumes about how desperate they were. A couple of them were junkies, more than a hand full were bass heads who scored rocks from the students they were supposed to be teaching, and a few of them were just trying to make it through the day alive. Those were the ones who packed heat of their own.

"Bone!" Savawn shouted. "What's happening my nigga?"

We rolled up on some of our partners from the hood. They were standing in the hall by the office blowing a fat blunt.

"Sup, my niggaz" Bone asked. We all exchanged handshakes and hugs. "What you niggaz gonna do this year?"

Bone was one of the dealers I was talking about. He dealt in rocks, but mainly sold weed. He was a B-Boy stuck in the eighties. He wore a big dookie rope chain, and always had his baseball cap turned to the side. He talked with a lisp, and slight New York accent, despite that fact that he was from the hood, and had never left the hood a day in his life.

"Shit we gonna wreck shop!" Savawn told him. "What kinda question that?"

Bone nodded. "I hear you, I hear you!" He took a puff

from his blunt, and blew weed smoke into the air. "We need to hook up on some of them games, and let a nigga hit it big on a point spread or something."

"Aw, nigga, ain't nobody shaving no points on no game!" Savawn told him.

"We blowing niggaz out, every game!" Dirty Curt added.

Bone extended the blunt toward us. "Y'all want a hit a this fatty?"

"Naw, nigga!" I told him.

Savawn took the blunt and pulled a long drag off of it. He blew weed smoke in the air, just as the principal was coming out of the office.

"Y'all wanna get to class?" the principal asked.

"We going," Savawn told him.

The principal waved his hand, clearing away some of the weed smoke. He shook his head and headed off. He was *overwhelmed*, like the rest of the administrators and staff. He didn't give a fuck about weed. He had homicides and gang fights and State Regulators and other important shit to worry about. Booker T. High was barely out of Federal Control, and the administrators were desperate to keep us from slipping back under the control of the federal courts. Yeah, *we were that bad.*

"Yo, we'll holler at y'all," I said, chunking up dueces. I

turned, and headed for my first period history class. Savawn and Dirty Curt trailed.

"I saw you on the field yesterday," Vashika said, rolling up on me.

"Yeah?" I said, trying to keep it moving.

She grabbed my arm and pulled me to the side. "And you was looking all tasty and shit."

The best way to describe Vashika, is the word gold digger. The second best word to describe her, would be loose. She was known to get extremely drunk at parties, and end up in bed with whoever put in a little effort and managed to get her to the nearest sack without her falling out. As a result, she had a reputation that wasn't cool. She was a flirt, and she used her body to manipulate guys into giving her what she wanted. Don't get me wrong, Vashika was fine as hell, but she had been ran through by way too many dudes. She had been trying to add me to her hit list since our freshman year, despite the fact that she knew I was rolling with Adanna.

"I wasn't doing shit," I told her.

"You was still looking all good," she said, licking her lips. "So, when are you going to come over and help me with my history homework?"

"I'm sure you can find a million guys to help you with your

history homework," I told her.

"Yeah, but they probably won't be as good as you with helping me with what I need, you know what I'm saying?" she smiled, and caressed my jaw with her finger.

"I can hook you up with my boy, Dirty Curt, he'll tutor you."

She recoiled, and shifted her eyes toward Dirty Curt and Savawn who were standing behind me laughing. "I don't think so."

"What about that nigga you got?" Savawn asked. "Ain't he from the Southwest? He's a big time baller, can't he hire your dumb ass a tutor?"

"See, I ain't even talking to your old busted ass!" Vashika said, snapping her fingers and craning her neck. The sensuality fled from her motions, and the Acres Homes came out in full force. "You need to get you some business."

"You need to wash your feet!" Savawn shot back.

It was no secret that Savawn and Vashika had hooked up on a few occasions. She was ghetto, and he was ghetto, and both of them were hoes. Savawn had a loose dick, that didn't discriminate. He would stick his dick in a trashcan if he thought it would feel good.

"You need to tell your momma to wash her funky ass pussy!" Vashika shouted.

"You need to tell your momma to stop leaving her bloody toilet paper all over the place!" Savawn retorted.

"Fuck you!" Vashika said. She came outta her shoes and tried to charge Savawn. He dodged her, and jogged away backwards while laughing.

"Busted ass, Beeyotch!" Savawn shouted from down the hall.

"Your momma is a busted ass beeeeyotch!" Vashika shouted.

"That's enough you two!" Mr. Davis told them. "Get to class! Savawn, get to class! Vashika, get to class! And the rest of you, the show's over. Everyone get to class!"

The gathering crowd started to disperse. If there was one teacher in the entire school that everyone was willing to listen to, it was Mr. Davis.

Mr. Davis was one of the school's counselors, and he also taught a couple of history classes. He was in his forties, which made him the same age as most of our pops. And what was so cool about him, was that he carried us like he *was* our pops. He was no nonsense, and he was tough, but it wasn't asshole tough. It was caring tough. He held us to higher expectations than anyone else in the school. He was also there to listen if you needed someone to talk to. If you had a problem in our school, you took it to Mr.

Davis, and you knew that he was going to go to bat for you. And so nobody crossed him, and everyone listened to him. He had our respect. And he had it for so many different reasons. Mr. Davis had two degrees mounted on the wall in his counseling office. Both were from Harvard. Seeing those degrees on his wall told each of us many things. One, if he could do it, we could do it too. It also told us that he didn't *have* to be here, but he was. He *wanted* to teach at the poorest school in Texas. Those degrees told us that he wasn't in it for the money, he was in it for *us*. And that's another reason why he got mad respect.

I started to drift away with the rest of the crowd. Until I felt an arm drape around my shoulder.

"Where are you going?"

I looked up, and it was Mr. Davis smiling at me.

"To class," I told him.

"Oh, now you want to go to class, huh?" Mr. Davis asked.

"That's what you just told us to do."

"Somebody has to tell you to go to class?" he asked. "You can't just go by yourself? Someone has to hold your hand, despite the fact that you've been doing this for the last three years?"

I couldn't do nothing but smile.

"So, how have you been?" he asked, pulling me to the side.

I nodded. I knew what he was talking about and why he

was asking.

"You sure?" he asked, lifting an eyebrow.

"I'm cool," I said, nodding.

"You didn't show up for Spring Ball, or summer workouts."

I shook my head.

"Why not?"

"Didn't feel like it."

"Why didn't you call me."

"Didn't need to."

"Don't bullshit me," he said. "You need to rap with somebody, you call me. You can talk to me about anything, you got that?"

I nodded. "Yes, sir."

"Augustine's death, was a terrible tragedy, son. It was an *accident*. A terrible freak accident. It could have happened to anybody, at any time, under any circumstances, you understand?"

I looked away and nodded. I wasn't trying to hear that bullshit. Augustine's death didn't happened to anybody, it happened to *him*. And it happened on the football field, and it happened with me holding him and telling him that everything was going to be okay. It happened on a play where I was supposed to be running the football.

"CB!" he said forcefully.

I turned my gaze back to him.

"Augustine's death was an accident," he continued. "I know you two were like two peas in a pod. You were like Amos and Andy. But let me tell you something, kid. Life goes on. You have to go on with your life. You cannot let Augustine's death be the end of *your* life. That boy loved you. And he would not want you to fuck your life off. You have to go on, and you have to live for the both of you, you got that?"

I nodded. "Yes, sir."

"Okay, you call me, or you come by my office if you need anything, you hear me?"

"Yes, sir."

"As a matter of fact, you come by latter on this week, and we gonna make sure that you got all your shit together for your college applications."

"Yes, sir."

"Okay," he said, patting me on my shoulder. "Now, you get your big ugly ass on to class."

I laughed, and headed off to class. Mr. Davis was cool as fuck. Without him, half of the niggaz in the school would have been dropouts. And for most of the niggaz on campus, he was the closest thing that many of us had to a father who actually gave a shit.

Baby Baller                    Caleb Alexander

# **<u>Chapter Five</u>**

Where you going, baby?" Big Momma asked.

I threw on my hoodie, and then began lacing my tennis shoes. "Going out for a quick run."

Big Momma dropped a few more pieces of her country battered, Southern fried chicken into her favorite skillet. The grease from the pan popped and sizzled, and the tasty aroma of Big Momma's cooking wafted through the air.

"Dinner a be ready in a little bit, so hurry back."

I finished lacing my shoes, leaned in, and kissed my Big Momma on her cheek. "I will."

"How was school today?" she asked.

"It was cool," I shrugged. "You know, the usual."

Big Momma stopped and faced me. "What is *the usual*?"

Again I shrugged. "You know. Just school."

"No, I don't know," she persisted. "What is *just* school?"

"Just the same ole stuff," I explained. I didn't want to say niggaz tripping, smoking weed, skipping classes, a school full of pregnant chicks, teachers not giving a shit, graffiti all over the school, roaches in the lockers, rats in the cafeteria, cars getting broken into after school, computers already missing from the computer lab, and fools are already getting into it and talking about blasting each other. The usual shit. But I couldn't say that to Big Momma.

Big Momma exhaled in frustration and turned her attention back to the stove. "Well, how was practice?"

"It was just the first day," I answered. And it had been. At least for me.

"How's the team looking this year?" she asked with a sly smile.

I really didn't know. But I nodded anyway. "About the same."

"Are we gonna win another state championship?" she asked, prodding.

"We're gonna try."

"Well then, that's about all you can do. Just try. As long as you give it all you can, then no matter where you land, you'll be a winner."

It was old school wisdom. Just try hard. Everybody is a

winner. It was classic Big Momma. Her optimism was boundless.
It was hard to *not* be optimistic when someone you love, was so full
of love.  She wanted me to talk about my day, because she knew
that I would be missing Augustine like crazy today.  She wanted me
to talk about football, so that she could give me some of her pearls
of wisdom. It was all out of love. And I loved this woman more
than life itself. I leaned in and kissed her on her wrinkled  cheek
again.

"We gonna get it done, Big Momma."

"Well all right!" she smiled.  "That's what I like to hear."

"I'mma go for a quick jog and I'll be right back."

"Dinner will be waiting, Sweety."

I turned, and headed out the door.  On the porch, I turned on
my iTunes, tossed my hoodie over my head, and started my jog. I
headed down the street, thinking about nothing but what was in
front of me.  I didn't want to think about football, or Augustine, or
the first day of school. So, I just tried to concentrate on some Drake
and Lil Wayne, while taking in the sites of the hood.

Acres Homes was rural, while at the same time, it was
ghetto.  To call the houses in my hood ramshackle, would be a
compliment.  Most were old, wood framed, white clapboard,
'shotgun' houses that had been thrown up in the '20's and 30's. A
few were built in the '60's, and a couple were thrown up in the 70's.

And that was about it. After the 70's, nothing else had built in the hood.

My hood was a place that saw its heyday in the 20's and 30's. And after the 60's hit, saw a steady decline. The brothers coming back from 'Nam, the racial tensions of the 60's, along with the introduction of smack in a major way, turned my hood into what looked like the remnants of an old Northwestern logging town. It was densely forested. With loose unclaimed chickens running around the hood. There were probably more horses than working cars in the hood. No sidewalks, because people didn't take sunny strolls down the streets. No drainage tunnels, because the water just soaked into the soil. No curbed streets, no street lights, nothing. Just a bunch of old ass, run down houses sitting on large overgrown tracts of land. That was it. A hood store here, a liquor store there, a couple of pawn shops, and plenty of dope spots. Run down apartment complexes, some seedy motels, and the 44 Bus line from H-Town was all we had. This was why the high school football team's winning season meant so much to the community. It was all we had to made us feel like we were a part of this world. It was all we had to make us feel like we were actually worth something. It was all we had to show the world that we were still here, and that we hadn't given up.

I jogged through the hood, taking it all in. The landscape

was surreal; The broken up pavement, the broken out windows, the dilapidated buildings, the graffiti riddled walls, the base heads that strolled around looking like zombies from *The Walking Dead*, all of it reminded me of one of those post apocalyptic movies on A&E. The difference of course, was that this was all real.

As I jogged through the hood, I spied a group of my homeboys hanging out at a local food mart. I knew what they were doing. My homeboy Quick lifted his hands in the air asking me what was up. I jogged in their direction.

"What up, fool?" Quick asked.

"What up, my nigga?" I said, greeting him. We clasped hands, and I leaned over and embraced him. That's right, I said *leaned* over. It wasn't because Quick was short, it was because Quick was confined to a wheelchair.

My homie Quick got his name on the football field, and on the jogging track. He could hit a 4.2 flat his sophomore year, and had been the hottest running back in H Town. He was even better at carrying the rock than Augustine. In fact, had Quick not taken a bullet to his spine, he would have been playing D-1 college football right at that moment. But like so many others, the hood took him under. He had been on the corner slanging yea-yo, trying to get money for his family's light bill, when some fools from the 3rd Ward rolled up and put a bullet in his back. He was through. Everything that he knew, everything that he had dreamed of, was over in an instant. He tried to kill himself at least six different times afterward. And then, once that failed, he made the decision to jump into the hood life ten toes down. He was in it for life now.

Quick had tatoos all over his face and neck now, and it wasn't uncommon to see him rolling down the street with a 12 gauge sitting on his lap, or an AK-47 attached to the side of his wheelchair. He no longer gave a fuck, and that's what made him so dangerous. The homies in the hood would lift him into the backseat of a car or the bed of a stolen pick up truck, hand him his AK, and then ride down on other hoods. He had a bigger reputation now, than he had when he was running the rock for the high school. His old reputation had him being the pride of Houston, his new one, had his being the scourge of the Houston community. In the three years since his injury, he had sent many a mother's son to a cold and lonely grave. He even had a black dress tatted on his neck now. The hood dealt shitty blows, and then it dealt *real* shitty blows. Quick was confined to a wheelchair, but the mothers of his victims paid for his shooting even worse, they had to bury their sons.

"So, what's the damn deal, my nigga?" Quick asked.

"Same, shit, different day," I told him.

Quick lifted a beer in the air. "You fuck wit it?"

I shook my head and waved him off. "You know I can't

fuck wit dat."

"Oh, that's right. You training and shit, old square ass nigga!"

"Fuck you!" I laughed.

He shook my hand and laughed. "You know I'm just fucking with you dog! So what's happening with the squad, fool? You niggaz gonna repeat or what?"

I shrugged. "We gone try."

Quick took a swig off his beer. "You gone try? Nigga, get that soft ass shit outta here! You either gonna wreck shit or you ain't! Which one is it?"

"I guess we gonna wreck shop."

"That's what the fuck I'm talking about!"

Our other homeboy, Lil Dirty, walked outta the store and handed Quick a pack of cigarettes. Quick peered at the cigarettes for a moment, before staring at Lil Dirty again.

"What the fuck is dis?" Quick asked.

"Some squares," Dirty told him.

"I don't smoke no motherfucking lights, nigga! Do I look like a bitch to you?"

Dirty smiled and nodded. "Yeah, you do."

"I got yo bitch!" Quick said, grabbing his dick.

"Here, ol' cry baby ass nigga!" Dirty said, snatching the box of squares out of Quick's hands. "I told that muthafuckin A-Rab that I wanted some muthafucking menthols, not no damn lights."

"Take them hoes back!" Quick told him.

"So what the squad look like?" Dirty asked me.

Dirty was another product of the hood. He was tatted up like Quick, but wore his hair in matted up dreads. And like most of the fools in the hood, he was grilled out with golds on his top and bottom teeth. His gold teeth blended perfectly with his golden skin, and his complexion made his tattoos even more noticeable. He had a big ass AK-47 tattooed on his neck with the words *I Kill Snitches* beneath it. Dirty had been selling dope and terrorizing the hood since he was seven. He had seven tear drops tatted beneath his left eye, symbolizing the number of bodies he had under his belt.

"Look the same as we did last year," I told him.

"Shit, not without ya boy," he said, pulling a blunt out of his pocket.

Quick nudged him. "Man, shut the fuck up."

Dirty fired up the blunt, took a long drag, and blew smoke into the air. "My bad, homie. How you feeling?"

I nodded, and peered off into the distance. "I'm good."

Dirty extended the blunt. "Here, you wanna hit this?"

Quick slapped his hand away. "Naw, fool! He playing

football. How you gonna offer that nigga a blunt, and he trying to play football and shit."

"What?" Dirty asked. "He can take a hit off the spliff."

"You a dumb ass nigga!" Quick told him. "This man try'na do something with his life. He ain't try'na end up like you."

"Aw fuck you, ol Paul Wall looking ass nigga!" Dirty shot back.

Quick smiled at me. "This nigga think everybody wanna be a muthafuckin criminal like his illiterate ass."

I laughed.

Quick reached for his strap, and peered at a car rolling by behind me. "That look like them 5th Ward niggaz."

Dirty pulled a .45 from beneath his shirt and cocked it. He too examined the car rolling by.

"Naw, that ain't them niggaz," Quick finally declared.

Acres Holmes and 5th Ward were apparently beefing again. It happened every so often. North Side niggaz and South Side niggaz had been beefing as far back as anybody could remember. And then, you had specific hoods on each side, that really hated one another. Acres Homes and 5th Ward was at that point right now. Blood had been spilled, and so it was on in a major way. This latest beef had been going on since the days of Club Northside, and Jamaica Jamaica, back in the early nineteen nineties. Back before most of us were even born.

"What's up with them fools?" I asked.

"Them niggaz tripping 'bout they punk ass homeboy getting beat up at the club," Dirty told me.

I shook my head.

"Roc pistol whipped that fool," Quick added.

"Aw, nigga, you was in on that shit too!" Dirty said laughing.

Quick laughed. "Fuck them niggaz."

Dirty slowly lowered the hammer on his .45 caliber Smith & Wesson semi-automatic. Quick spun around in his wheelchair.

"You lucky they won't let me back on that bitch ass football field," Quick smiled. "I still got some moves for they ass!"

"Your old ass ain't got no eligibility left!" Dirty told him.

"Nigga, you can't even spell eligibility!" Quick shot back. He clasped my forearm and pulled me in closer. "Say, fool. Ya'll first game is against Cinco Ranch right?"

I nodded. He surprised me a little. I didn't think that he still kept that close of a tab on high school football to know our schedule.

"They trying to blast y'all out the gate with a tough ass schedule," he continued. "They trying to give y'all some early losses, and take y'all spirit away. Don't even trip, fool. Y'all got them niggaz."

I was really surprised now. I knew that our team's playoff run had rallied our community, but I didn't know that Quick had paid any attention to it. And now that I thought about it, it had to have been hard on him. He should have been out there on the field with us, leading us to victory last year. I was really feeling uncomfortable talking to him about the upcoming season.

"Let me tell you something," Quick said, after taking a swig off his beer. "All y'all gotta look out for, is number 24. That got damned running back they got is the truth. And that QB they got is all right too. But y'all can get 'em. And as far as they defense go, they got that one DB who is decent, and they got that one lineman who's going D-1. But they soft up the middle, fool. That nigga they got playing middle linebacker, sucks. He can't go left."

Dirty pulled off his blunt and blew smoke into the air. "How the fuck you know that, fool? This nigga just talking!"

"Cause the muthafucka had surgery on his right foot!" Quick shouted.

"So what the fuck that got to do with the nigga going left?" Dirty asked, rolling his eyes.

"Cause the muthafucka ain't never been able to go left, since we was kids!" Quick shouted. "And the muthafucka got turf toe last year, and ever since then, he ain't been able to cut off his right foot and make lateral movements to the left, nigga!"

Quick had hit me hard with that one. I was really feeling fuck up. His heart was still in the game. His heart was ready to play, but his body no longer could. It was a lesson that hit me hard as fuck. He would give anything to be out there on that field again. *Anything*. And so would Augustine. And here I was, feeling sorry for myself, not knowing if I wanted to play again. I felt like shit, because I had that option. Neither Quick nor Augustine did.

"Yo, I gotta get back to the crib," I told them.

"Grams cooking it up, huh?" Dirty asked.

I smiled and nodded.

"Give her my love," Quick told me. We clasped hands briefly. He pulled me in closer again. "It's candy up the middle, fool. Hit the hole hard, and then cut to your right. He can't get to you. And then it's one on one with that safety. He's a white boy, so you can do him all day long."

I laughed.

Quick nodded. "Listen to your boy! I'm telling you."

I nodded, put my ear buds back in my ear, and jogged off. On the way back to the crib, I thought about Quick. Not just about his advice, but about the passion that I saw in his eyes when he was giving me advice. He was an athlete in his heart. The hood shit, was superficial. It was him lashing out, because his first and only love had been denied him. It was him being pissed off at God about the hand that he had been dealt. I thought about how many niggaz would still be alive, if Quick could have still played football. I thought about my life, and about my future as well. Everybody was telling me to go on, that Augustine would want me to. After talking to Quick, I realized it wasn't just my hood's hopes and dreams that I was carrying on my shoulders, and it wasn't just Augustine's. It was Quick's as well. It was all of the victims whose lives had been taken by him. It was for the families that they left behind as well. I had an obligation to take Quick's anger, and fury, and vengeance, and turn it into something else. I had an obligation to turn his actions, into something that would uplift and give hope to my community. I had an obligation to inspire the next generation of kids playing street football in the hood. I had to give them a choice. They could be me, or they could be Quick. They could heal a community and bring joy to it, or they could hurt a community, and bring pain and sorrow to it. For the first time in my life it really hit me, that everything that was going on, was so much more than just football. It was about life. On the individual level, it was about choosing what type of life we were going to have. Were we going to be healers, or hurters. And on the community level, it was about what type of community we were going to be. Everyone here was desperate to tell the world that we weren't about violence and destruction, but that we could be so much more. In our own little lane, in our own little way, we too could be the best at something.

# **Chapter Six**

Our first football game came faster than I expected. It seemed like one minute I was talking about it, practicing for it, and the next minute, we were here. It was game time, and I definitely wasn't ready for it.

Our first game was against Cinco Ranch. They were a bunch of rich ass niggaz and White boys from the far west side of the city. Cinco Ranch was a land of big ass brick houses, beautiful lakes, plenty of parks, and beautiful manicured lawns. It was everything that Acres Homes wasn't. They were the poster children of upper middle class life.

The fact that we were playing them said a lot about the Texas University Interscholastic League. Cinco Ranch was a football powerhouse in division 6-A high school football. And to put them on our schedule as our first game, told us that the UIL wasn't happy with a bunch of ghetto ass niggaz winning the state championship, and being the face of Texas high school football. They were trying to knock us out of the box early, and they were counting on a tough ass schedule to get it done. We had Cinco Ranch, we had state football powerhouse Katy, and we had Fort Bend Hightower all on our non district schedule. It was crazy. No other team in the state had to play a gauntlet schedule like that. All of the teams on our non district schedule were undefeated in the regular season last year, and all of them were ranked in the top ten this year. They even cooked it so that all of the games with these powerhouses would be away games, so we had to play at *their* stadiums. It was bullshit.

"You ready?" Big Matt asked, patting me on the back.

We were inside of the visiting team locker room at Cinco Ranch's brand new, state-of-the-art, eighteen thousand seat, sixty-five million dollar stadium. It was nicer than most college stadiums, and a far cry from the circa 1960 stadium that we called home.

"As ready as I'll ever be," I said, lacing up my cleats. I threw on my Under Armour girdle, and then pulled my shoulder pads over my head and buckled them on. My nerves had me shaking like a leaf.

My shaking hands had nothing to do with first game jitters,

or the quality of our opponents, or the massive monolith that they called a stadium. I could hear our six thousand fans being out-shouted by their twelve thousand fans, and I knew that the atmosphere inside of the stadium was electric. But I had been at big games before. Our state championship game had been played at Cowboy Stadium, in front of sixty thousand screaming fans, and televised live to a national audience on ESPN. So, what was it that had me shaking? I couldn't figure it out for the life of me. I seated myself back down on the bench and contemplated the answer to that question.

This would be my first game without my boy Augustine. But what did that mean, I wondered? Is that what had me shaking? And if so, why? It was another game. I had played hundreds of football games. And if you count the pick up games in the hood, perhaps even thousands. So why was I shaking?

I lifted my hand in the air and examined it. It was trembling uncontrollably. I had always thought it was bullshit when I heard people say things like that. I thought that it was psychological. That all they had to do is tell their body to do something, and it would do it. And now that my body was tripping out on me, I had a new appreciation for that type of shit. It was game time, and I needed to get control of myself.

I leaned back against the locker, and I thought about last

year's games. What was so different? I don't ever remember feeling that way before a game. I knew that my boy was gone, and that *had* to be the difference. We had a pre-game ritual that we went through, and I guess it was this ritual that calmed me, and made each game seem so routine. And now that it was absent, I guess it was getting to me.

"Ready, CB?" Savawn asked, walking past and patting me on my shoulder pads.

"As I'll ever be," I replied.

The team was heading out of the locker and gathering in the tunnel. From the tunnel we would walk out onto the corner of the field together, gather at the giant banner, and then break through it and walk out onto the field together. It was here. I can't believe that another season was finally here. I don't know why it came as a surprise to me. I don't even know why I felt a little bit pissed off about it. Augustine was gone, and yet, everyone just carried on like it was nothing. Like he was never here, like he was never among us. Was life really that fucking meaningless? Do we just step over our dead and keep on moving?

"Let's go, Baby Boy!" Dirty Curt shouted, slapping me across my shoulder pads. He was trying to get me hyped up for the game. "Let's go get this, baby! Let's go! Let's go show them fools what time it is!"

He wasn't going to go away, so I knew that my thinking time was over with. And maybe that was for the best. I was depressing myself before the game.

"You ready to go get these fools?" Dirty Curt asked.

I lifted my helmet and put it on. "Let's go."

"Yeah! That's what I'm talking about!"

Dirty Curt followed me out of the locker room and into the tunnel, where the rest of the team had gathered. Coach Beckwith was standing in front near the entrance. He turned and faced us.

"Is that everybody?" Coach Beckwith asked.

Coach Gaines peered out over the gathered players. "Looks like everyone."

"This is it," Coach Beckwith started out. "This is what we've been training for, this is what we been practicing for, sweating for, and some of us, bleeding for. This is what we endured 5 A.M. practice for. This is why we went through two-a-days in the 100 degree August heat. This is it!"

Coach pointed out toward the field. "They have doubted each and every one of you, since the end of last season. They called your championship a fluke. They questioned how you could have won. They went through our records with a fine tooth comb, trying to find ineligible players. They have done everything that they could do, to take away what you worked for, and sweated for, and bled for. Are you now going to go out there and just give it away?"

"No, sir!" we shouted in unison.

"I can't hear you!" Coach shouted back.

"No, sir!" we shouted thunderously.

"They are stacking the deck against you!" Coach continued. "We didn't ask for this schedule, but this is the schedule that the Interscholastic League gave us. They are trying to knock you out of the box early. They want to crush your spirits, they think that you'll lose, and go home and quit. *That's what they think of you!* That's who they think you are. And now, it's time for us to once again, show them who we *really* are! Show the world what we're really about. It's time to show them that last year's championship wasn't a fluke! It's time to show them that what resides inside of each and every one of us, is the heart of a champion! Are you with me?"

*"Yes, sir!"*

"I said, are you with me?"

*"Yes, sir!"*

"Then let's go out there and shock the world, gentlemen! Let's go out there and win another championship! Let's show them that no matter what they do, no matter how they rig our schedule, that we'll play with anybody, anywhere, at anytime! Let's show them that we are…"

*"Booker T!"* we shouted in unison.

"Who are we?"

*"Booker T!"* came our thunderous reply.

"Let's get 'em!"

We charged the field whooping and hollering and shouting at the top of our lungs. Coach had everyone hyped. The crowds cheered and clapped when we exited the tunnel. We gathered again at the banner, where we locked arms. Most teams ripped through the banners and ran to their sideline. We ripped through our banner, and walked arm in arm to our sideline like we were cool as fuck. It intimidated the other teams like crazy. We looked like it was just another day at the office, and we were about to handle our business. The media hated it. They called it arrogant, and unsportsmanlike. They just didn't understand our program, or what we were about. They didn't understand what Swag was.

We arrived at our side of the field.

"Huddle one, get ready!" Coach shouted. It meant our starters. "Special teams, take the field."

We ran out onto the field and got ready to receive the kick off. We had won the coin toss and elected to go on offense first. We always took the ball if we won the toss. Another thing that teams didn't like about us. And again, they called us arrogant for it.

The opposing team kicked the ball off, and Dirty Curt caught it. He returned the ball down all the way to the fifty yard line, giving us a short field to work with. The game was crunk, and the atmosphere was crazy. We were ranked number two in state, and they were ranked number four. Our cross town rivals, Katy, was ranked number three, while Allen High School up near Dallas was ranked number one. Trinity, another Dallas area school was ranked fifth, while The Woodlands, another Houston area team was ranked sixth. We would pretty much have to go through all of them to repeat our championship. In fact, we had Katy the week after next. The powers that be, wanted to make sure that we lost.

The first play of the game, was a hand off to me. It was a basic, up the middle play, just to get everyone's nervous jitters to go away. Usually after a play or two, everyone calmed down, and just got down to playing football. So coaches usually called it vanilla on the opening play. I took the hand off, shot through the middle, and got to the forty yard line. First down.

I looked to the side line where the play callers were using hand signals to give us the plays. We usually used three signal callers; two of them were fake, and one was live. Only we knew which one was live. In this case, our offensive coordinator, Coach Gaines was the live signal caller. He called in another plain Jane running play. It was a QB read, which in my case, meant that I was pretty much going to get the ball, even though the QB had the option to keep it, or throw it. We were a running team.

"Hike!" the QB called out. He rolled out to his left, and then pitched me the ball. I shot around the outside linebacker and zipped past the corner. The safety took me out, sending me flying out of bounds. But it was another first down.

I lined back up in my position, and then we all looked to the sideline to get the play. This one was a hitch and go. The QB would throw the ball out to the slot receiver, who would then pitch it to me as I ran past him full steam. It was one of my favorite plays, because it allowed me to be running at full steam before I got the ball. And the slot usually pitched and then took out the cornerback for me., who was usually closing in on him anyway. It was a money play, and it usually got us big yards.

We set up, the guard hiked the ball, and QB threw it to our slot receiver, who then pitched the ball to me. I was already at full steam. Our slot didn't have to take out their corner back, because he was no where to be found. Now, it was just me and the safety. And that fool thought that he had an angle on me. I waited until he got right on me, and then I spent off of him, and basically strolled into the end zone. The crowd went wild.

"Yes!" I shouted.

My team mates rushed me and surrounded me. Our right tackle lifted me into the air.

It was my first touchdown of the season. I was happy. I

raced to the sidelines looking for Augustine so that we could leap into the air and do our chest bump. I took off my helmet and peered around excitedly. And then , it hit me. I had gotten lost in the game, and I had forgotten for that brief moment of ecstasy that Augustine wouldn't be celebrating with me. I had forgotten that my friend was gone.

I pulled off my helmet, threw it onto the ground, and raced off of the sidelines and back into the locker room. I seated myself on the old wooden bench in front of my locker, lowered my head into my hands, and balled like a baby. Augustine's death hit me harder than at any other time during the last nine months. No longer would there be any celebrations or chest bumps after a touchdown. No more secret handshakes, or signs to throw up in the air. No rebellious yells, or quick two man dance routines. For the first time in my life, I finally realized what my heart had been struggling with my mind to deny; My best friend was gone, and he wasn't coming back.

# **Chapter Seven**

"You okay?"

I turned. Adanna was standing just behind me. I placed my book bag inside of my locker, retrieved my gym bag, and slammed my locker door shut. Adanna rested her hand on my shoulder.

"St. Claire, are you all right?" she asked again.

I nodded reluctantly. "I'm okay."

She knew me well, and she knew that I wasn't. *I* knew that I wasn't. We both knew that I was putting on a brave face. She knew that something was bothering me, because I left the game, went home, and shut myself off from the world. I usually called her after the game, and many times, even sneaked out and met her in the park, or even near the train depot. But Friday night had been different. Augustine's death hit home hard. It had been my first football game since his death, and I needed to shut myself off from the world and deal with things my own way.

"What's the matter?" Adanna asked, caressing the side of my face.

She knew what it was, I suspected. She was just trying to get me to talk about it. Maybe she was right, maybe I did need to talk about it. Shutting myself inside of my darkened room the entire weekend hadn't helped. Staring at posters on my wall, pictures of me and Augustine, staring into the darkness of the room, or at the moonlight reflected off of my closet door hadn't helped. I had tried to hold a conversation with God, but found it one sided. He wouldn't answer the question that I had begged Him to answer for the last nine months; *Why Augustine?*

I could have gone into the game, I should have gone into the game. Why didn't He allow me to be the one to go into the game? Why?

"You've been thinking about Augustine?" Adanna asked.

I lowered my head and nodded. She was my girl. I needed to let her in.

"Talk to me," she said softly.

I swallowed hard. I didn't know where to begin. "It was just the first game, you know..."

A look of realization quickly spread across her face. She was smart, and held wisdom beyond her years.

Adanna nodded. "It was the first game since his death."

I nodded.

She wrapped her arms around me and pulled me close. "I'm so sorry. St. Claire, why didn't you call me? Why?"

"I just wanted to be alone," I told her. "I just needed to think about some things."

She peered into my eyes. "You don't have to face this alone. You never have to face anything alone. I am here for you."

I nodded. "I know."

"Baby, when you need to talk, you call me," she continued. "I don't have to say anything, I can just sit and listen."

Again, I nodded.

"You miss him," she said matter-of-factly. It was a statement, and her tone indicated a measure of sadness.

I lowered my head and nodded.

"I miss him too," she said softly. "I miss his loud, brash ways. I miss his shouting, his boisterousness, his braggadocio, his bravado. He could always make a person smile."

I smiled. I leaned in and kissed her cheek. "You can too."

"Me?" she asked, returning my smile.

"That British accent of yours. Braggadocio? We don't use those type of words in America, girl. Especially not in the hood."

She laughed. Her laughter was infectious, it made me smile.

Augustine meant a lot to her as well. He meant a lot to us all. He was the wild one. The one always cracking jokes, doing crazy shit, making everybody laugh. He could walk into the room and instantly light up the atmosphere. Somehow, I kept forgetting how much he meant to so many others. I always thought of my best friend as being *mine*, and *mine alone.* I knew that his death left a hole in my chest where my heart should be, but I never thought about how it had affected anyone else. Adanna was right, he *had* been her friend as well. I needed to share my pain with her. Perhaps we could work through it together.

Adanna rested her hand on my chest. "Well, you Americans should. Your English is horrid. Churchill often said that we are two peoples, separated by a common language."

I laughed politely at her British humor. Adanna was educated beyond belief. She was in all GT Classes, taking college courses at the local community college, and online. I could only imagine what she thought about our educational system here, especially in our poor ass school district. It must have been laughable to her.

The school bell rung, and again, I kissed her cheek. "I gotta get to athletics."

"You're going to be late," she shouted, as I rushed off. "Your coach is going to make you run!"

I rushed down the hall, and ran into the gym. I hurried across the gymnasium floor and into the boys locker room. Just as I opened my football locker, Coach Beckwith approached.

"Baptist!" Coach Beckwith shouted. "C'mere for a minute, son."

"Shit!" I exclaimed in a hushed tone. I hurriedly threw my gym bag inside of my locker, and followed Coach into his office. There was gentleman seated inside of the office waiting for us.

"Baptist, this is Coach Fletcher, one of the offensive coordinators for Texas A&M," Coach Beckwith said, introducing us. "He wanted to have a word with you before practice."

"How ya doing, son?" Coach Fletcher asked, with a deep Southern drawl. His accent was pure Texan.

"I'm good, sir," I answered.

"I've been hearing some good things about you," Coach Fletcher told me. "We're had you on our radar screen for a good while now, and we like what we see."

"Thank you, sir," I replied.

"Your coaches all speak highly of you, and your talent speaks for itself," Coach Fletcher said.

"Thank you, sir."

"A&M is looking at you for a couple of positions," Coach Beckwith said, jumping into the conversation. "They've seen you play both sides of the ball."

"But we are mainly interested in you as a running back, and a slot receiver," Coach Fletcher declared. "Coach Beckwith said you're pretty good as a safety and a line backer."

I nodded. "Yes, sir."

"And you do kick return and punt return?" Coach Fletcher asked, lifting an eyebrow. "There's no doubt you're a natural athlete, son. And that's what we're looking for. Ever considered playing for A&M?"

Was he shitting me, I wondered? Playing for Texas, or Texas A&M was the dream of every kid in Texas. It was what we dreamed about from the first day we began to understand the game. While most other kids pretended to be cowboys or indians, we pretended to be Texas Longhorn football players, or Texas A&M Aggies. Of course I considered playing for A&M. My heart was focused on TCU, because the Dallas - Ft. Worth area was where Adanna was heading, and because Texas and A&M were so damn hard to get into. They garnered recruits nationally, and if you weren't the best in the nation at your position, they didn't even look your way.

"Yes, sir," I answered, swallowing hard.

"Good!" he said, slapping my leg. "Because we are definitely interested in you. Coach Beckwith tells me that you're going to be participating in the Army All American Game."

"Yes, sir," I said, nodding.

"And he's a McDonalds All American," Coach Beckwith added, while smiling at me.

Coach Fletcher nodded approvingly. "So, how are your grades?"

I shrugged. "They're okay."

Coach Fletcher lifted an eyebrow. "Okay?"

I nodded. "I mean, they're okay, I guess."

"What's okay?" Coach Fletcher asked.

"I guess I make B's and C's," I told him. "I got a couple a A's."

"Let me guess, an A in athletics, and an A in health?" Coach Fletcher asked with a smile.

I nodded. He knew the game. Athletes got candy classes to boost their GPA's. It wasn't nothing new.

"How many C's?" Coach Fletcher asked.

"We talking last year, right?" I asked. "Because this year really just started, and grades ain't came out yet."

He nodded, and then gazed into space. "What I'm trying to figure out here, is if you're a B student, or a C student. Football is only one aspect of attending our university. You have to be able to cut the mustard academically, son."

Again, I nodded. "I will."

"Have you taken your SAT's yet?" Coach Fletcher asked.

I shook my head. I hadn't taken them. In fact, I had been dreading the day when I would *have* to take them. I had heard so much about that test. It was supposed to be a test of everything you've learned in all your years in high school. How the fuck was I supposed to remember all of that? Remembering algebra formulas from my freshman year was out of the question. Remembering some fucking Civil War battle that occurred hundreds of years ago, or some fucking European monarch who died a thousand years ago was virtually impossible. Who could actually remember all of that shit? So, no, I wasn't hyped about taking that fucking test. But I knew that the day was coming when I would have to.

"No, sir, I haven't taken it yet," I told him.

"Well, you need to get that scheduled," Coach Fletcher said. "Depending on where your GPA is, the test is going to count for a lot."

I nodded.

Adanna had been pressing me about studying for the test. Some say that you can't really study for the test, but Adanna insisted that she saw some SAT study guides in the library that could help me. I planned on taking her up on it. Whether I ended up at TCU, or Texas A&M, I still needed to do well on the test. I would have to get serious about studying for it.

"We going to be keeping an eye on you," Coach Fletcher
told me. "That was a great run on Friday."

"Thank you, sir."

"Go on and get suited up for practice," Coach Beckwith told
me.

I nodded, and extended my hand to Coach Fletcher. "It was
a pleasure to meet you, sir."

Coach Fletcher shook my hand. "I'll get your number and
email address from Coach Beckwith before I leave. Remember,
we'll be keeping an eye on you."

I turned, headed out of the locker room with a big ass smile
on my face.


*****


My trip home after practice took me through the hood,
where I ran into the homies once again. As usual, they were
standing on the corner hustling. Quick was seated in his wheelchair
with a Forty on his lap, while Dirty was serving a customer in a beat
old Honda Accord.

"What up, my nigga?" Quick shouted, once he saw me.

"What up?" I said, exchanging handshakes. I leaned over

and embraced him briefly.  "What it do?"

Quick took a swig from his forty ounce.  "Same shit, different day.  What it look like this year?"

I shrugged.  "You already know."

"Oh yeah?"  Quick said nodding and smiling.  "You think y'all gonna win state again?"

"Hell yeah," I told him.

"What it be like?"  Dirty shouted, walking up.  We embraced briefly.

"Same shit," I told him.

"When you gonna get some of that scholarship money and get you a whip?" Dirty asked.

"Old dumb ass nigga!" Quick proclaimed.  "You can't use no scholarship money to buy no damn car, nigga!"

"What the fuck?" Dirty asked.  "When do a muthafucka get paid?"

"You?  Never!"  Quick told him.

Dirty pulled out a fat ass wad of rolled up twenty dollar bills.  "Muthafucka I'm already paid!"

Dirty slapped hands with me and laughed.

Ishmael and Rasheed, two of our other homeboys from the hood, strolled up to the cut.  Rasheed held a fat blunt between his lips, while Ishmael held a forty ounce of Olde English.

"Running Back Baby!" Ishmael shouted. We slapped hands. "What's good, my nigga?"

Ishmael was another former football standout. He even actually got to leave the hood and go up to Ranger Junior College and play football for a minute. His grades and too much partying caused him to have to return home. He even managed to get back into shape, get his grades right, and make it onto the team at Prairie View A&M, a historically black college just outside of H Town. That shit didn't work out either. He said it was too many fine ass bitches on campus for him to concentrate, and being broke wasn't his cup of tea. He came back and started slanging. That was months ago, and he still hasn't made the big time come up. Like so many others in the hood, he was another broken dream, another cat filled with promise, who just couldn't see past the hood. And now, he was corner hustling.

Rasheed started acting like he was trying to break down and tackle me. "You still dodging muthafuckas on the football field, nigga?"

"I'm trying to," I told him.

"Here, this a make you faster," Rasheed said, handing me the blunt.

"He don't want none a that shit!" Quick told him, knocking his hand away. "He trying to do something wit his life, old negative as nigga!"

I laughed.

"Nigga, you act like you his muthafucking daddy or something!" Rasheed countered. "That man can hit the blunt if he want to! Here, my nigga!"

I lifted my hand and waved him off.

"Old bad influence, crab in the bucket ass nigga!" Quick told him. "Want everybody to be a fucking pot head like his ass."

We all broke into laughter.

"This shit make you run faster," Rasheed said, taking a long pull off the blunt.

"That shit make you dumber, muahfucka," Quick told him. "You living proof of dat."

"Fuck you, old wheelchair bound nigga!" Rasheed told him.

"Yo mama like it!" Quick told him. He turned to me. "Y'all got Hightower next, huh?"

"Yeah?" I said nodding.

"What y'all gonna do?" Quick asked, with his eyes lighting up like a child on Christmas morning.

"Win," I said with a smile.

"How you gone do that?" Quick asked, leaning back in his wheelchair, taking me in.

"I'mma bust they ass," I said, confidently.

"No," Quick said, shaking his head. "You score, and then they score, and then you get into a scoring fest. I'mma tell you two things, and you better listen. You hear me?"

I nodded.

"First, their offensive line is soft up the middle," Quick said, leaning in. "The center is one of the coach's son. His ass shouldn't even be on the field right now, let alone starting. He's a big ass sophomore, who should still be playing JV. Tell your boys to blow through the middle every play. Every single fucking play, shoot through the A Gap. You'll disrupt their offense every play. And their quarterback is a pocket QB, he can't scramble worth shit. You're going to stop them from scoring. You do what I tell you to do, and they'll go three and out every single time."

I smiled and nodded. "How the fuck..."

He waved his hand cutting me off. "Another thing, the head coach's son is playing corner. He's another sophomore, who shouldn't even be on the fucking field. Y'all can use and abuse his ass, every play on offense. They playing Daddy Ball over there, putting their sorry ass kids in the game as starters, when they shouldn't even be on the field in the first place. Take advantage of that shit."

He was telling me shit that wasn't even on the film. He was *dying* to still play. I lifted my hand, and Quick clasped it.

"Thanks, homie," I told him.

"Do what I told you," Quick said, nodding.

"I will," I said, nodding. "I'mma head on to the crib. I'mma get with y'all later."

"All right, my nigga," Quick said, exchanging handshakes.

Me and Dirty, and then me and Ishmael, and finally me and Rasheed all exchanged hugs and handshakes. I walked off, heading home. My thoughts shifted from SAT's, and Friday's game, to Quick. I went from feeling sorry for myself, to thinking about how fortunate I was to still be able to play. Life dealt us shitty hands, and dealt some of us even shittier hands. I had no right to complain about my life, because I still had the ability to make it better.

# **Chapter Eight**

Saturday came quick, I rose, and headed out the door to meet Adanna. It was the one day a week that we could both get away and spend time together. It was the day we sat aside to relax and chill, and just hold each other. We had a special meeting place. It was on a small hill high above the main rail yard. It was a place that meant so much to each of us, as it was the place of leaving.

We would lay on a blanket, picnic, watch the trains pull out, and dream that we were on board. Where it was going, we didn't care, we let out imaginations run wild. We dreamed of a snow filled Alaska, where the sun never truly sat, of a lake filled Minnesota, where we would live in a log cabin and fish for food, and chop wood and build fires for warmth. Our imagination had taken us to Oregon, where we ran through tall forest while being soaked by gentle rain showers, we had gone to California, where we walked on Venice Beach and watched the skate boarders perform unimaginable tricks and feats that defied gravity. We went to New York, where we were dazzled by the bright lights of Time Square. We went to Memphis and took in the music on Beale Street, and we had thrown beads from the balconies in New Orleans during Mardi Gras. We sat high above that train yard, and we left Houston, and we dreamed of a better life, a life that we would build together. I was anxious to get to her, I was anxious to see where we would go today.

On the way to the train depot, was the hood store, where to my surprise, the homies were already posted up and hustling. It was as if they had never left, as if they never slept. It was deja vu, they were a constant presence, and everyday, must have looked just like the previous one. I thought my life monotonous, their days must have seemed like a continuum from years ago. They, like so many others in the hood, were living ground hogs day. I couldn't live like that, I couldn't imagine the thought of my entire existence being the hood, the corner, hustling. It would be suffocating. I was determined to get out, I was determined to not be one of them. As much as I loved my homeboys, I wanted more.

Quick lifted his hands into the air. "What up, my nigga?"

"What up?" I asked, lifting my hands in the air as well.

"You ready?"

"Always!" I shouted back.

I stood at the corner, ready to cross the street and kick the breeze at the hood store with them for a few moments. My crossing was halted by a car that pulled up to the stop sign just in front of me. I didn't see the passenger side of the vehicle, but I did see the homies reactions. They scrambled. All except Quick, who was wheelchair bound. He pulled out his weapon and the shooting commenced.

I hit the ground.

The sound of the gunfire sent sharp, thunderous booms throughout the hood. I had never heard anything so loud, so deafening. Sure, I had heard gunfire before, it was almost a constant in the hood, but I was always inside the house when it went off. Today, I had gotten caught in the middle of it, and my ears were paying the price.

I can't describe the sound to you except to say that it was ear splitting. It sounded louder than a lightening strike. It sounded as if the air around me was one giant sheet being ripped apart. The air was heavy, as if the discharge of the weapons were filling the air with gunpowder. At it was. The acrid smell of gunpowder filled my lungs. It was a sweet smell, like someone was burning some species of sweet wood. But their was nothing delicious or nutritious about the lead that was flying through the air. I could hear bullet striking the blue Impala in front of me, and I could even hear the sounds of the bullets flying over my head and striking the wall of the building behind me. The constant violent ripping sound of the air being torn apart was eventually supplanted by the sound of squealing tires. I could see in my peripheral vision the car racing away. And although it seemed like the gun battle had lasted an eternity, I knew that it hadn't. It was over, just as quickly as it had began, and now, we were left to deal with the aftermath. My ringing ears left me daze and confused, and I found myself struggling to gain my bearings and get up off of the concrete. I placed my fingers inside of my ears and wiggled them around in an effort to stop the ringing. Next, I ran my hand over my body, checking to see if I had been hit. I didn't feel like I had been, but I guess it was just something that humans did. My next thoughts were of my homie Quick. I knew that he couldn't get down, he couldn't duck, he couldn't run, he couldn't hide. I was hesitant to look to the place where he was before the shooting began. I just knew that I would find his wheelchair tipped over, with him lying on the ground in a pool of blood.

Slowly, I rose. I dusted myself off, and then peered across the street toward the store, the place where my homies had been chilling before the shooting started. Quick's wheelchair was there, but it wasn't overturned, and he was sitting in it. A smile was spread across his face, and his still smoking handgun was sitting in his laps.

"You all right, homie?" Quick asked, shouting across the street.

A smile spread across my face. I was happy that he was okay. I was happy that we were all okay. Dirty was standing and smiling as well.

"I'm cool," I said, shouting back.

"Old bitch ass niggaz from the 5th!" Quick shouted.

"I'mma teach them hoes a lesson!" Dirty said, nodding. "They gone learn tonight!"

I walked to where Quick and Dirty were, and I shook hands and each of them in turn. I held Quick's a little longer than normal.

"I'm good, home boy," Quick said, reassuring me. "What you doing out? Y'all fools got film today?"

I shook my head. "Naw, we gonna do film on Monday morning. I'm heading to meet up with Adanna."

"All right," Quick said, shaking my hand again. "You betta get ya ass outta here. Them folks a be here in a minute."

We could all hear the sirens in the distance. Quick handed his gun and dope to Dirty, who carried it into the store so that the clerk could hide it behind the counter for them.

"I'mma get with you later!" I said, raising my fist and

starting off.

"Be careful, homeboy!" Quick shouted, lifting a fist in unity as well. He wheeled off the curb, and headed down the street. I turned, and continued on to my destination. Yesterday, there had been shooting, today there had been shooting, and more likely than not, tomorrow there would be shooting in the hood. Everyday, was the same. There had to be something else, some better. There had to be another life out there. I just had to get to it.

*****

When I got to the hill overlooking the rail yard, Adanna was already there. She had everything set up. Our picnic blanket was spread out on the ground, and she was seated on top of the small cooler that she brought to hold our drinks and sandwiches. She completed her text and peered up at me from her phone.

"Are you okay?"

Apparently bad news in the hood traveled fast.

"Yeah," I said, nodding. "I'm all right."

"I heard they were shooting at the store?" she asked, peered up at me. Even through her dark sunglasses, I knew that her eyes were fixated on me, trying to gauge my face for the truth.

Again, I nodded. "Yeah, some fools from The Nickel."

"You were there?" she asked.

I knew that she already knew the answer to the question.

"I was across the street," I answered. "They were shooting toward the store."

Adanna shook her head. "Fools. Blacks killing other Blacks. And for what? For what?"

Her British accent became less pronounced and more Nigerian when she became excited or angry.

"It's all because that's what their minds have been programmed to do!" Adanna continued. "They look in the mirror, and they hate themselves, and so they look at one another, and they hate them as well! They have the spirit of this country in them, and lack the spirit of their ancestors, and the knowledge of their history!"

I laughed and lifted my hands. "All right, calm down. Calm down, baby."

"This country, was set up, to keep the Black race subservient," Adanna huffed. "It was all about keeping the slaves in bondage, and the rich, White, landowners on top. And when King George wanted them to pay more taxes, they rebelled against him as well. They want their money, and their slaves, and they want to feel good about themselves."

"Are we going to have this conversation today?" I asked. I

knew, that she would rant and rave for half an hour if I didn't try to stop it now.

"You've never been to the Capitol Building in Washington, D.C., St. Claire," she said. "I have. You should see the images on the wall. You should see the friezes around the Capitol Dome, depicting the history of this country. It's a ludicrous farce. America's idea of itself, indeed!"

The fact that she called me St. Claire told me that she was upset. The fact that her accent was reverting back to it's natural British state told me that she was calming down a little. It was my chance to change the conversation.

"I saw my father at the game," I said softly.

She turned and faced me. "Did you speak with him?"

I shook my head. "I saw him in the crowd. I turned, and I ran into the locker room after the touchdown. I looked for him after the game, but I couldn't find him."

Adanna caressed the side of my face. "You have to talk to him. You have to reach him. He needs you. The two of you need each other."

I nodded. I had tried to reach him. But it seemed like I was trying to reach the unreachable.

"I call to him, and he just rushes away," I told her. "He won't speak to me. He won't say anything."

"He's hurting," Adanna said. "His whole life came crashing down. Everything that he had, everything that he knew, was gone in an instant. That would break even the strongest people in this world. He lost the woman that he loved more than life itself."

I thought about my father, and about my mother. I remembered them together. They had loved one another since kindergarten, my father would say. I could see him placing a Cameo, or Al Green, or Barry White, or Commodores, or Luther Vandross, or Earth, Wind, and Fire record on his old record player, pulling my tired Mother close, and dancing until she became butter in his arms. No matter how tired Momma was from working all day at the hospital, my Dad could put a smile on her face. They way he looked at her, and they way she looked at him, it seemed as if they were the only people in the universe. Sometimes I felt that way when Adanna and I were together. Sometimes, it felt like it was just me, her, and the stars in the sky. I could lay on the picnic blanket, stare off into the night sky, and just hold her forever. And I know, that what I felt, was only a piece of what my Dad felt toward my Mother.

"I worry about you," Adanna said, out of the blue.

"Why?" I asked.

She shrugged. "I worry about you, when you're not with me. I worry about you walking home, I worry about you constantly."

"For what?"

"Because you're young, and Black, and you're a target."

I swallowed hard and closed my eyes. I thought that we had moved past this conversation.

"I'm okay," I told her. "I'm going to be okay."

"I know you are," she said, smiling. Adanna laid back on the blanket. "You're going to be all right, because you have me."

I laughed.

"We are going to finish school, St. Claire," she said, without looking at me. "We are going to finish school, and we are going to go to college. And you are going to go off and be some big American football star, and I am going to go to Oxford, and study law, and you will marry some White bitch and have little half breed babies."

I laughed out loud.

"Probably one of those Kardashian bitches," Adanna said, rolling her eyes.

"They're all taken," I said, kissing her on her cheek.

"I'm going to get you through school, and then, you're going to run and marry one of them," she said laughing.

"If I marry a White girl, she's going to have an ass like pow!" I said, spreading my arms wide.

"You marry a White girl, and you're going to hear a pow all right," Adanna said smiling. "But first, you'll hear a snip, because I'm going to cut it off first."

I pulled my baby close, and held her in my arms. She liked to tease me, but she knew, just like I knew, that there was no other woman on this planet that I was going to be with. She was my heart. I don't know how, or why, or exactly when I fell in love with her, all I knew was that I was madly in love with her. She was my air.

Caleb Alexander

# **<u>Chapter Nine</u>**

The best thing I could say about Mr. Stock's class, was that it only lasted an hour. It was English Lit, and he was one of those teachers who had given up a long time ago. He even stood in front of the class at the beginning of the year and told us that most of could barely speak English, so he wasn't going to torture us by making us read some classic Victorian or Elizabethan bullshit that we wouldn't understand, and would forget about as soon as we walked outta his class. And so, he usually spent most of the period sitting behind his desk surfing the internet, checking out chicks on Instagram and messaging his friends on Facebook. He didn't give a fuck, and so we didn't give a fuck either. And in most of the people at Booker T, that made him a cool teacher. I thought of him that way at first, and then Adanna ranted and raved about it for hours and got me to understand that what he was doing was some bullshit. He was setting us up to fail. Mr. Stock wasn't cool, he just didn't expect shit out of us. In his mind we were all headed straight to prison or the cemetery.

"Running Back Baby!" Flip shouted, as he entered into the classroom.

"RBB!" Dice shouted, as he strolled in just behind Flip.

The three of us exchanged handshakes, and Flip and Dice pulled a pair of desk closer to where I was seated.

"What up, my nigga?" Flip asked.

Flip was one of those cats who was hood happy. He was happy to be in the hood, he was happy being from the hood, and was just happy to be. All he wanted was to just exist. In fact, that was how he earned his nickname. He was constantly asking the dope boys in the hood to flip his money. He didn't want to come up, he didn't want to score bigger and bigger amounts, he just wanted to flip his money so that he could have a little extra for beer and weed, and some fresh clothes and kicks every once in a while. He was happy with that and no more. He could hustle with the best of them, and many of the homies in the hood who were on top offered to front him and help him come up, but he just wasn't interested. All he wanted was a flip.

My dude Dice came upon his name the same way. He was a

hustler, but unlike the dope boys, his main hustle was gambling, and his choice game was craps. He could shoot dice like nobody else in the hood. Everyone accused him of using fake dice, loaded dice, and dice with magnets, and all kinds of other tricks, but the simple fact of the matter was, he was lucky. He was a helluva crap shooter, and he could seven-eleven the biggest ballers in the hood until he left the game with everything they walked in with. I just hoped that Dice's luck never ran out. I knew many a hood cat who had caught a bullet because a sore loser accused them of burning the dice. Losing ten, twelve, fifteen, twenty, and even fifty thousand dollars on a dice game was no laughing matter. And the fact that Dice liked to talk shit while he took their money didn't help either. I hoped that he made enough to get up out the hood before he ended up on First 48 with a bullet in the back of his head.

"So, what the deal on the game?" Dice asked, sucking on a lollipop. It was his trademark.

"What do you mean?" I asked.

"What's the line?" Dice asked.

"Line?" I asked. "Ain't no line!"

"Are y'all gonna win?" Dice asked.

"Yeah," I said, nodding. I wasn't one hundred percent sure, but I was confident that we could win.

"By how much?" Dice asked.

I shrugged.

"Let's say, you make it two touchdowns," Dice said, leaning back and pulling a wad of money out of his pocket. "You guarantee me a win by two touchdowns, no more, no less, and we can make some serious money, Baby Boy!"

Flip nudged Dice in his ribs. "He ain't fixin to shave no points for your crooked ass!"

Dice held up his money. "There's some big money in it for you."

"Man, don't listen to this nigga!" Flip said, waving his hand and dismissing Dice's offer. "Man, just do your thing. Get as many touchdowns as you can."

"Nigga, what's the deal?" Dice asked. "A win is a win!"

"This man is trying to get a scholarship!" Flip told him. "He ain't fixing to fuck up his scholarships for your two bit hustling ass!"

"Two bit?" Dice asked. "Your ass constantly falling off, and you calling my shit two bit?"

"Man, they pretty tough," I said, stopping their argument. If I didn't they would trade barbs with each other for the remainder of the class. "Who knows, we might win by a touchdown, or maybe even a field goal or an extra point. They ain't playing this year."

"Yeah, but y'all ain't playing neither, my nigga!" Dice said. "C'mon, my nigga, I know you can blow them fools out. I just need you to let me know by how much, and then make it happen."

I shrugged. "I don't know how much, or even if we gone win. Ain't no guarantees. They good."

Dice leaned back in his seat disappointed. He stuffed his wad of money back inside of his pocket.

"Yo, Mr. Stock, can I go to the restroom?" Dice asked.

"Nigga, you ain't going to no restroom!" Big Deebo said, calling him out from the back of the classroom. Everybody in the class laughed.

"Mind your muthafucking business, old square ass nigga!" Dice shouted.

Deebo stood.

"Nigga, I'll shoot you!" Dice shouted.

Deebo headed to where Dice was seated.

Dice started laughing. "Deebo, go on! Quit playing, wit yo old Cro-magnon, caveman looking ass!"

Everyone in the class laughed. Deebo lifted Dice's desk, with Dice sitting inside of it. "Bitch, I'll toss you out the window!"

"Deebo, quit playing, nigga!" Dice shouted, holding on to his desk.

Deebo lowered the desk, dropping it the last few feet,

causing a thunderous crash. Mr. Stock didn't even look up from his internet chat session. Dice rose from the desk and headed for the door. It was only then when Mr. Stock looked up.

"Where are you going?" Mr. Stock asked.

"I told you, I gotta hit the john," Dice told him.

Mr. Stock peered up at the clock on the wall in the back of the classroom, and then back at Dice. "Can't you hold it for a little while."

Dice grabbed the front of his pants. "Man, I gotta piss."

Mr. Stock shrugged. "You get caught in the hallway, it's on you. They ask me, I'mma say you skipped my class."

"What?" Dice asked, smacking his lips. "Man, that's some punk ass shit."

Mr. Stock shrugged. "Why would you care? It's not like you would show up for detention anyway. Just tell 'em you got locked up on the weekend, and couldn't make detention."

Oooohs and ahhhs went through the classroom.

"Mr. Stock," Dice said, again grabbing his privates.

"What?" Mr. Stock asked.

"Fuck you!" Dice said, pointing his middle finger.

"You'll probably really be in jail this weekend," Mr. Stock told him.

"Naw, I'll be at your crib, making sure your wife never

fucks with another White boy again!" Dice said, walking out of the classroom.

Mr. Stock grabbed an eraser off of his desk, and threw it at Dice. The eraser hit the door, just as Dice was slamming it shut.

"You little punk!" Mr. Stock shouted. "Don't you fucking come back into my classroom!"

It was another day at Booker T. I was surprised that they didn't actually exchange blows. That's the way it usually happened. The teacher and the student would exchange blows, and depending how things worked out, either the teacher would quit, get fired, or retire, or the student would get kicked out and maybe even arrested and charged with assault. We even had student pulled pistols out on teachers, and teachers pull pistols out on students. Booker T was the Wild West as far as high school went. It was the lowest on the totem pole, and nobody gave a shit. The state took us over for a little while, but that was just to prevent the Department of Education from taking us over. And as soon as our test scores ticked up a percentage point, the state tossed the district back the keys, and said good riddance. The only people who cared about Booker T, were the teachers who needed to keep it open in order to get a paycheck, and the poor hoods that it served, because the next closest high school was in Pearland, and no one wanted to travel that far to go to school. If there was any hope for Booker T, it came from the football team.  It was our championship football team, and our all Black band that was going to make people pay attention to us.  It was our football team who was letting people know that we're still here, and that we still had fight in us.  It was our football team that was bringing pride to our community, and making everyone feel better about themselves, and where they were from. We were the hope of the school, and the last hope for our long dead community.

# **Chapter Ten**

I needed to clear my head. We had a tough game coming up, and the last thing I wanted, was to run out of the stadium and leave my team hanging in the wind. And so I did what I always did when I needed to think, I went for a jog.

Jogging in H-Town this time of the year meant humidity, and it also meant heat. Football season in the rest of the country meant cool weather, or at least mild temperatures. The beginning of football season in Texas still meant heat, and sweat, and sometime 118 degree heat on the football field after a particularly hot day. And if it's one think that the heat brought out, it's people. People left the inside of their homes and ventured outside in the evening to get some fresh air, and to escape the sauna like temperatures inside of their homes. At least those who couldn't afford air conditioners. And in Acres Homes, that was pretty much most of us. We were still on 'fan in the window' status in my hood.

Everybody was out and about. People were sitting on their front porches, kids were playing in the front yard, or in the street. Some playing football, some hooping, a few with real basketball goals with no nets, while others used banged up metal garbage cans. A few families had turned on the garden hoses and were letting the kids cool themselves off by playing in the water. This was my hood, and even though we didn't have much, we made do with what we did have. And if it's one thing I can say about Acres Homes, it was that we were still a community. Everyone knew everyone, and everyone looked out for everyone else's kids. If you needed some eggs, you could run next door and borrow some, and everyone else could do the same. Milk, bread, eggs, sugar, a pack of Kool-Aide, those were the biggies. We also shared lawn mowers, weed eaters, rides to the grocery store, a mistrust of the police, and a desire to make it through life. That was what most hoods were about, I suspect, people just doing whatever they had to do, to get by. Even though it was all good in the hood, I still wanted more, I still saw myself doing more, being more, reaching for something more. I stared at my neighborhood, and I knew in my heart, that there was more to be had than this, I knew that I had a different destiny than just being a standout football star in the hood. I didn't want to be one of those cats sitting on the porch, reminiscing about the glory days. Something inside told me that these were not my glory days, and the best parts of my life were yet to come.

I jogged and jogged, and soon I found myself picking up speed. My jog picked up in speed, as my thoughts turned to my mother, and then to my father. I was running. I don't know if I was running toward my mother, away from my past, chasing my father, or away from my hood. I just knew that I had started running.

My mother was strong. She had been one of those loving types, who gave and gave and gave, and when you thought she had no more to give, she gave some more. I could see her smile. That's the one thing that I could always see clearly. I remember her always smiling. I always saw her wearing her nurse's scrubs, and I always saw her with her hair cut short, with that big, wide, loving smile on her face. It was a smile that told me that she loved me, and in her eyes, I could do no wrong. I was her baby, and her smile let me know it.

My father on the other hand, kept most of his smiles reserved for my mother. It was as if his smiles were locked in some secret chest, that only she could open. He stared at my mother, like they were the only two people on Earth. He loved me as well, but didn't verbalize it as often as she did. I could probably count the number of times he said it to me on one hand. And though he rarely said it, he showed it daily. He showed it by teaching me football, by tossing the ball with me out in the yard, or by working with me on my hand offs. He took me to football games, he helped me with my homework, cooked dinner for me every night while my mother was at work. I remember my father showing me how to ride a bicycle, I remember him teaching me how to ride without training wheels, and then bandaging my knees or elbows whenever I fell. I remember him being my football coach when I played little league, and then consoling me after a loss. He never said it, but he show it in so many ways. We didn't have a lot of money in the NOLA, but we had each other. And I would trade anything to have my life back the way it was before Kartrina. I imagine many others would as well. If there had been no Katrina, then my mother would still be alive. If there had been no Katrina, Augustine would still be alive. So many people died that night, and for the survivors, the ones that had to bury their loved ones, bury their dreams, and bury the lives that they had before, Katrina had been worse than death. For people like my father, people who lost everything they owned, everything they built, their life partners, it was even worse than that. Shifting through the rubble for pictures of the people you love, for remnants of the life you had built together, for shards of a fractured past that had been whisked away by a stormy thief in the night, had to be the hardest thing in the world. I knew that I needed my father, but at the same time, I could understand in a way what had happened to him. The foundations of his mind had been ripped away, like the foundation of so many houses in the NOLA. I didn't blame him, and I wasn't angry with him, I just needed him.

My run through the hood led me to the hood store, where I stopped to get something to drink. I was sweating like a South Carolina slave, and I needed some Gatorade to replenish my system. As usual the homies were hanging out. The heat and humidity, also brought out the rock boys in the hood.

"My nigga!" Quick shouted, lifted his arms into the air.

"Hold on, I'mma grab some Gatorade," I told him.

Quick wheeled himself into the store and up to the counter. He pulled some money out of his pocket and tossed it onto the counter. "Abdul, this is for my homeboy. Let 'em get whatever he wants. I'll get the change from you later. And you better not try to cheat me you crooked ass muthafucka."

The Arab store clerk smiled. "I won't cheat you. Why you always accusing me of cheating you?"

"I know how you muthafuckas are!" Quick said, smiling. He wheeled himself out of the store.

I took my Gatorade to the counter.

"That's it?" Abdul asked. "Get some more. Get some Skittles."

"Naw, I'm good," I told him.

"Your friend, he already paid for it," Abdul said, lifting a bag of candy from the counter trying to tempt me.

"I'm good," I said, smiling.

I walked out the store to where Quick was hanging out. The usual suspects were all around. Somebody was banging some Screw out of their car's stereo system. Dirty pulled up in a Impala sitting on some thirty-inch rims, and hoped out with bags of food. Half the bags were from Timmy Chan's, and the other half were from A Fish Place.

"Gimme my shit, nigga!" Quick shouted.

"Wait, old bitch ass nigga!" Dirty shouted. "Either that, or come and get it. I ain't serving your ass like I'm your bitch."

"You are my bitch!" Quick said, laughing.

The homies tore through the bags looking for their orders. Dirty handed quick his two orders. One from Timmy Chan's, and the other from A Fish Place. Quick handed me a Styrofoam container from A Fish Place.

"You can have my fish and shrimp, homie," Quick said, peering up at me.

I waved off his offer. "Naw, I'm good."

"Here, nigga!" Quick said, offering up the food again. "We ain't about that shy ass shit. Eat, my nigga!"

"I'm good," I said, again waving off his offer. "I already

had some grub. Besides, I'm just passing through."

"Granny hooked it up?" Dirty asked with a smile. "What she cook?"

"Some gumbo," I told them.

Dirty rubbed his stomach. "Damn, I should have went over to your crib and ate."

"For real, my nigga!" Quick said, sitting the platter down in his lap. He placed his Styrofoam Timmy Chan platter on top of the fish platter and opened it up. He pulled the plastic wrapping off of his plastic utensils and started shoveling chicken and fried rice into his mouth.

"So, who y'all got next?" Quick asked.

"The Woodlands," I answered.

Quick smiled and shook his head. "That's some bullshit. They trying to knock y'all out the box early."

I returned his smile and nodded. "They trying to take our spirit, make us lose early. And then they figure that the no pass- no play rule will fuck us up too."

"They counting on you niggaz to fail," Dirty added.

"Man, you got to tell them niggas not to be bullshitting, and to make sure they keep they grades and shit up," Quick said, chewing his food.

"They figure that if we can lose a few games, get hit by no

pass-no play, then we'll be in trouble when district play starts," I told them. "I'm pretty sure they hoping for some injuries as well. If we lose any of these pre-district games, they gonna knock us out of our number two ranking in the state's polls."

Quick shook his head. "Damn, they really trying to fuck over y'all."

"As usual," Dirty said, nodding. "White folks fucking over Black folks. As usual."

We all laughed.

"They soft on the inside," Quick said. "But even more than that, they slow on the outside. At least compared to you. You get to the outside. Make them beat you to the outside. Have your tight end lead that corner away from you, and then hit it. It'll be you and the safety, and you can make a highlight reel off of that fool every play."

We all laughed. Quick held out his hand and I gave him five.

"You can have a field day on them slow ass White boys," Dirty added.

"What the fuck you know about football?" Quick asked, peering up at Dirty. "Old drop out ass nigga!"

Again, everyone around broke into laughter.

We were all so busy laughing, and most of them so busy

eating, that none of us saw the Ford Explorer rolling up on us. It was full of Black faces. Dirty was the first one to peep them.

"What the fuck?" Dirty asked, squinting, and trying to make out the vehicles occupants. He went for his pistol. "It's a hit!"

Everyone gathered around tossed their food and went for their weapons. And since I didn't have any food to toss, I hit the ground.

Gunfire erupted all around. The loud explosions from the numerous weapons going off around me, was ear splitting to the point of being almost deafening. I placed my hands over my ears, and the sparks from the bullets flew off of the concrete all around me. Shell casings by the dozens fell on top of me and all around the spot where I was laying. The thunderous raport from the guns played havoc on my ear drums and my brain, causing me to become disoriented slightly. I rolled over, and I could see the occupants of the SUV firing out of their window. I rolled over in the other direction with my fingers still in my ears, and I could see Quick firing his forty caliber Glock. The black handgun spit smoke and flames from its barrel, as he squeezed the trigger in rapid succession, sending massive rounds towards the occupants of the SUV. Dirty and the others had taken cover, and were returning fire from covered positions, while Quick remain next to me in his wheelchair, firing away. It was as if he were determined not to hit the ground, not to roll away and seek cover. It was clear that he was over me, covering me, protecting me, yelling, shouting, firing his weapon, like a wild banshee.

Soon, I heard the squealing of tires, and I saw out of the peripheral that the Explorer was speeding away. My homies came out from their positions, raced into the street, and kept firing at the vehicle, as it hit the corner and disappeared.

"Fucking bitches!" Quick shouted.

"Old bitch ass niggaz!" Dirty shouted.

I rose, and shook my head. I was still disoriented, and my disorientation caused me to waver slightly, before catching my balance.

"You all right, fool?" Dirty asked, grabbing my arm and steadying me.

I nodded, placed my fingers inside of my ears and wiggled them around.

"That's them ho ass niggaz from the Northside!" Quick said, angrily. "Them ho ass niggaz rolling with them niggaz from the Fifth!"

"They want some, they can get some too!" Dirty said, nodding.

The war between Fifth Ward and Acres Homes had spread.

Third Ward and South Park had joined in, on the side of Fifth Ward. While South Acres had linked up with my hood.

Dirty reloaded his weapon. "They call that bitch The Bloody Nickel, well, that bitch is fixin to be real bloody tonight."

Quick and Dirty slapped hands. They were about to go and handle some business. My thoughts weren't on riding or getting revenge, but rather on them coming back and getting revenge for my hood getting revenge. And then my home boys would have to ride again, and then they would have to come back and retaliate. Where would it end, I wondered? When did it stop? I knew that it was easy to get caught up in that type of cycle, and I was determined not to. I loved my hood, and I loved my home boys, but I wanted something different. I wanted to live my life another way.

"Bitch ass niggaz made me waste my food!" Quick proclaimed.

The rest of the home boys broke into laughter. It relieved a little bit of the tension in the air. In reality, all of the home boys had their blood running, and the tension in the air was still thicker than a cup of syrup. They were ready to ride and kill, and you were either with them, or you weren't. Walking away right now, could have possibly sent the wrong message. Walking away would have made them think I was scared to ride, like I was a coward, or like I wasn't down for them or the hood. It could have even caused bad blood, an argument, anything. And seeing as how they were all armed, and I wasn't, and how they were all in a mood to kill, things wouldn't have gone in my favor. I was more scared of walking away than of riding. But still, I knew what I needed to do.

"Man, I'm outta here," I said, leaning over and embracing Quick.

Quick wrapped his arms around me for a couple of seconds. "All right, my nigga! Yeah, we all need to roll out. One time will be here in a little while."

"I can hear then hoes sirens right now," Dirty said.

I knew what they were doing. They were giving me the cover I needed to leave. And I knew what Quick had done for me while I was lying on the ground covering my ears like a scared little girl. If he had left me, I would have been an easy target. But he didn't, he stayed with me, he protected me, he made himself a target, and he spit lead back at the people shooting at us. It's hard to shoot directly at a person shooting right back at you. We were all humans, and none of us wanted to die. And Quick had made sure that I would be going to a football game on Friday, instead of a morgue that evening. I owed him my life.

I held up the deuces, turned, and walked away. I knew that once again, I had been given a chance. I had been spared a few times in New Orleans, I had been spared from Katrina, and I had been spared a couple of times in Houston. And with this latest chance, it only reaffirmed that I had to do something with my life. I owed so many people so much, and I knew that I couldn't let them down. I owed my Mother, my Grandmother, Adanna, Augustine, Quick, and a few others. I was determined to make it out of the hood. I was determined to do something with my life to make a difference. And until I knew what that was, I was going to use the gift that God had given me. I was going to put a football in my hands, and I was going to run.

Baby Baller                              Caleb Alexander

# **Chapter Eleven**

I woke up the next morning, and I felt like I had been through a world war. Everything seemed surreal. I couldn't blame it on my ringing ears, or the tone that resonated between my ears for much of the previous evening. I had my senses back for the most part, but still, it seemed as if the world was moving in slow motion. As if we were all stuck inside of some great, invisible glob of molasses. I climbed out of bed and headed down the hall and into the kitchen to fix me a bowl of cereal. I had been up for some time, but had lain in bed, hesitant to climb out and face another day. I was anxious to move forward, but time was an enemy at this point. My days were long, and I was anxious to begin a new chapter in my life. Any chapter, as long as it was different from the one I was stuck in at the moment.

To my surprise, Big Momma was there, finishing up

breakfast.

"What are you doing here?" I asked, rubbing the sleep out of my eyes.

"I just thought I'd fix us a little breakfast this morning," she said with a smile.

"I thought today was the day you go under the bridge with the church to feed those homeless people?" I asked.

"It is," Big Momma said, placing some pancakes on a plate, and setting them on the table. "But I thought I'd have some breakfast with you this morning instead."

I knew a set up when I saw it. Something was on her mind. I had a suspicion about what it was. The news of yesterday's shooting had not only went through the community like a wild fire, but even made the evening news. Furthermore, the home boys from my hood had apparently handled their business later that night, because the news also reported a major shooting in the Fifth Ward, with multiple casualties. No one was stupid, and the entire city knew that the two hoods were beefing. I wondered if my grandmother knew that I had been at the store at the time of the shooting.

I sat down at the table, and Big Momma placed a bottle of Mrs. Buttersworth pancake syrup on the table in front of me. She also placed a plate of hotlink sausages on the table as well. Big

Momma seated herself across from me, and I reached for one of the still smoking sausages.

"I don't think so!" Big Momma said, slapping my hand. "You better say grace first!"

I smiled sheepishly, interlaced my fingers, closed my eyes and bowed my head. "Lord, thank You for this food we are about to receive. In Jesus' name we pray. Amen."

Grandma opened on eye and peered over the table at me. "That's it? That was a quickie."

"I'm hungry, and I got to get to school," I told her. Again, I reached for a sausage.

"Always make time for the Lord, St. Claire," Big Momma told me. "You always thank Him for His blessings. He don't have to put food on the table, and He don't have to place His mighty hands over you and keep you safe."

I knew where the conversation was going.

"Been a lot of stuff going on in the neighborhood lately," Big Momma continued. She began fixing her plate. "People shooting, and getting shot up. Just a bunch of craziness. Glad you safe."

I nodded. "I'm safe."

"Ain't nobody after you, is there?" Big Momma asked.

I smiled and shook my head. "No, Ma'am."

"How are things going in school?"

"Pretty good," I said, nodding.

"School pictures are coming up."

I nodded.

"Have you already signed up to take them?"

I shook my head. "We don't need to waste no money on that kind a stuff."

"St. Clair Baptiste! Have you lost your damn mind! Don't you worry about my pocket book, do you hear me?"

I didn't say anything.

"I said, do you hear me?"

"Yes, Ma'am."

"You don't know what I got, or what I've been saving up for, understand? This is your senior year, and I've been waiting my entire life to put a picture on my living room wall, of my grandbaby in his cap and gown, and you are not going to deny me that pleasure! Do you understand me?"

I smiled. "Yes, Ma'am."

"Sign up to take your senior pictures!" Big Momma ordered. "And you go to JC Penny's, and you get sized for your class ring."

"Big Momma…"

She lifted her hand stopping me in mid-sentence." It's already paid for. All you got to do, is take the receipt, and let them size your finger! Do you hear me?"

"Yes, Ma'am."

"We are all right, and we are always going to be all right!"
Big Momma said, resuming her breakfast. "The Lord has my back.
Always has, and always will."

I felt bad about costing my grandmother so much money. In
fact, it made me feel lower than low. I was supposed to be easing
her burden, not becoming one.

Big Momma reached into her housecoat and pulled a wad of
money out of her bra. "I won big at bingo the other night. You
need some money?"

"Big Momma!"

"I told you, the Lord will provide." Big Momma peeled off
a couple of twenty dollar bills. "Take that pretty little girlfriend of
your to the movies or something. Get out a little. Have some fun.
Be young. There's a whole other world out there, outside of a
football stadium."

I rose, leaned over the table, and kissed my Big Momma on
her cheek. "Thank you, Big Momma. I love you so much."

"I know. And I love you."

I wolfed down the remainder of my food, and turned to head
back to my room.

"Claire," Big Momma said, softly.

"Ma'am?"

"You be careful out there, you hear me?"

I knew that she had known more than she had let on. I nodded. "Yes, Ma'am."

"I can't lose you, baby."

"You won't, Big Momma. I promise."

"So many times, I've seen young boys get so close to finishing school, and then they drop out, or get hurt, or go to prison," Big Momma said, rising from her chair. "Don't be one of them, baby. It's when you get so close, that the devil's work increases. You walk with Jesus, and you keep The Lord with you at all times. And you don't let nobody or nothing lead you into temptation. You go on, and you make me proud, and you make your momma proud. You don't get caught up in all of these worldly things, baby. You have the anointing on you."

"Yes, Ma'am."

It was a message that my Big Momma constantly gave me. I had the anointing on me. She had been telling me this since I was a child. She swore up and down that God was going to make me a preacher. That God was going to use me for something special. Prepare yourself to be an instrument of God, she would always tell me. The Man Upstairs had a plan for me. She believed it, and most of the time, she had me believing it. That was Big Momma's power. The ability to instill faith, where there was none, to increase it, where it was lacking, to give hope, when all seemed hopeless. Big Momma swore that I had the anointing on me, but if there was anybody who had a direct line to the Man Upstairs, it was her. She was the one who had played the piano in church for over thirty years, she was the one who had sang in a church choir since she was five, and she was the one who ran down to the jail house to administer the gospel to the prisoners. Big Momma tithed what little she had, she stayed up under the bridge feeding the homeless, and volunteering in the shelters, taking food to elderly people who didn't have any, and giving rides to the grocery store to people without any transportation. She was the one who kept a worn Bible by her bed that she read at least three times a day. I, on the other hand, had big time issues with the Man Upstairs. I had doubted Him, cursed Him, challenged Him, and disobeyed Him in every way possible after the death of my mother. Despite Big Momma's insistence that I allow our tragedy to bring me closer to Him, I allowed it to tear me away. I was mad at God, and I still had issues, along with plenty of questions. Why take my mother, and allow all of these killers running around town to live? Until we reconciled that, I wasn't really trying to get too close, and I definitely wasn't going to be any kind of preacher. And because of my love and respect for Big Momma, I kept all of my thoughts about God to myself.

"I don't want to be late," I said, kissing Big Momma on her cheek. I walked back to my room to get dressed, and grab my book bag and gym bag. Football practice was going to be tough today. We had to get ready for the big game against The Woodlands.

\*\*\*\*\*

I arrived on campus, thinking I was going to make to my first period athletics class on time. Mr. Davis had other ideas. He cornered me in the hallway.

"Mr. Baptiste!"

Instantly, I became deflated. Teachers and school administrators loved to call a person by their last name when they were in trouble. I wondered what I was in trouble for now.

"Yes, sir?" I asked, as I stopped and turned to face him.

"A word, Mr. Baptiste?"

I exhaled, adjusted my back pack that was slung over my shoulder, and walked to where Mr. Davis was standing. He waited a few seconds for the hallway to clear.

"I heard there was an incident in the neighborhood yesterday," Mr. Davis started off. "Want to talk about it?"

I shrugged. "Nothing to talk about. It didn't concern me."

Mr. Davis stared at me and nodded. "I hear that you were right in the thick of the action."

"I was at the store, and the incident happened at the store," I said, hoping to clarify my role."

Mr. Davis crossed his arm and eyed me. "Sometimes, were think that we have something to prove, when in reality, we don't have to prove a damn thing to anybody but ourselves."

"I never said that I had nothing to prove," I told him.

Mr. Davis shook his head. "You don't have to prove that you're still down, son. You don't have to punch in a hood clock, or put in a requisite number of hours to show your loyalty."

I shifted my weight to one side. "What are you talking about?"

"You were hanging out at a place you shouldn't have been."

*"In my own neighborhood?"*

Mr. Davis nodded. "Yeah, *in your own neighborhood.* Especially when the spot in your neighborhood is *the* drug spot, and especially when that spot is frequented by cats who aren't doing anything with their lives. You have a choice, St. Claire. You can get caught up, you can catch a bullet, or you can make the right decisions and do something with your life."

*"I'm not getting caught up!"* I said, turning up my palms in frustration.

"Do you know what you mean to this community?" Mr. Davis asked.

"What?" I asked. I was confused.

"Do you know how much you mean to the football team, and how much this team means to this community?" he asked.

I lowered my head and nodded. I understood. I understood clearly how much the team meant, and how much pride we brought to our hood, and the other hoods feeding in to the school.

"This team, is the best thing that has happened to this community in a long time," Mr. Davis continued. "It's brought a sense of pride, a sense of renewal, and a feeling of rejuvenation. Graffiti is being painted over, trash is being picked up, and windows are being fixed, and signs are going up saying Booker T. Washington Pride. This team, is bringing this community together, and this team can't win without you. You mean more to this school, and more to this community than you know. Think, St. Claire. Since this team started winning, how many young men have been killed in this community, by someone else from this community? You want to know the answer?"

I stared at him with a blank expression. I didn't know.

"Zero," Mr. Davis said, holding up his hand. "None, nada, zilch, zero. Not a single one. And that's because everyone is screaming about Booker T. Washington. Your life is valuable. You are *saving lives.* And if you don't want to keep your ass out of jail for your own selfish reasons, then do it for selfless reasons. Do it for the mothers who haven't had to march to the cemetery and bury their sons. Do it for all of the other young men on your team who need to win in order to get college scholarships and make it out of the hood, do it for all of the kids who are watching your every move, trying to emulate you, be you, and who dream of making it out of the neighborhood by walking the path that you are forging for them. A lot of people's hopes and dreams and futures are riding on you. *And you better not let them down.*"

I lowered my head, because I knew that everything he was saying was true. I had a lot riding on my actions. I had a lot of people looking to me, and I owed a lot of people so much. I owed my mother, my father, my grandmother, my teachers, and the entire city of New Orleans. I had to do it to strike a blow at everyone who called us refugees. I had to do it for Houston, the city who took us in and gave us a home. I had to do it for Big Momma, who believed in me, and my Momma who dreamed that I would do great things. And I would also do it for myself. I wanted a life away from here. I wanted a life with Adanna, and that life was only to be found away from her brothers. I had to survive, and I had to watch my every move. My Big Momma was right. There were so many of us who got so close to the end, only to end up a statistic. The only statistics I planned on being affiliated with, was breaking Texas high school football records.  As hard as I knew that it would be, I knew what I had to do.  I would have to walk away from hanging with the homies in the hood.  As much as I loved my homies, I knew that the choice was clear.

# Chapter Twelve

Football practice came, and my mind was flooded with thoughts from earlier in the day. It was obvious to all that I was simply going through the motions.

"Baptiste!" Coach Gaines shouted. "Get your head out of your ass! Aww, forget it! Desmond, go in!"

I exhaled, knelt, and then sat on my but with my left leg extended forward. My hamstring was feeling tight, so I decided to stretch it out. At least it would look like I was interested in practicing that day.

I stretched out my left leg, and then changed positions and stretched out my right. I rose from the ground, dusted myself off, and then continued my stretching by leaning as far to the left as I could, and then doing the same to my right. I finished up my brief stretching exercises with a quick jog in place, and a couple of sit ups. It had been enough to satiate Coach Gaines.

"Baptiste, are you ready?"

"Yes, sir," I responded.

"Get your ass in there. Run a counter."

I lifted my helmet, and placed it on my head as I jogged on to the field. I ran into the huddle. "Coach wants to run a counter."

The guys all nodded, and then headed for their positions. I lined up just behind and to the right of the quarterback. He clapped his hands, and the ball was snapped. He handed it off to me, and I raced around my blockers, heading for the corner. I shook the corner back, and then cut up field, where it was one on one with the safety. I made quick work of him with a quick shake and then a spin, causing him to get tangled up in his own legs and fall. Ooohs and Ahhs could be heard throughout the practice field. I ran into the end zone, where I jumped up and dunked the football over the field goal bars. I was quickly surrounded by my teammates on offense.

"Baptiste!" Coach Gaines shouted at the top of his lungs.

I knew that he didn't like showboating, at least in practice against our own teammates. But he had pissed me off by sending Desmond in as a starter over me at the beginning of practice. Never mind that my heart and mind wasn't in it, I was the starting running back on this team. I just wanted to remind him of that fact.

"Baptiste!" Coach Gaines shouted again. "Get your ass over here!"

I jogged to where Coach was standing. Two unfamiliar faces were standing on either side of him. Upon approaching them, I could tell who they were by the logos on their clothing. They were college scouts.

"Baptiste, this is Coach O'Malley from Notre Dame, and this is Coach Neely from Alabama."

I extended my hand, and exchanged handshakes with each of them in turn.

"How are you doing, sir?" I asked, with each greeting.

"Pretty impressive out there, son," Coach Neely said, with a deep Southern drawl.

"Thank you, sir," I told him.

"We sent you a packet, did you get it?" Coach Neely asked.

"Yes, sir," I said, nodding.

"I put my phone number in there, and told you to give me a call," Coach Neely said. "I wanted you to call me, and give me your number so that we could stay in touch. I wanted to make sure that you were interested so that I could put you on our official prospects list."

I nodded. "Thank you, sir."

"Crimson isn't his color," Coach O'Malley declared. "This

man would look fantastic where a golden dome.  Tell 'em, son.
Blue and gold is your favorite color!"

I laughed.

"Yeah, South Bend in the winter?" Coach Neely asked with
a smile.  "What's it like, a hundred below up there?"

"Better than Alabama in the summer time!" Coach
O'Malley countered.  "It's what?  A hundred and twenty degrees in
the shade?  No, this young man wants to come and run the ball for
the Fighting Irish.  Tradition,  T.V. time, a famous, powerful,
influential alumni network. "

"Tradition doesn't go any deeper than 'Bama, son!" Coach
Neely declared.  "Bear Bryant, and the 'Tide?"

"Excuse me, Coach," I told them.  I started off towards the
stands.  He was there, and even from a distance, I could tell that it
was him.  My father was sitting at the far end of the field on the
edge of one of our rickety old wooden bleachers.  It was my chance
to talk to him.

My steps toward him gained in pace despite the weakening
of my knees and the wobbliness in my legs.  I wanted to see him, I
wanted to look into his eyes, despite the fact that I had no idea what
I would say to him once we were face to face.  Maybe I was hoping
that he would know what to say.  Maybe I was hoping that once he
saw me, once he looked me in my eyes, he would come home with

me to Big Momma's house. I knew that he was living here and there, in shelters, on the streets, under the bridge, in the park. I just needed him to come in from the cold, and maybe, just maybe, we could help each other. I needed my father, and I knew that he needed me. Sure, Big Momma was family, but my father was the only *immediate* family that I had left. We needed to be together. We needed to support one another, we needed to be able to talk to each other, or even just sat silently and think about my Mother. We were the only ones who knew what each other was feeling. We lost everything, we lost our home, we lost the life we had together, and we *both* lost her. I needed him.

My father saw me coming, and rose from the bench. He quickly headed in the opposite direction. I quickened my pace, and he quickened his.

"Dad!" I shouted.

He continued to scurry away.

"Dad!" I shouted again, this time with my voice breaking.

My father rushed off, and hit the corner. Apparently he still wanted nothing to do with me. In a way, I knew how he felt. Running away from a hurtful past, was a lot easier way to deal with it, than having to face it and re-live it each and every single day. Even though I understood his not wanting to see me, I still needed to see him. I needed to wrap my arms around my father, to hug him, to hold him, to tell him that I love him. That wasn't going to happen today. I turned, jogged off the field and into the locker room. Adanna met me at my locker.

"Are you okay?" she asked, rubbing my back.

I nodded, and then quickly wiped away the tears that had formed in the corners of my eyes.

"Hey, don't worry about it, okay?" Adanna said, leaning in. "He'll come to you when he's ready."

I slammed my locker closed. "When will that be? Another year, two years, ten years, when?"

"It may be next month, it may be next year, it may be never," Adanna told me. "But it will be on *his* time, when he's ready. You can't rush him, or force him, or trap him into being ready. And until he is, you have to keep living *your* life, you have to keep moving forward."

"I can't…" I said stuttering. "Adanna, he's a part of my life. How can I move forward, knowing that he's out there, knowing that he's in *that* condition? I can't even talk to him, so I can close *that* God damned door!"

"Who says that you have to?" she asked. "Everything is not neat and clean and pristine. You can't wrap everything up in a neat little package just because you want to. Life isn't neat, it isn't organized, it isn't something that you can compartmentalize! It doesn't always fit! And some doors will never be closed!"

I closed my eyes and rested my head against my cold metal locker door.

"There is a very famous book in my country, called Things Fall Apart," Adanna continued. "It was written by a famous Nigerian author named Chinua Achebe. Have you heard of him?"

I shook my head. "No."

"In this book, the protagonist, he lost so much, and to him, it seemed as though his whole world had turned upside down. His village was changing, society was changing, fate was not kind to him. Hence the title, Things Fall Apart. He went from a man who had so much, to a man who lost everything. Fate deals us all shitty hands, it's what we do when *things fall apart*, that defines who we are. Do we give up when things don't go our way, or do we persevere? What are we going to do, C.B.?"

Without lifting me head off of my locker, I nodded. She was right of course. She was always right.

Adanna caressed my back. "C.B., you have to go back out there. Go out there, and finish practice. Face it head on, and overcome it. What happened in the past is always a part of us, and to some extent our experiences define us, but we cannot let them dominate us."

I turned, stared into her eyes, and then leaned forward and

kissed her.  She was my strength.

# **Chapter Thirteen**

Game time came, and we were ready. In fact, we were more than ready. At least I knew that I was. I needed this game to relieve the stress and tension that had been building up in me the last week. I needed this game to get my mind off of the hood, off of my father, and off of all of the bullshit that had been going on lately. The football field was my world, and as crazy as it may seem, it was my sanctuary. The bright lights, the roaring crowd, the booming band, the shouting cheerleaders, somehow, it all brought a peace and calm to me that I was able to find in few other places.

My adrenaline was high, and yet, it was almost as if the world had slowed. My mind had somehow tuned everything out. I could feel the heat of the giant stadium lights, and I knew that the capacity crowd was on its feet roaring. I could see the cheerleaders shouting, and I could see the band members playing, but still, I could hear nothing. It was my game mode.

We elected to receive the ball first. They kicked the ball off, and Desmond managed to get the ball down to the forty yard line, giving us pretty good field position. I don't know why I said managed, because despite the fact that I hated him for taking Augustine's position, he was a pretty good running back. That, coupled with the fact that we were playing against The Woodlands, a team of White rich boys from far north Houston, meant that each and every one of us was subject to break a long one at any given time during the game because of our superior speed. This game was going to be about our speed and athleticism, versus their discipline and technique. Many would say that a well disciplined and well coached team would win this match nine times out of ten, but the truth of the matter was, we were that tenth time. We were hungry and fast, and we were playing with a chip on our shoulder. Our slowest, biggest lineman ran a 4.8 in the forty yard dash. Most of our linemen were running 4.7, while our linebackers were running 4.6 and 4.5. Our corners and safeties were running 4.4's, while our running backs and quarterback were down in the 4.2 range. And we were all athletes.

Our first play was always a hand-off to me, or it was a quarterback keeper. We did this to get used to the snap, to get the quarterback's legs under him, and to get that first snap over with. It was to get everyone acclimated to game time speed and to get all of the nervous jitters out of everyone's system. We all looked to the sideline, where the coach was calling the play. We used cards sometimes, and sometimes hand signals. We switched up our signal calling to throw the other teams off. Today we were keeping it simple, and coach was just using hand signals. Of course, we had two other people using hand signs to help throw the other team off as well. Only we knew which coach was live, which meant that he was the one giving the real play calls. In this instance, it was Coach Marshal. We looked to coach, and he called a Twenty-Three Left, which would send me up the middle, with the full back as my lead blocker. Not a problem.

The quarterback clapped his hands three times, and the ball was snapped, He dropped back, and then turned and handed the ball off to me, just as the full back ran past. I clutched the ball and followed the full back through the hole that the linemen had made. The fullback, Marquise, hit the hole at full speed, and took out the middle linebacker. That was all I needed. I flew past the middle linebacker and leaped over him and Marquise who were falling to the ground. I could hear the crowd's reaction to this stunt, and that put a smile on my face. I knew that I was going to give them something else to gasp about.

The safety from The Woodlands came at me full speed.

That meant that the highlight reel I was about to get off of this fool was partly his fault. He was a big, tall, White boy, about six-two, and I guess he was one of the fastest cats on their team. But the fastest cat on their team, meant that he wouldn't have been a safety on ours. I let him race toward me, and then as soon as he got within arm's reach, I spun to my left causing him to fly by. He tried to correct and turn, but it only caused his tall, lanky, awkward body to slip and fall. I could hear the crowd going wild. I slowed to a jog, held the ball out, and strutted into the end zone. I was back in show mode. My teammates raced into the end zone, and grabbed and hugged me. I even leaped into the air gave Marquise a chest bump. This was a tradition reserved for me and Augustine, and it was hard for me to do it with someone else, but in a way, I knew that I needed to. Augustine would always be with me, and in many ways, he still was, but I knew that I needed to go on. He would want me to keep it moving. His last words to me were to keep going and to live for both of us. I wasn't ready to let go, and I would probably never let go, hell, I didn't *want* to let go, but I needed to keep going. My touchdowns were his touchdowns, my glory was his glory. I lifted my arms toward the heavens giving my dude a shout out, and then I dropped down to my knees for a quick prayer.

We kicked the ball off to the other team, and once again, our defense did their thing. We were too fast for them. Our defense swarmed like bees; *Africanized* killer bees to be precise. The frustration on their faces was clear. They were used to scoring and dominating other teams from the onset. With us, they were down 7-0, a position they weren't used to being in, and nothing they tried was working. They couldn't run on us, because our line backers were too fast. They couldn't pass on us, because our safeties and corners were like gazelles. We were all over the place, and it must have seemed like we had twenty guys on the field. That's what our speed did for us; that was the benefit of having a team of niggaz from the hood who grew up playing football in the street. They went three and out, and had to punt the ball.

Desmond again got us descent yards on the return. This time, he got the ball down to the fifty, and nearly broke on for ninety yards. Their kicker got the angle on him, and that's the only thing that prevented him from taking the ball all the way to the house. But giving us the ball on the fifty yard line, was nearly the same as giving us the ball on the twenty yard line. This was going to be easy.

Our offense took the field, and again, the first play was usually a hand off, or a quarterback keeper. We stood, stared at the sideline, and watched as Coach signaled in the play. I was getting the ball once again.

We got set, and again, the quarterback clapped his hands,

giving the snap count. The center hiked the ball on three, and we went into action. The quarterback shoved the ball into my gut, and again I headed up the middle. This time, they were ready. They brought the safety down to close the hole, so I spun and headed out of the hole and around the right side of my line. My wide receiver took out their right corner, and that gave me the room I needed. The fact that they had brought their safety down to help plug the middle, meant that once I cleared the corner, it would be virtually impossible for dude to catch me. He tried to take an angle, and I could have shifted into another gear on his ass and got ghost, but I was in show time mode. Instead of racing past, I hit the brakes, stopped on a dime, and allowed his clumsy ass to fly by me. I then hit the accelerator and got ghost on all of them. I showed them what a 4.24 in the forty looked like. In fact, I was running so fast, and chopping so hard, that I could feel my heels hitting the back of my ass. I got to the end zone and dove in, despite the fact that absolutely no one was around me. We were in clown mode, and we wanted to embarrass those fools.

My teammates ran into the end zone and lifted me off of the ground and surrounded me. Again we chest bumped, high-fived, and even acted like we were posing for pictures. It was what they expected of us, so we gave it to them. They treated us like niggaz, and so we decided that we were going to act like niggaz. Of course we got a celebration penalty from the refs, but we didn't give a shit. We were going to send the rich White kids back to their million dollar homes with a loss. The world outside of the football field belonged to them, but the world on the turf belonged to us. And for all of the doors that they would shut once we were done with high school, we wanted to deprive them of similar opportunities in the here and now, while we were the masters. Maybe this was a lesson they would take with them and remember. Perhaps they would take with them the lesson of glory denied, of humiliation in front of their family, of wanting something so bad, and not being able to achieve it. They would have to leave their unblemished record on the field tonight, we were determined to make it so.

I raced back to the sideline with the rest of the offense, and was met by Savawn and Dirty Curt, who slapped hands with me.

"Easy money, Baby!" Savawn shouted.

"Easy money!" I said, rubbing my fingertips together.

We kicked the ball off again, and again, our defense was brutal. We didn't even have to take the field for a new offensive series, because our defense picked off their quarterback's pass and returned it for a touchdown. With the score 21-0, and judging by the ease with which we were scoring, it soon became obvious that this was going to be a blowout. The vaunted Woodland High School, which was supposed to give us our first loss of the season, was about to get the score ran up on them. Our crowd even got into the act, and started cheering, *"Over rated!"*

All of us had joy on our face. I took a seat on the bench and started taking it all in. My teammates were all smiling, the crowd was cheering, and taunting the other team, and it seemed as if the entire community was having a wonderful time. I stared at the faces in the crowd and for the first time, it really hit me. This team really did mean so much to the community. We really were bringing them together, and we really were giving them something to cheer about. For three hours, they were able to forget that the utility bill was overdue, or that the cable was about to get cut off. They were able to forget that their boss was an asshole, or that they were out of stamps and that their Lone Star Cards weren't going to be refilled until the first or the fifteenth. We took them away from their day to day problems, and we gave them hope and renewal. We showed them that their children were winners, and by extension, they were winners. Taking in the individual faces in that crowd helped to renew my spirit as well. I had been so focused on death, and what had been lost and destroyed, that I had paid little attention to what had been spared and what was alive. Life was happening, and it was all around me. I saw children clapping and cheering, and I saw smiles on the faces of their mothers. Life went on.

My staring into the crowd brought me to a familiar face as

well. He was here. My Dad had never missed a game, even in his current condition and state of mind, he was always there. Sometimes I could spot him in the crowd, and sometimes I couldn't. But even on the times when I couldn't pick him out of the crowd, I knew that he was there. I could *feel* his presence. I felt less alone. For a brief second, I thought about jogging off of the field and into the stands to see if I could catch up to him, and to see if I could get him to say something to me. But I decided against it. This moment wasn't about me, it was about them, the cheering crowd. It was at that moment, that I knew that I was a part of something greater than myself. I felt small, but connected. The scar that ran across my heart when Augustine died, was slowly starting to heal.

# <u>Chapter Fourteen</u>

My joy from Friday night's 72-0 rout of The Woodlands turned into a fucking nightmare on Monday morning.  After the game, the team went out and celebrated, and of course, a bunch of students from our school joined in the festivities.  Adanna was one of them.  We celebrated until two thirty that morning, and then I made sure she got home safe.  Despite the fact that she was a senior in high school, and that it had been a Friday night, and that there had been dozens upon dozens of parents celebrating with us, her brothers didn't take her staying out so late too kind.  They blamed me for it, and they grounded her, and again, for the hundredth time, forbade her to see me.  And if that wasn't enough, they waited for me on my route to school.

"Hey Cockroach, I thought I told you to stay away from my sister!" Wilson shouted from the driver's seat of his BMW 750iL as they pulled up along the side of me.

I should have known that they meant trouble, because they pulled ahead of me and parked. I should have run away, but instead, I kept walking. They climbed out of the car in all of their muscular glory and blocked my path.

"What are you, retarded?" Nelson asked, shoving me. "Are you stupid, deaf, hard of hearing, what?"

I adjusted my back pack, and tried to go around them. Wilson grabbed me and slung me on the ground, causing my back pack to fly off of my shoulder. Some of the contents spilled onto the sidewalk.

"Keep your fucking hands off of me!" I said, hopping up off of the ground and balling my fist.

"What are you gonna do, Cockroach?" Nelson asked.

"You have a good time with my sister Friday night?" Wilson asked.

"I told you to stay away from her," Nelson declared.

"She don't need no third world refugee trying to turn her into a baby momma," Wilson added. "Putting her on welfare, and giving her your Haitian AIDS and shit."

Edward, Adanna's third brother, who also looked the part of a world champion bodybuilder moved in closer, and stole me across my cheek. The blow was so powerful, that it dropped me instantly.

I was stunned by the blow, and it took me a while to get my bearings and shake it off. Sure, I had been hit hard before, but it was always while wearing and helmet. This was a direct blow with a fist to the side of my face. I was really shaken up.

I tried to place my hands beneath me and get up, but my effort was thwarted by a powerful kick to my stomach. The air rushed from my body, and I collapsed back down onto the ground. I don't know which brother landed the kick, but I do know that another punched me in the back of my head, causing my face to scrap against the hard concrete sidewalk.

"Muthafucka!" I shouted at the top of my lungs. "You sorry muthafuckas!"

A kick was delivered to my side, causing pain like I had never felt before. I just knew that my ribs had been broken.

I could see Nelson leaning down so that I could see him.

Stay away from my sister, Cockroach!" Nelson shouted. "This is your last warning!"

He delivered his warning with a punch to my jaw. At and that was it. I don't know if I dozed off temporarily, or if I went to sleep at all, but I do know that it took me forever to get up off of the ground. And when I did finally pick myself up, I felt pain like there was no tomorrow. My face hurt, my legs hurt, my ribs hurt, my entire body hurt. I slowly gathered my belongings, put them back inside of my back pack, and stumbled on to school.

The last person I wanted to see when I got to school, was the first person I actually saw. That was how it always seemed to work wasn't it? When you were looking for someone because they owed you money, you couldn't find them anywhere on the planet, but when you were desperate to avoid a person, they seemed to gravitate toward your ass like the two of you were magnets. I saw Mr. Davis step out of a classroom just down the hall, and immediately, I pivoted and headed off in another direction. It was too late.

"Baptiste!" Mr. Davis said, calling out to me in his booming staccato voice.

Despite the fact that he could probably be heard in every nearby hallway, I acted as if I didn't hear him and I kept walking.

"St. Claire!" he shouted a little louder. "Mr. Baptiste!"

I was trying to make it to the next hallway so that I could hit the corner on his ass, but it wasn't going to happen. I stopped and turned, so that I could face him.

"I know you heard me calling you!" Mr. Davis said, with a little bit of an edge in his voice. "What are you doing roaming the halls right now? You're supposed to be in class. Wait a minute, did you just get here? If so, then you need to go to the attendance office and check in."

And then, Mr. Davis noticed the blood and bruising on my face.

"What the hell?" Mr. Davis clasped my chin and turned my face up examining it. "You been fighting? *Are you fucking kidding me?*"

I yanked my face away from him.

"You've been fighting?"

"Not exactly."

"Not exactly? *What the fuck's that supposed to mean?*"

I shook my head.

"You need to come to my office," Mr. Davis said angrily. "You're going to tell me who you've been fighting with, and why. I want names, and I want them now. I'll suspend all of your asses!"

"I ain't been fighting with nobody at school!" I shot back.

"Who you been fighting with then?" Mr. Davis asked, pursing his lips and shifting his weight to one side. He thought I was lying.

"I was on my way to school, and I got jumped," I told him.

"Jumped?" he asked, folding his arms. *"You got jumped?"*

"Yeah," I said nodding.

"By who?" he asked, clearly growing exasperated. "Who in *this* neighborhood would jump *you*?"

I turned away for a few seconds to gather my thoughts. I didn't know if I should tell him what happened, and why, or who. Would it make me a snitch to say that I got jumped by a bunch of old ass niggaz because they didn't want me fucking with their sister?

"I got jumped..." I said hesitating. "Look, I don't want no trouble."

"Do I need to call the police and make a report?" Mr. Davis asked, frowning.

"I don't want this to go no further than between us," I told him.

Mr. Davis shifted his weight once again. "I can't promise you that. I need to protect this school, and I need to protect my students, and that includes you."

I nodded. "Fair enough. But I need this to stay between us."

"Let's hear it."

"Adanna's brothers don't like that we're together," I explained.

A look of realization spread across his face and he slowly nodded. "I see. And you're telling me that these grown ass men jumped on you?"

I nodded.

"My better judgment tells me that I should call the police and make a report," Mr. Davis said, again crossing his arms and staring into space.

I shook my head. "I won't report it."

"You need to, before this gets way outta hand."

I peered at him with my busted lips, and bloody nose. "It's already out of hand."

"Yeah," he said nodding. "And it could get worse. Next time, it won't just be a bloody face and some black eyes."

"There's not going to be a next time," I said, shaking my head.

"Yeah? And what's that supposed to mean?"

I shook my head and looked away.

"Son, don't go do anything stupid," Mr. Davis told me. "You're too close to the finish line. Don't throw it all away."

"I'm not leaving Adanna," I told him.

"Call the police," he told me. "We'll have these guys picked up, and they'll be prosecuted. And, we'll get a judge to issue a restraining order."

I looked at him like he was stupid and laughed. "They just rolled up on me and whipped my ass. Do you really think that these are the type of guys who'll honor a restraining order? Besides, how would that come off to my girl, if I had her brother's locked up?

And if they were all locked up, where would she go, huh? Who would take care of her? Man, it's too much bullshit involved in this, and I'll not going to lose her."

Mr. Davis nodded. He now was beginning to understand my situation. I'd be damned if I did, and damned if I didn't. I would just have to ride things out.

"I don't want to see you get hurt," he told me. "What if I brought them in here and talked to them?"

I shook my head. "Then I'd get my ass whipped for snitching."

"And maybe if they knew that you'd told somebody, then they'd leave you alone. Or at least not kill you. They don't know how may people you told, or if there is a report about the incident. And if you showed up dead, then at least they'd know that they'd be the prime suspects. It would keep you alive, son."

I nodded slowly. Maybe he did have a point. Maybe it would keep them off of my ass, or at least keep them from putting a bullet in it.

"Let me think about it for a little while?" I asked.

He stared me in the eye for several seconds before nodding.

"You need to go to the nurse's office," he told me. "She's going to take plenty of pictures, and she's going to swab your fingernails, fingertips, and hands for DNA, that we're going to send to the hospital. And, she's going to treat your wounds. How do you feel?"

"Like shit."

"You look like shit."

"I feel like I got hit by an eighteen wheeler."

Mr. Davis nodded. "You know what, forget the nurse. Forget school policy. I'm taking you to the hospital."

"What?"

"I want them to go ahead and X-Ray you just to be on the safe side. And they'll also be able to monitor you for a concussion."

Mr. Davis nodded for me to follow, and I did. I would follow him anywhere, as a matter of fact. Mr. Davis didn't just talk the talk, but he walked the walk. He didn't give a fuck about his job, or school policy, or getting fired, he was worried about *me*, and he was going to risk it all to drive me to the hospital. He cared. He was a Black man who cared about all of us, like we were all his children. I had always listened to Mr. Davis, and I had always respected him, but my respect for him shot up astronomically. He had once again showed me and everyone else, what a *real* Black man looked like. He didn't give a fuck about nothing but doing what was right.

I came to a conclusion that day, that no matter what happened in my life, no matter what twist and turns it took, I wanted to be like Mr. Davis. I wanted to be the next Mr. Davis, and I wanted everyone in my community to look at me, like we all looked at him. I guess at the end of the day, the main thing that most of us needed was to see a real Black man, in order to know what one looks like. And because we had one in our lives, we all could see what we were supposed to do, how to behave, how to act, how to carry ourselves. He was a role model, and we were all blessed that the Man Upstairs had sent him to us.

# **Chapter Fifteen**

After the trip to the hospital, Mr. Davis took me back to school, so that I could finish the day, grab my homework, and even make it to practice. Football practice had been a light one for me, as Coach Beckwith saw how fucked up I was. My eyes both had contusions on them, and I also had a contusion on my forehead. My nose turned out to not be broken, and I sported a bandage on it, as well as my lips. My ribs were not broken, but they were bruised. I had several contusions on my back from being kicked brutally, but all-in-all, I was okay. And the pain reliever and muscle relaxer that the doctor injected at the hospital helped tremendously. I was still feeling the effects of the high.

Speaking of high, I rolled up on the homies kicking at the hood store on my way home. They tripped the fuck out when they saw me.

"What the fuck happened to you, my nigga?" Dirty exclaimed.

Quick wheeled up to me and examined my face. "What's up, kinfolk? What the fuck happened?"

I waved my hand dismissing the incident. "Punk ass niggaz."

"Who did this, kinfolk?" Dirty asked, frowning. He was ready to ride. "Show me who them niggaz is."

"Man, just tell me who they are, and I'll get with them fools later on today," Quick told me.

Dirty moved in close and examined my face. "Man, they fucked you up!"

I laughed.

"Naw, seriously, my nigga, who did that shit?" Quick asked angrily.

"Man, Adanna's punk ass brothers," I told him. "They don't want me fucking with her."

Quick, Dirty and the others exchanged glances.

"You want us to ride on them fools?" Dirty asked.

I shook my head. "That would just fuck shit up with Adanna."

"She ain't gotta know," Quick declared. His face was red and flush with anger. "We can take care of all of them ho ass niggaz tonight!"

"I don't need that right now," I told him.

"Nigga, you ain't gonna be there!" Dirty said smiling. "We gone roll up on them fools with some choppers, and I guarantee you they won't ever fuck with you again."

I smiled. The thought that they were willing to kill for me, blew my mind. We were all cool, and had been since we were little, when I had been coming to H-Town to visit my Big Momma during the summers. I loved Quick and Dirty like they were my brothers, but still, the thought of them getting down on my behalf was overwhelming. I wasn't one to give in to emotion, but I could feel a lump forming in my throat.

"I'mma just let it slide for right now," I declared. "Fuck them niggaz. They can't stop me, and they *ain't* gonna stop me from seeing my girl."

"That's all well and good, but you don't let nobody put they hands on you and get away with it," Dirty told me.

"I ain't even seen my girl yet, and told her what happened," I said, peering off into the distance.

"Damn, that shit is fucked up," Quick said, frowning. "When this shit happen?"

"This morning when I was on my way to school," I told him. "They rolled up on my ass and jumped out and tripped."

"Man, maybe you don't need to be walking to school by yourself in the morning," Dirty said. "Or least, carry some protection."

Dirty reached into his waistband, pulled out a large nine-millimeter Taurus semi-automatic pistol. He pulled back the slide, checking to make sure there was a round in the chamber. He then de-cocked the gun, turned it around, and held it out for me to grab. I was stunned into inaction.

"Here, take it, nigga!" Dirty said, extended the pistol even further.

I knew that if I took it, things would change. The potential for things to get even worse, would rise astronomically. Did I really need to be carrying around a pistol? Did I want to? If I took that gun, I would be making a choice. And I knew that taking that gun, would be a bad choice. I could get stopped and searched by the police at any moment. I could get searched by campus police. And then, there were the metal detectors at the school. There were the locker searches, the drug sniffing dogs, and all of the other bullshit that went on. And what if them fools did roll up on me again? Would I pull out the gun? Would I be able to squeeze the trigger? I shook my head. Nothing good could come of it.

I waved off Dirty's offer to take the pistol. "Naw, I appreciate it, but I'm good, kinfolk."

"Nigga, you don't need to be out there getting caught slipping," Dirty told me. "Here, you can have this one. I got plenty more."

I smiled. "Don't need that on the football field."

"You ain't on the muthafucking football field twenty four seven, nigga!" Dirty said, laughing.

"How you feeling?" Quick asked. "I see they fucked up your face. They break anything?"

I shook my head. "Naw, I went to the hospital. They did X-Rays and shit. I'm straight, nothing broken. I'll be ready to play this weekend."

"That's good," Quick said nodding. "Your ass better be ready. Y'all got Hightower this Friday."

I nodded.

Quick nodded for me to follow, and slowly began to wheel his chair away from the rest of the guys standing around in front of the hood store. He wanted to talk, and apparently he didn't want them to hear what he was about to say.

I followed Quick a little ways down the street, and once we were away from the others, he stopped, turned toward me, and took a swig from his 40 ounce of Olde English.

"Yo, dude, are you straight?" he asked.

"What do you mean?"

He nodded up toward my face. "I mean, with this shit here. You know, with them niggaz."

I nodded. "I ain't worried about them fools."

"You should be" Quick told me. "Them African muthafuckas into all kinds of shit. And they'll get down for they shit, homie. I know you ain't really down with all of the bullshit, so if you need me to handle things for you, just say the word."

I shook my head. "Naw, I'm good."

"What you gonna do about it?" Quick asked, taking another swig off of his beer. "You just can't ignore the shit. They don't want you fucking with they sister, that shit ain't just going to go away."

"I ain't cutting her loose."

Quick shook his head. "Then you have a dilemma. What are you going to do?"

I shifted my gaze toward the concrete and shrugged. I had no idea.

"You can't duck and dodge these fools forever," Quick continued. "You gonna run into them again one day. And when you do, they gonna be pissed that you still fucking with Adanna."

"I know," I said nodding. "So what do you think I should do?"

Quick laughed. "You know what I think. I think you should

let me smoke them fools, and we'll call it a wrap."

I laughed.

"So the doctor said you straight?" Quick asked. "No breaks, no cracks, no hairline fractures. You got to be real careful about them hairline fractures, homie. You could be running the ball, cut the wrong way, and then it's all over with but the shouting."

"I know," I said nodding. "But they did an MRI because of my ribs, and they didn't see anything. I think I'm straight."

Quick took a drink from his beer and peered off into the distance. "When it first happened, they told me that I was going to be all right too. I came out of surgery, and I swear, I swear, homie, I could feel my legs. I could feel pain all over, pain in my back, my arms, my knees, everywhere. I thought that I had made it. I thought that I would be back on the field, leading my team to a state title."

I stood quietly, taking it all in. I didn't know what to say, of even if there *was* anything to say. Quick and I had never had this conversation before, in fact, I don't think that it was a conversation that he had ever had with anybody. I felt numb. Listening to him talk about the day he came out of surgery took me back to the night at the hospital when Augustine died. The waiting, the false reassurances that everything was going to be okay, and then getting hit with the news that everything wasn't going to be okay. It felt like I had been slammed into a brick wall, or hit by a locomotive.

Even though the doctor had spoken the words softly, the news that he was gone hit with the loud, cataclysmic force of a category five hurricane. I couldn't even begin to imagine Quick being hit with the news that he would never run again, walk again, play football again, or even be able to have a family of his own.

Quick took another swig from his beer, while continuing to stare off into the distance.

"The doctor came into my room and asked my how I was doing," Quick continued. "I told him that I was fine. I felt fine. Or maybe it was just that I *wanted* to feel fine. Maybe I was fooling myself, because I was just happy to still be alive."

Quick paused for a moment, drew in a deep breath and held for a few seconds before exhaling and continuing.

"The first bullet struck my lower back, causing severe thoracic injuries. That was the bullet that severed Th-8. The second bullet struck lower, causing severe lumbosacral injuies. That was the bullet that severed Th-12 and L-1. It pretty much disintegrated my spinal disk. The hematoma damage was so great that my cells produced fluid for months before the even began to think about healing. I remember my mother coming to visit me, and I remember trying to sit up. That was the first time it really hit me. I just wanted to sit up. And no matter how hard I tried, no matter how much I stared at my legs, no matter how much help I tried to give them..."

I had never saw Quick cry before. So when I saw that lone tear fall from his eye and roll down his cheek, I didn't know what to think. I didn't know what I was supposed to do. Was I supposed to reach over and embrace him? Was I supposed to pat his shoulder? Hug him, hold him, what? I did know, that I felt my own tears welling up in my own eyes.

"I just wanted to play football, homie," Quick said, wiping away the tear. "All my life, I had been playing football. All my life, I had been told how fast I was, how good I could catch, how accurate I could throw. I was an athlete. A pure athlete. I could play any position on the field, on *both* sides of the ball. And I was going to use that, to get my Moms up out the hood. I was going to use my speed, to run away from this muthafucking hood, right into college, and right into the muthafucking NFL. I used to dream, homie, dream about draft night. I used to dream about hearing my name called, and walking up onto that stage, and putting on the fucking Dallas Cowboys baseball cap, and then taking pictures with my moms. I saw that shit like it was real, kinfolk. I *felt* that shit. I *knew* that it was going to happen. I remember sitting in front of the TV watching the Cowboys play, and I remember turning to my mother and telling her that one day, I was going to be a Dallas Cowboy, and that one day, I was going to be playing football on TV.

And she smiled at me. She just smiled at me and told me that she knew that I could do it. And I promised her, and I promised myself, that I was going to do it, I was going to make it to the pros, and I was going to buy my mom a big ass house out in Lake Olympia, or Sienna Plantation,, or Kingwood, and I was going to buy her a clean ass Benz, and she wasn't going to have to work no more, or worry about money no more. I promised her. And then those dirty, low-down muthafuckas took everything away from me. They shot me in the back and they took *everything* away from me. Ho ass, coward ass niggaz! They couldn't hit me in the front, no, they had to shoot a nigga in the back."

My own tear rolled down my cheek. "It ain't over, homie."

Quick smiled. "I know God damned well it ain't over. It's far from over. When one door closes, another muthafucking door opens. I might not be able to get it in one night, by signing a contract, but believe you me, I'm getting it. Dope money spends just like draft night money."

I wiped away my tears and laughed.

"I got to get it how I live," Quick told me. "But you still got a shot, homie, you still got a chance to get that lump sum from them White folks. But it's all about you now, it's all about the moves you make. Remember, it's not how you start, but how you finish. And I've seen plenty of niggaz get within sight of the finish line, and come up short. I'm one of them. I'm still in the race, but I'm moving like a turtle instead of a hare. I'm grinding, and it's coming, but there's a price to pay for the way I got to get it, you feel me? You can get it legit. Just watch your back, my nigga. Don't fuck up, and don't lose sight of the prize."

"I can't give up my girl, Quick," I told him, now realizing where he was going with the conversation.

"Do what you supposed to do, homie," Quick told me. "Do what you feel you have to do, but just be careful. I ain't saying you gotta carry a strap twenty four seven, but just keep your eyes open, and your mind clear. You can always keep her in pocket, but just make them niggaz think that y'all done broke up. Y'all can hook back up in college, and it's all gravy from there."

I nodded.

"Get your paper, homie," Quick said, extending his hand. I shook it. "I'm gone get mine. Maybe we can both buy up a couple a cribs next door to each other over in Riverstone. Or maybe buy us a couple of cribs up in River Oaks, and be chilling with the old money."

I laughed. I could imagine Quick living in River Oaks. "Maybe we can do that."

I held on to Quick's hand a little longer than normal before finally letting it go. I don't know whether it was because I was letting him go, letting the hood go, or what? I knew what he was saying when he was admonishing me to do what I had to to, and to keep my eyes on the prize. Staying focused, and staying out of trouble, also meant staying away from those who were getting into trouble. He was selling dope, and getting into all kinds of shit, and he knew that by me stopping by the hood store and hanging out with them, I was putting myself at risk as well. In his own way, Quick was telling me that we would hook up again in better times, under better circumstances. Maybe we would live down the street from one another in Sugar Land, or Missouri City, or somewhere else out in Ft. Bend County. Maybe.

"I'mma head to the crib, homie," I said, leaning over and embracing him. He embraced me tight.

"All right, kinfolk," Quick said, with a knowing smile. "Get out of here. Do what you need to do. You close to the finish line, so you keep your eyes on the prize, and you don't let nothing and nobody slow you down, and keep you from getting it."

I nodded, gave him a pound, and then headed off to the crib. On the way home, Quick weighed heavily on my mind. He just wanted to play football, he just wanted to get his mother out of the hood. He wanted to do, what me and Augustine, and so many other wanted to do. He wanted to provide a better life, for the people that he loved. We weren't so different. We were all one bad night, one wrong turn, one gunshot wound from being in the same situation.

I had no illusions about Quick. I knew who he was, the things that he had done, the monster that he had become. The hardest part to reconcile, is that I knew why. I knew him before he had been confined to a wheelchair, I knew him when he still had hopes and dreams of making it to the pros, and when those hopes and dreams were obtainable. I don't excuse him for anything that he's done, but I can say that I know what happened to him. I think that the scariest part of the situation, was that his life had been decided by inches. One inch to the left, he still walks and runs, and plays football, and so many mothers sons would still be alive. One inch to the right, and he still walks and runs, and plays football, and so many mothers sons would still be alive. The same thing with Augustine. If he would have been hit an inch to the left, or right, or an inch lower, then his neck doesn't snap, and he would be alive today. They've always said that football, like life, is a game of inches. Perhaps that was the scariest thing of all. An inch, a second, a moment in time. A wrong hit, and tiny bullet on a cold Houston night. Life changes, life is so fragile, fate so fickle. I thought of Quick, and I thought of chance, and I thought there, but for the Grace of God, go I.

# **<u>Chapter Sixteen</u>**

I saw Adanna the next morning. It was the day we set aside for morning tutoring in the school library. She was helping me brush up on my math skills, and my knowledge of world history. Truth be told, she also helped me with English, and Chemistry as well. We hadn't seen one another since I ran into her brothers, and my beat up and banged up face was a complete surprise to her. She leaped from the library table she was seated at upon seeing me.

"C.B!" Adanna shouted. "What the hell happened to you?"

She placed her hands on my cheeks and examined my face. I cringed from the pain of her touch.

"I ran into your brothers yesterday morning."

"What?"

"Shhhh!" the librarian behind the desk hissed, admonishing us.

"Are you kidding me?" Adanna asked in her Nigerian accent. It was the accent that came out and replaced her normal British accent whenever she was angry. "Tell me that you're joking."

I tilted my head to the side as if to asked if she were serious.

Adanna rested her hand against her forehead. "Please tell me that you're lying, please tell me that my brothers didn't do this to you."

"I wish I could, babe," I said, making my way to the table she was seated at. I placed my book bag down next to her belongings.

Adanna pulled me close and kissed my forehead. "I'm so sorry." Adanna sniffled, and began to cry. "I'm so sorry about this. Please forgive me."

"Hey, hey, hey, you didn't do this," I said, wrapping my arms around her. "This was not your fault, and you had nothing to do with this. Don't blame yourself for one second."

"Why?" she asked, turning up her palms.

"Because, they don't want their sister with a cockroach," I said smiling. "And you can't blame them. They're just looking out for you. They know that you're too good for me."

"Don't say that!" Adanna said, wiping away her tears. "You're no fucking cockroach. And I'm not better than you, no one is. Don't you ever say that, or think that again."

I clasped her shoulders and stared into her eyes. "You are. You are better than me. You're better than them. You better than everyone else in this fucked up world. You're the best thing that's ever happened to me."

"They had no right!" she shouted, pulling away. "This is *my* decision! They have no right to interfere in my affairs!"

"They're your legal guardians, remember?"

"That doesn't give them the right to dictate my life, and it doesn't give them the right to go around battering people. They've crossed the line!"

Adanna began to gather her belongings.

"Whoah!" I said, lifting my hands and halting her. "Where are you going?"

"I'm going home to kick some ass!"

"No, you're not!"

"Yes, I am!"

"Hey, don't worry about them," I told her. "They didn't stop anything. They can't stop anything. We're here, right?" I pulled her close once again. "We're still doing all of the things we were doing before, and we still have a plan. They can't stop us, they can't stop our plan. We have a future together. They're in the past."

Adanna pulled back, and examined my face closely. Tears

fell from her eyes, as she caressed all of the wounded parts of my face. With her fingers she traced my black eyes, my busted lips, and busted nose. She traced her finger around my bruised and swollen cheeks, and then she leaned in and kissed my lips.

"It's not your fault," I said softly.

We sat down at the table. Usually we would jump right into our tutoring session, but today was different. I could tell that she felt awkward, like it was her fault that her brothers had done this.

Adanna rested her head in her hands. "I wish that we could just leave right now. I just wish that graduation was here, and that we could both leave."

"Me too," I said softly.

"As soon as school is over with, let's leave."

I nodded.

"I mean, let's not wait until August, or until the end of summer, let's leave right away," she continued.

"We both have enough credits to graduate," I told her. "TCU would love it if I reported for the spring ball. I could leave in January."

"But that would leave me stuck here."

"You have more than enough credits," I told her.

"I know, but I can't leave in January," Adanna said softly. "I need to complete the classes I'm enrolled in, so that I can graduate at the top of my class. If I just blow those classes off, then I won't be Valedictorian. And you know how important that is to me, and to my parents back home."

I nodded. I understood completely. She had been taking about graduating number one, since the day we first met.

"I'm not leaving without you," I said with a smile.

"I know," she said nodding. "We can leave the day after I walk the stage. The very next morning, we can be on a bus to Dallas."

"Sounds like a plan," I told her.

"I can't wait to start a life together away from here," Adanna said, resting her forehead against mine. "I can't wait to be away from here, to be free, and away from them."

"It's going to happen, babe," I said softly. "I promise you it's going to happen. I give you my word."

"Please keep your word," she whispered. "I want to live out the rest of my life with you."

"I will keep my word," I told her.

*****

My school day went by faster than normal it seemed. I breezed through my classes with thoughts of Adanna and leaving for Dallas. I worried about what she would say to her brothers once she got home, and I worried about what they would do once they found out that she and I had talked. I had a big game coming up on Friday, and I still felt pain in my side, and on the bruises spread over my face. My eyes were blood shot from the broken blood vessels, and they were surrounded by a purple hue because of the bruising. I had a lot on my mind, to say the least.

After school I found myself simply going through the motions during football practice, and then muddling through the streets on my way home. I barely noticed the homies hanging out at the hood store, and only came to acknowledge them when Dirty called my name.

"What up, kinfolk?" Dirty shouted, lifting his arms into the air.

"What's up?" I said nodding. I walked to where they were, and exchanged handshakes. Quick wheeled himself out of the store and slid across the soft gravel and sand like he was drifting in a small Japanese sports cars. He stopped just short of clipping my legs. "Watch out, fool!"

"You should have told them niggaz to watch out when they was beating your ass," Quick said, laughing.

The others joined in the laughter.

"Fuck you!" I said, laughing as well.

"What's the deal, my nigga?" Dirty asked. "You seen them fools again?"

I shook my head. "Naw, I ain't worried about them niggaz."

Dirty pulled a blunt from behind his ear and lighter from his pocket. He lit up the cigar and took a couple of long pulls from it, before offering it to me.

"You know better than that," I said, waving him off.

"Stop being the devil," Quick said, snatching the blunt. "Always trying to tempt muthafuckas into doing wrong."

"You *are* the devil," Dirty told him. "And smoking blunts ain't wrong. They stimulate young minds and bring clarity to young entrepreneurs such as myself."

"Spell entrepreneurs, nigga!" Quick said, puffing on the blunt. The others broke into laughter.

"D-i-r-t-y!" Dirty told him. "So fuck you, and you, and you!"

Again, there was more laughter.

The homies in the hood always seemed to lift my spirits. They kept everything real, and kept everything grounded. Life was simple; they hustled, and they survived. It put a lot of things into perspective for me. No matter how tough things got, I realized that I always had tomorrow. There would always be a chance to make things better. I still had the sweet curing balm of hope.

"Check them, check them, check this car fool!" Dirty said, reaching for his pistol.

All of the homies turned, and spied the car, just in time to see the tinted windows slide down, and barrels of a couple of assault rifles come out. I admit, I froze like a deer in a pair of headlights.

The loud pops and rattles of assault rifles filled the air, as smoke and flames poured from the barrels. The flames that the rifles spit were so long, that they seemed to be able to reach out and touch the people that they were spitting rounds at.

"Get down, fool!" Quick shouted.

I felt Quick yank my arm, pulling me down, and then when that wasn't good enough, I felt him push himself up from off his wheelchair and dive on top of me. We both fell to the ground, with him on top of me.

I could hear all of the homies returning fire from various positions around the hood store, and after a few moments, I could hear the screeching of tires, and then nothing but silence. I knew that it was over with.

"Damn, kinfolk, your ass is strong!" I said. I tried to scoot from beneath Quick, so that I could get into position and help him back into his wheelchair. Dirty ran up and helped. He started to lift Quick.

"C'mon, nigga, help push or something!" Dirty said, placing his arms beneath Quick and trying to pull him up. "Fuck!"

Dirty pulled his hands from beneath Quick, and Quick fell back down. Dirty's hands were covered with blood. I looked down at my shirt, and my shirt and pants were bloody as well. I hurriedly climbed up off of the ground.

Dirty rolled Quick over. There was a massive hole in Quick's sternum. His lips were purple, and his face was slowly turning blue.

"Fuck!" I shouted.

"No, no, no!" Dirty shouted.

The rest of the homeboys gathered around and began to freak out. I dropped down to my knees, lifted Quick's head, and placed it in my lap. Blood was pouring across his once clean, crisp, white t-shirt, turning it a deep, dark, crimson.

"Quick!" I said, shaking him. "Quick!"

He was alive. He stared up at me and focused for a few seconds, and then allowed himself a smile.

"Will somebody call the fucking ambulance!" Dirty shouted.

"Quick!" I shouted, shaking his head. "Stay with me! Stay with me! The ambulance is on its way! Just breathe, kinfolk! Breathe!"

There was nothing romantic, or heroic about Quick's death.

There was nothing poetic, and even remotely glorious. His eyes rolled back, and he simply died in my arms.

# Chapter Seventeen

I didn't sleep at all that night. Not only was Quick's death bothering me, but the fact that he died saving me hung heavily on my mind. I had questions, and yet once again, God had seen fit not to answer any of them. Why Quick, and why not me, was one of them. Why Quick period, was another one. Why not one of the other cats that were around yesterday? What if I would have kept going and not stopped to rap with them, would Quick be alive? What if Dirty hadn't called me and I had kept walking?

I laid in my bed staring into the darkness, not wanting to contemplate what came next. I knew that school was looming, but climbing out of bed to face the day was something I wasn't going to do. I couldn't do. I needed a respite from the world, if only for a day or two. I needed to check out. Emotionally I was exhausted, mentally I was fatigued. I had spent the entire night in tears, mourning the loss of my friend. If wasn't fair, I kept lamenting. Why, was the question that I needed answered.

I knew that Quick wasn't exactly an angel, and I knew that he had done so much dirt in the world, but still... He had been broken. His hopes, his dreams, his humanity had been stripped from him. Was it his fault that he became a monster, or was it the fault of The Man Upstairs who allowed that bullet to strip away so much of his life? Was it the fault of the trigger man? Was it the hood's fault? A monster had been created, so whom was to blame? Was the Frankenstein monster at fault for being created, or was it the fault of Dr. Frankenstein, his creator? I felt for Quick. I felt every molecule of his pain. I knew what it was like to want something so bad, and to know that it was not to be. I wanted my Mother, I wanted my Father, and I wanted our old life back in New Orleans prior to that bitch Katrina. Quick wanted to be able to play football, to keep his promise to his mother, to get his family up out of the hood. Neither of us could have what we wanted. My life wasn't coming back, my mother wasn't coming back, and Quick's life was not coming back. We had both been dealt some really fucked up cards.

I rolled over and stared at the bloody clothing piled on my bedroom floor. My clothes were stained with my friend's blood. I had taken them off, tossed them on the floor, and then climbed into the shower and cried the entire time I was showering. I couldn't believe that he was gone. I couldn't believe that God would let this happen.... *again.* Quick had a mother, and three little sisters to look after. And three girls growing up in the hood without a father or a big brother to look after them, were subject to becoming prey at an early age. Getting pregnant at sixteen was the norm. Not only had Quick been dealt a shitty blow, his sisters had been dealt one too. Even if one looked at it philosophically and thought that maybe, just maybe, Quick deserved his fate, what had his sisters done to deserve the life that they were now facing? It was all fucked up to say the least.

My mind wondered why Quick had to die while saving me? What did that mean? Why did Augustine die on a play that I was supposed to go in on? What did that mean? Why did everyone keep dying around me? Was I being sent a message? Was I being punished? What had I done, and what could I do to make amends with The Man Upstairs?

Slowly, the door to my room crept open, and Big Momma stuck her head inside.

"Claire."

I didn't answer.

"St. Claire," she said, calling out to me softly. "It's time for school, darling."

Again, I said nothing.

Big Momma switched on my light, shooting unwanted rays straight into my retina. The light felt like it was searing my eyeballs, and transmitting headache inducing forces straight to my brain. I lifted my arm, shielding my eyes from the light, and let out a grumbling disapproval at her actions.

"I got some breakfast waiting in the kitchen," Big Momma said softly.

"I'll eat it later," I told her.

"You have to eat it before you go to school," she said.

"I'm not going to school," I told her.

Big Momma stepped inside of my room. "Why not?"

I shook my head. "I don't feel like it."

"What's the matter?" she asked, lifting her arms. "Are you sick?"

"You could say that."

Big Momma nodded. "Something tells me, that it's not the kind of sickness that a doctor could cure though, is it?"

I burst into tears.

Big Momma walked into my room and began to wipe away my tears. *"He will wipe away every tear from their eyes, and death shall be no more, neither shall there be mourning, nor crying, nor pain anymore, for the former things have passed away."*

I peered up at my Big Momma, I didn't want to hear any quotes from the Bible. I was so angry with God, angry for letting this happen, still angry about him taking Augustine, angry about Him taking my Momma, *and* I had so many questions.

Big Momma seated herself on the edge of my bed, causing me to scoot over and make some room for her. She continued to wipe away my tears.

"*For everything there is a season, and a time for every matter under heaven: a time to be born, and a time to die; a time to plant, and a time to pluck up what is planted; a time to kill, and a time to heal; a time to break down, and a time to build up; a time to weep, and a time to laugh; a time to mourn, and a time to dance; a time to cast away stones, and a time to gather stones together; a time to embrace, and a time to refrain from embracing.*" Big Momma leaned over and gently kissed my forehead. "I know its hard, St. Claire. I know you don't understand, and you have a lot of anger in you, and you find yourself questioning The Lord. But trust in *His* judgment St. Claire. Know that He has a plan for you. Know that He is with you, and that He has never left you or abandoned you. Everything happens for a reason. *The Lord is near to the brokenhearted and saves the crushed spirit. He heals the brokenhearted and binds up their wounds.* In time, He will heal your heart as well. We all have our own races to run, baby. Your friend Quick, he just finished his race a little early. No one promised that we was all gonna finish our races together, just that we were going to finish. The Lord said "*I am going to The Father, for The Father is greater than I. And I have told you before it takes place, so that when it does take place you may believe.*"

Big Momma rose from the bed, placed her hand on my head, closed her eyes and began to pray. "Father God, we come to You and ask that You ease the pain that weighs so heavy on our hearts today. Dear Lord, You said come to Me all who labor and are heavy laden, and You will give us rest. We come to You today, Father God, with burdens unbearable, with pain so great that it clouds our judgments. We know that you Mighty Father, the Great Comforter of Zion, are the Master Comforter. You are our rock, our fortress, our deliverer, our God, our strength, in whom we trust; our buckler, and the horn of our salvation. You are our high tower, Father, and we know that there is nothing that You cannot speak into existence."

"We come to you today, All Mighty Father, to ask that you Bless Quick, and his family. Please comfort them in their time of grief, and ease their pain. You said, Dear Lord, that we are crucified with Christ: nevertheless we live; yet not we, but Christ liveth in us: and the life which we now live in the flesh we live by the faith of the Son of God, who loved us, and gave Himself for us. So we ask that you open up Your glorious kingdom for Quick, and walk him into one of the many mansions prepared for him by Your son, our Holy Savior Jesus Christ. Let him sing the new song, Heavenly Father; let him understand that he is worthy to take the book, and to open the seals thereof. In Revelations it says; *for thou wast slain, and hast redeemed us to God by thy blood out of every kindred, and tongue, and people, and nation.* So we ask that you welcome this young man into Your kingdom, and bring peace to those who he leaves behind. Let them know that they should rejoice in the coming of the Lord, and that they will see this loving child again. Remind them that Jesus said I am the resurrection and the life. Whoever believes in me, though he die, yet shall he live. And remind them of Thessalonians, where it is written that *through Jesus, You will bring with Him those who have fallen asleep. For this we declare to you by a word from the Lord, that we who are alive, who are left until the coming of the Lord, will not precede those who have fallen asleep. For the Lord himself will descend from heaven with a cry of command, with the voice of an archangel, and with the sound of the trumpet of God. And the dead in Christ will rise first. Then we who are alive, who are left, will be caught up together with them in the clouds to meet the Lord in the air, and so we will always be with the Lord."*

"We ask you these things in the name of Your beloved son, Jesus Christ. Amen," Big Momma said. She made the sign on the cross on my forehead, and then leaned down and kissed me.

I wasn't feeling well even after her prayer. Nothing had changed. Quick was still dead, and my heart still felt like it had been ripped from my chest.

"C'mon in here and get something to eat, baby," Big Momma told me.

"Big Momma, I don't feel like eating."

"St. Claire, you have someone in the kitchen who wants to see you, baby," she said with a smile.

My curiosity was piqued. I couldn't imagine who would be waiting for me in the kitchen this time of the morning. The only person that I could think of, was Adanna. And I would love to have seen her. I felt like I *needed* to see her. I needed to wrap my arms around her and hold her.

I followed my Big Momma into the kitchen, and to my surprise, Mr. Davis was seated at my breakfast table.

"Good morning, sleepy head," he said, smiling at me. "I know you're not going to school in your undies."

He made me crack a smile.

Mr. Davis waved for me to take a seat at the breakfast table. Big Momma already had my plate out. I sat down and immediately bit off a piece of my toast. Big Momma disappeared into her room.

"I came by to give you a lift to school," Mr. Davis started

off. "I figured you could use a ride today. Maybe even have a chat."

"Appreciate that," I told him.

"You know, we all come to a major crossroads in life, CB." Mr. Davis said. "And it's this critical crossroads that determine what the rest of our life is going to be like. So of us make really good decisions, some of us make okay decisions, and some of us make really poor decisions. I believe you're at that crossroads right now CB."

I bit off a piece of hot link and nodded.

"So, what are you going to do, St. Claire?" Mr. Davis asked.

I didn't really have an answer for him. It was too soon, *way too soon.* Quick was still laying on a cold slab in the morgue at University Hospital, and my mind wasn't on making any major life altering decisions right now.

"I don't know," I said, shrugging my shoulders.

*"Well, you better know!"* Mr. Davis said. "You *need* to know. You need to make a conscious decision right now, what you are going to do with your life. You need to set a path, and stay on it, no matter what."

It was the same thing Quick had told me the day before he died.

Mr. Davis leaned in. "There's a monster out there, CB. And

it's a monster that likes to feast on young Black men. There is a
system in America that is set up, so that you can fail. It's
institutionalized, it's engrained in the American fabric, there a
hierarchy in this country, and you don't factor into it. We, as a
people, have *never* factored into it."

"What happened to the land of opportunity?" I asked.

"It's the land of opportunity for some," Mr. Davis said
sitting back in his chair. "But not for people of color. This country
was founded by, for, and because of, rich, White planters and
business interest, who didn't want to pay their taxes. *That's* what
America is about. That's what America has always been about. It's
an economic system, and it's set up so that the rich get richer, and
everyone else serves *their* interest. And the only role we play in this
system, is to keep the cogs moving. To work in the factories and
serve as cheap labor. To sweep the streets and collect the trash. To
keep the trains running so that the wealthy can move their goods
from coast to coast and across the globe. And in order to ensure
that you stay on the bottom, they have devised a set of laws to
entrap you. They have set up a police state, to remind you of your
precarious position in this country. They have set up factories in
prison, so that you can work for 30 cents an hour, and they can
make billions of dollars off of your labor. The system is set up to
control what you learn, to control what you are exposed to, to

control *your* kind, and to make sure that you devalue one another, and remain in a position of servitude. What's going on in Chicago, and in Black communities all across this country is not an accident, it's all part of a well orchestrated plan."

"So what am I supposed to do?" I asked, lifting my arms and turning up my palms.

"You're supposed to *not* become a statistic," Mr. Davis said. "You're supposed to educate yourself, and you're supposed to break the chains, and then help other young Black men do the same."

*"I'm only one person!"* I shot back.

"And that's how they want you to look at it," Mr. Davis said with a smile. "They want you to feel overwhelmed, like the problems too big for any one person to make a difference. And then they make sure that we never get together, by sewing distrust within our communities. But trust me, if you do your part, and another young man does his part, and every other young man does his part, then soon, together, we will have made a difference."

"What's that?" I asked. "What's my part?"

"First off, son, you have to *survive,*" Mr. Davis said shaking his head and leaning in. "You have to keep breathing. You can't go out there and contemplate revenge, and get yourself killed, or caught up in the system. You have to walk that stage, you have to go to college, and then you have to turn back and extend a hand and help another young man do the same. You understand that, son?"

I peered down at the table and thought about what he was saying. It was all a part of my plan anyway. I was going to make it, I was going to go to college, and I was going to do what I could do to help my community. I nodded my head, letting him know that I understood what he was saying.

"Good," Mr. Davis said nodding. "Now, finish up your breakfast so we can get to school. I have a first period class I have to sub for this morning."

# **Chapter Eighteen**

My football game came. I had forgotten all about it,
because of Quick's death. At first, I felt like I didn't want to play.
But the closer we came to game time, the more I thought about
Quick, and the advice he would always give. The closer we got to
game time, the angrier I became. By the time kickoff came, I
wasn't speaking to anyone, and I was seeing nothing but red. I had
transformed into a raging ball of anger and hatred, and I intended to
take out my anger and frustrations on the other team.

I walked out onto the field, shoved one of my teammates to
the other side, and lined up. Normally, on kickoff, he was on the
right side of the field, while I was on the left. However, during film
it had been pointed out that the other team's kicker had a habit of
kicking the ball to his left, which was our right, and I wanted the
ball. I wanted it more than any other time in my football playing
career. I had a point to prove, I had anger to release. I wasn't so

much as playing the game *for* Quick, as I was playing it to *avenge* him. I wanted vengeance because his life had been taken away from him, because he couldn't be in the stands or be able to talk about the game afterward. I wanted vengeance, because he couldn't play the game that he loved with all of his heart. Quick was dead, and the other team was going to pay for it.

  The kicker kicked the ball toward me out of habit, and I moved under it and caught it I knew that he wasn't going to make that mistake again for the rest of the game. Already, his coaches were shouting at him. They knew what kind of mistake he had made.

  I took off full throttle down the sideline, and as soon as I saw most of the other teams players trying to make a bee line for the side line to intercept me, I cut back toward the middle of the field. I picked up a couple of blocks from my teammates, and that was all she wrote. I hit an extra gear and I channeled my anger into my stride. Usually when I ran angry, it was about running over some fool, or trying to stiff arm or punish some idiot in front of me. This time, I changed my anger into steam power. I could feel my legs pushing me forward harder and faster than they had ever pushed. I knew that I had just broken a record with this run. Not only was it a ninety-nine yard run, but it was a ninety-nine yard run in full pads, that had been accomplished in just over ten seconds.

Running a sub ten second time without pads was ridiculous, running it in just over ten seconds in football gear was unheard of. I knew that I was flying. I closed my eyes and I felt like I was back in New Orleans; barefooted, running through the projects. I was young again, times were good, Katrina was years in the future. I could see my friends in front of me, I could see my friends chasing me, I could see girls in pig tails smiling and laughing, I could see white linen hanging on the clotheslines throughout the projects, and I could smell fried chicken, gumbo, collard greens, and the salt from the ocean breeze. No one could touch me.

I heard the roar of the crowd, and snapped out of it, just in time to cross the goal line and see the line judges lift their arms and signal a touchdown. I had ran back the opening kickoff for a touchdown. I turned and stared at my sideline, my teammates were going crazy, my coaches were going crazy, and the stands had been whipped into an uncontrollable frenzy. The flashing lights from the camera were blinding. And they were not just from digital cameras, or cell phone cameras, but from news cameras. Some local, some state, and some national. I didn't know what to do. I was breathing so heavily that my chest was heaving up and down visibly. Normally I would jump into the air and chest bump, or act like I was ripping open my shirt and showing everyone the S on my chest. Tonight was different. Not just record setting different, but surreal different. I wasn't in a celebratory mood. I was still angry, and my mind was on Quick. I was reflective. And so I did something that I hadn't done since Augustine's death. I tossed the ref the ball, ignored my teammates, tuned out the roaring crowd, and knelt down in the end zone.

God and I weren't exactly on good terms. I had been angry since the death of Augustine, and even angrier since Quick's death. I had questions, and He didn't see fit to answer them. So why I knelt down in prayer was beyond me. I couldn't explain it for the life of me. All I know is that I knelt down, and said a prayer. I didn't pray for a safe game, or thank the Lord that no one was injured on that play, or thank Him for a touchdown, or ask for a good game. No, I prayed for Quick. I asked God to forgive Quick for everything that he had ever done, to understand what had happened to him, and to accept him into His kingdom. I wanted Quick to go to Heaven.

After my prayer, I rose, and jogged to the sideline and joined my teammates. The coaches slapped me on the ass, my teammates embraced me, patted my back, slapped my shoulder pads, while I walked past them to the bench to take a seat. One of my coaches handed me some oxygen, which I gladly took. I placed the mask on my face and breathed in deeply. My rest on the bench however, was short lived.

Running back a touchdown on the opening kickoff, normally did two things; one, it put the opposing team in an awkward position. It made them desperate to respond in order to regain the momentum, and to keep the team from a letdown. They needed to send a message that this was going to be a game, not a blowout, and the coach needed to keep his team's head together. This caused mistakes. The second thing that it did, was embolden the scoring team. We had scored easily. Usually the first drive is to feel the other team out, but now we had a touchdown that we hadn't counted on, and our entire offense was still fresh. This also got our teammates hyped, especially our special teams players. Coach was now in a position to try something risky.

Coach Beckwith called for a bounce kick, which was not exactly an onside kick, but a short kick to keep the ball out of their return man's hands, and get it in the hands of one of their slower players up front. And usually, those slower players up front were blockers, not used to handling the football. Coach Beckwith's gamble worked beyond his intentions. The ball hit one of the blockers on the other team, bounced off of his shoulder pads and onto the ground. One of our special teams guys dove on the ball, giving us possession once again. Our crowd and our team went wild.

"Baptiste!" Coach Gaines shouted. "You ready?"

I pulled off the oxygen mask, grabbed my helmet, and raced onto the football field. My last touchdown had been as a part of special teams, and so my offensive line hadn't had a chance to hit the field, and neither had my quarterback. They were all fresh.

As usual, the first play out was a run play. Coach usually called a simple hand-off for the first play so that our quarterback can get the snap right, so the receivers can gauge the speed of the guys guarding them, so that our lineman can get some initial contact, so that our quarterback can feel the ball in his hand, and for dozens of other reasons. The play was sending me straight up the middle.

The quarterback called the snap count, the center snapped the ball, and I was handed the football. I tucked it away, and blasted through the middle of the line, right between the center and the guard. They had opened up an enormous hole for me in the middle, and the fullback blasted their middle line backer. My tight end's hunted their outside line backers, while my receiver's handled their corner backs. That left me, and two safeties to deal with. I cut left, immediately causing their safety on my right to try to cut me off before I got to the the end zone, while their safety responsible for guarding the left side of the field made a bee line straight for me. It was one on one.

Despite all of my anger, all of the frustration that was

penned up inside of me, I managed a smile. They were idiots. The right side safety had taken himself out of the picture by trying to cut me off, leaving me one-on-one with the remaining safety. I cut left again, then right, causing him to trip over his own feet. I immediately headed for the now empty right side of the field.

The safety who was supposed to be guarding this side, but who had headed to the left to cut me off, quickly changed directions and tried to cut me off before I got to the end zone on this side of the field. I was way too fast for this fool. I would be through the end zone and sitting on the bench before he got anywhere close to me. Had I ran straight into the end zone, that would have been enough. But it wasn't. I was angry, and I was out to humiliate these fools. I looked behind me to make sure that nothing was coming, and once I was sure that everyone else had pretty much given up on the play, I changed direction and headed toward the safety that was coming toward me. I could hear the crowd screaming no, and I could see my coaches going ballistic on the sidelines. I raced toward the safety, and just as he got close, I stopped instantly. He tried to overcompensate for his speed, and found himself sliding across the field and out of bounds. I lifted the football into the air and walked into the end zone triumphantly.

The crowd exploded, the refs knew that it was bad sportsmanship, but didn't know what to call. I hadn't taunted, I hadn't acted like I was doing the Superman, I had simply humiliated another player by avoiding his tackle and making him slide out of bounds. They looked at one another confused as hell. The coach for the other team was going ballistic screaming for a penalty flag to be thrown. While my teammates once again surrounded me and congratulated me. I knew that my coaches were beyond livid, but fuck them. I was giving them what they wanted, and I was giving the crowd what it had come to see. I felt like Maximus in the movie *Gladiator.* I wanted to lift my arms to the crowd and ask them if they were not entertained. That what it felt like to me on this night, a blood sport. I was hurting, and yet they cared little about my pain. And so, I was out to inflict humiliation and pain on the other team, regardless of how the other players would feel after the end of the game, regardless of what scouts were there watching them, regardless of how many college scholarships and opportunities that I ruined that night, I was out for blood.

I went on to score seven more touchdowns that game, before coach pulled me from the game. I had tied a high school record for most touch downs in a single game. I would have owned the record, had coach not pulled me. But my antics on the field had grown with each touchdowns. We were beating the other team by fifty points, so leaving me in the game would have been completely ridiculous and unsportsmanlike on his part. He pulled all of his

starters, once the lead was more than thirty points. Sitting on the
bench gave me time to search the crowd thoroughly. I knew that he
was here.

My father never missed a game. Despite what he was going
through, despite all that had happened, he still managed to make
each and every one of my games. Rain, sleet, snow, or sunshine, I
could always find him sitting high up in the stands if I really
searched. I found him tonight.

I tossed my helmet and raced for the stands. He had stood,
and started to mill out with some of the other members of the
crowd. For all intents and purposes, the game had *been* over. Most
of their crowd had left at half-time, while the majority of ours
stayed to watch the show. But now that it was the fourth quarter,
even our die-hard faithful thought it better to beat traffic, than to
wait for the last few minutes to tick off the clock. We were down to
our fourth string players now, and if coach could have pulled
cheerleaders off the bench and suited them up he would have. Guys
who only touched the field during blowouts were now getting
massive amounts of playing time. They were even getting
exhausted.

I climbed over the rail, and raced through the stands trying
to find him. I needed him, *I needed to talk to him. I needed him to
acknowledge me.* I was hurting, and I couldn't go to my Mom, so I

was searching for the next best thing, my Dad.

I spotted him in the distance. He was wearing the same tattered brown jacket that he normally wore on cool evenings. His hair was uncut, and he wore it in a small untrimmed graying afro. He also had a scruffy un-kept medium sized beard on his face.

"Dad!" I shouted.

He kept walking.

I imagine no one had called him that in years, and so he probably no longer answered to it.

"Dad!" I shouted again. I raced toward him, and the crowd, upon seeing me in my football uniform, parted for me. I raced up to my father, jogged in front of him, and stopped just before him. He searched my eyes.

"Dad," I said, calling out to him softly.

My father could see the tears welling up in my eyes. He was that kind of man. He could sense pain, and he always knew the right words to say to make things better. I needed that ability from him on that night.

We stood face to face, staring at one another for several moments. The tears falling from my eyes, brought water to his own.

"I need you," I told him.

My father nodded. "I know."

"Come home," I told him. "Come to Big Momma's. You don't have to be on the street."

Again, he nodded. "I know."

"I need you," I pleaded. They were the words that kept popping into my head.

"I'm sorry," my Dad said softly.

I shook my head. "Don't be sorry, *just be there.*"

He turned his palms up. "How can I? Look at me!"

"I need you!" I said more forcefully, with my tears flowing more heavily.

"How can I help you?" he asked, in an almost pleading tone. "How can I be of any help to anybody?"

"You can help me, by coming home."

My father shook his head. "I don't have a home. Not anymore."

"Home is where *we* are," I said pleading. "You once said, that home is where we are when we're together."

My father nodded, and wiped the tears from his eyes. "We're not all together, son. Not anymore. Not anymore..."

My Father walked past me and headed for the exit.

"*You and I are still here!*" I shouted. "*We can re-build together!*"

He stopped, hesitated for a moment, and then turned to face

me. "I'm sorry about your friend."

He knew about Quick.

He turned out his palms. "I can't help you, son. I wish I could, but I have nothing left to give."

"You can give me your love," I told him.

He shook his head. "I never took it away."

"You can come home, you can be there for me, we can re-build our life together."

"I'm broken, son," he said, with tears pouring down his face. "How can I re-build, when I'm still broken?"

"I miss her too," I said softly.

My father turned and headed for the exit.

*"She would want us to be together!"* I shouted. *"She would want us to be strong, to work through this together."*

My father paused at the exit for a moment, and then continued on, getting lost inside of the exiting crowd.

# **Chapter Nineteen**

My record breaking performance may have been one for the ages, but I still felt like shit the entire weekend. Seeing my father, and seeing the state he was in, bothered me more than I could began to explain. His eyes were glassy, like a crack head, even though he wasn't a smoker. He still had those eyes, those eyes that seemed to stare through you, or to stare at life without seeing it, without partaking in it. As if he were a real walking, talking, breathing zombie. I had heard about the cats coming back from Vietnam with what they called a thousand yard stare. Like they had seen shit that was too horrific to believe, to much to take in or digest. They had seen the pale horse, and they were different for having done so. That was the look in my Father's eyes. He had seen the most horrific things in life, and he was worse off for it.

The thought of seeing him that way played over and over

again in my head the entire weekend. Was there any hope of bringing him back? What could be done? What could I do? Was it even to late at this point?

I sat in the school library daydreaming about my situation, until my thoughts were interrupted by Adanna.

"A penny for your thoughts?" she asked with a smile.

I shook my head. "Just thinking about my father."

"It was hard seeing him the other night," she said shaking her head. She rested her hand on top of mine. "You have to believe that everything will work itself out."

"That's easy for you to say."

"It's easy for anyone who has faith to say," she shot back. "You just have to have a little faith."

I shook my head. "Faith implies that there is someone listening. My prayers haven't exactly been answered these last nine years."

"Just because you can't see a plan, doesn't mean there isn't one," she replied.

"Man, miss me with all of that," I said, slashing my hand across my throat. "I'm not trying to hear that shit right now."

Adanna pushed my SAT study guide toward me. "Okay, then let's focus on this."

I pushed it away. "I'm really not trying to focus on this

either right now."

Her mouth fell open. "Really?"

"Yes, really," I said, mocking her British accent.

"You do want to get a great score, don't you?" she asked, growing upset. "You do remember the plan don't you. Oh, that's right, you don't believe in plans."

I exhaled, sat back in the plastic library chair and stared at her. "Are you serious? Are we really doing this right now?"

"I can't tell what we're doing!" Adanna snapped. "We were supposed to be here studying. But instead, you've chosen to wallow in your misery."

"Wallow in my misery?" I asked, sitting up. "My Mother's dead, my Father is living on the streets, my home was destroyed, not one, but *two* of my best friends are dead, and yet I wallowing in my misery.  Sorry if I'm boring you, Princess.  But you know, some of us have real problems here.  We don't have parents back in the United Kingdom with a bunch of stolen loot from the Nigerian people.  Corrupt government contracts must have been pretty sweet to have, Princess."

Adanna took her palm and slapped me across the side of my forehead.

"Fuck you, asshole!" she shouted.

"I'm sorry."

She rose, and I clasped her arm.

"I'm sorry!" I repeated. "Don't go."

"You know, you can be a real asshole sometimes," she whispered through clenched teeth.

I lowered my head and nodded. "I know."

"Let me go!" she said, snatching her arm away.

"Me, me, me! It's always all about you, always about *your* grief, about what *you're* going through, what *you're* dealing with. *You self-centered bastard!* There are millions of people all over the world who would trade places with you in an instant! You're going to university next year, St. Claire! *Next year!* Do you know how many people would kill or die to have that opportunity? Faith isn't just about praying to some invisible god in the sky, it's also about hope! Hope for a better tomorrow, hope for a better future! It's about bringing hope to your community, about giving hope to your grandmother, it's about giving hope to the next kid from South Acres who comes along and wants to do something with their life. *It's not always about you! Get over yourself!*"

"I'm sorry," I whispered.

Adanna rose and began to collect her belongings.

"Please, don't go," I pleaded.

"You should have paid more attention in history class, and you should have read those book I gave you on African history. It's obvious to me now that you didn't."

I lowered my head. She gathered her purse.

"The history of your people is one of faith. Before there was a God of Abraham, there was *your* people, kneeling, bowing in worship, thanking the Almighty Creator for all of the blessing the He had bestowed upon them. The history of your people is about hope. About never giving up. No matter how hard times got, or how desperate things appeared to be, nor how dire the situation became, they endure because of faith. Their faith in one another, their faith in a better tomorrow, their faith in a better world. The skin that God blessed them with, was His covenant with them, and yet, you have the faith of an empty milk carton. People look at you on the football field like you're a god, little do they know that you have the faith and the courage of a coward."

Adanna banged the desk in front of me and leaned in. "A man has the courage of his convictions, he has the strength to lead his woman to a better tomorrow. He has the strength to lead his people to the promised land. How can you lead your woman to a better life, or lead your team to victory, when you can't even lead your own emotions? Call me when you, the *old* St. Claire, is ready to dream big again. Call me when you finish wallowing in self pity, and are ready to move forward with our life together."

Adanna turned and strutted out of the library leaving me

alone with my thoughts. She was right. I had been focusing so
much on my own grief, that I had thought little of anyone else. I
hadn't checked up on Augustine's girl in a while, or checked up on
his mother. I had been so focused on how *I* felt, that I had lost track
of my community, and what they had riding on the season. I needed
to get my shit together, and I was glad that I had a real ass chick to
put me back in check whenever I needed it. Adanna's ability to
keep it real, and to put shit in perspective was one of the reasons
why I loved her so much. She took my sorrow, and made me feel
like shit for thinking about myself. There were millions of people
around the world who would love to have the opportunities that I
had. No matter how bad I thought my situation was, things could
have always been worse. The fact that I had colleges pursuing me,
meant that I had choices. And with choices, came hope. And where
there was hope, their was faith. I had been stupid and blind. And
now, I needed to go and get my girl, and I needed to crack down on
my studying to make sure that I kept all of my opportunities open.

I rose from the library table, gathered my belongings, and
ran after my woman.

# **Chapter Twenty**

After school practice came quick. The recruiters sitting in the stands had grown exponentially. I couldn't officially commit to any school until February, on National Signing Day, so all of the schools felt like they still had a chance to win me. I had kept my cards close to my chest, so no one but Adanna knew where I was really heading. Again, it all depended on my SAT scores.

Savawn's crazy ass grabbed a football and whistled. "Running back baby! Go long, Baby!"

Savawn motioned down the field with his hand, and I took off down the football field. We were just messing around. I wasn't being recruited as a receiver, and Savawn wasn't being recruited as a quarterback, but all eyes were on us. Savawn launched the football through the air, and I ran under it. It was a sixty yard pass, and I never broke stride. I could hear the whistles and the comments from the dozens upon dozens of recruiters on the bench. And now it was my time to show off. I lobbed the ball back down field to Savawn, and hit him right in his chest. The recruiters went crazy. All of them immediately began scribbling notes and tapping on their laptop keyboards. It was hilarious. It was just shit we did on the streets in the hood. Lobbing passes back and forth. Any kid in the hood could lob a pass down the field accurately. I guess the only problem was, recruiters went to football games to scoop up talent, not pick up games in the projects. That was too bad for a lot of brothers.

Savawn threw me another pass, this time to the opposite side of where I was standing, forcing me to have to run across the field to catch it, which I did.

"Whew!" Savawn shouted. "It's those QB skills, Baby!"

"It's my catching skills, nigga!" I shouted back. I returned the favor, by lobbing a pass back down field, but this time, I sent it to the other side of where he was standing, also forcing him to have to run across the field to catch the ball. Savawn caught it with one hand.

"You can't fade me, nigga!" Savawn shouted. "That's skills, nigga! I got hands like Super Glue! Whew!"

"That's cum from jacking off all night, nigga!" Big Matt shouted.

Everyone on the field laughed.

"I don't touch my own dick," Savawn told him. "Ya momma won't let me!"

Ooohs and Awwws, accompanied by laughter shot through the field.

"I got something for you when I catch your ass!" Big Matt told him.

"Same thing yo mamma said!" Savawn shouted.

Everyone broke into laughter.

"Fuck you, nigga!" Big Matt shouted.

"Baptiste!" Coach Gaines shouted, while waving for me to come over.

I walked to the side line, where Coach was standing and talking to a couple of unfamiliar faces. I assumed they were recruiters, like all of the other unfamiliar White faces around campus this time of the year.

"What's up, Coach?" I asked.

"This is Coach Harmon from Auburn, and this is Coach Lambert from Florida State," Coach Gaines said, introducing the two men.

I nodded at them.

"Some arm you got there, son," Coach Harmon said. "Ever play quarterback before?"

"Just when I was a kid," I said, shrugging. "Some in middle school. Played a little bit my freshman year when our two starters got hurt."

Coach Harmon nodded, leaned over, and spit out some chew.

"Baptiste is a true stud," Coach Gaines told them. "He's a true athlete in every sense of the word. He can run, catch, throw, and pretty much do it all."

"He's got the build of a running back, thick calves, solid, but the height of a DB," Coach Lambert said, examining me."

"Well, you know we like 'em big these days," Coach Harmon said smiling. He had a deep Southern drawl that made me feel uncomfortable. "The days of the small running back are long gone. These days, we like 'em muscular, but we also like some height on 'em."

"How tall are you son?" Coach Lambert asked.

"Six three," I answered.

"Well, turn around," Coach Gaines said, twirling his finger. "Let 'em get a good look at ya."

I recoiled at first, and then I spun slowly. Coach Harmon knelt down and began to squeeze and examine the muscles in my calves.

"Oh yeah, he's ready," Coach Harmon declared. "And we

gonna get you even bigger than that by the time we all done with ya."

I felt humiliated, dirty. I was pissed at myself for turning around and showcasing my muscles.

"Go ahead, get ya pads off," Coach Gaines told me.

I hesitated.

"Take 'em off son!" Coach Gaines said excitedly.

I unbuckled my shoulder pads, and then pulled them over my head. I let them drop to the ground. I was wearing a wife beater that had been cut off midriff. My abs were exposed, my shoulders, arms, upper back, and neck. Coach Harmon thumbed the muscles in my upper arm, while Coach Lambert jotted down some notes on a pad he was carrying.

"Solid as a rock!" Coach Harmon said, laughing. "You already built for college."

"What I tell ya?" Coach Gaines asked with a smile.

Listening the the three of them with their deep Southern drawls, talking about how muscular I was, how fast I could run, how well I could catch, all the while poking, and prodding, and squeezing my muscles and jotting down notes, was the most humiliating experience I had ever been through. I had on my pants, but still, I felt naked. I felt like a slave on the auction block. They stood in front of me and talked about getting me ready for the NFL, and how the boosters would love the fact that they had brought in another legitimate NFL prospect. How much money the schools got from former gads who went on to the NFL, and how much having legit prospects on the team brought in money from the schools alumni and how much it help get them TV time on the networks. They examined me, and then they ignored me like I wasn't even there. It was like a group of overseers talking in front of a buck they were going to buy and then groom for the field and use for breeding. I had value to them, in so much as what I could do for them. No one mentioned school, or education, or graduation. It was a foregone conclusion that I would declare early for the draft, drop out of college, and go into the NFL. They knew my future. It had been well mapped out, because they had seen it thousands of times over their careers. Black bucks from poor areas of the country always took the money and ran. That's why we were there. We were the entertainment, the help, the property. They were the owners. We preformed, they got payed, the crowds were entertained, and everyone was happy. I felt more than dirty, I felt violated. I needed to hit the showers. In fact, I needed to get away from these men, before they saw the tears that had formed in the corners of my eyes. I turned and walked away.

\*\*\*\*\*

I hit the showers and exited the locker room. Only to run into Mr. Davis waiting outside. I had spotted him in the stands during football practice, along with a group of other teachers. It was like that now, we were undefeated and even the teachers were coming out to practice and to the games. The entire community was electric with excitement.

"What's up, my man?" Mr. Davis said, greeting me.

I shook my head.

"Team looking good," he continued. "And that was quite a performance you put on the other night."

"Thanks," I told him.

"That wasn't a compliment," he said flatly.

I stopped and stared at him.

"Humiliating the other team like that," he said shaking his head. "How did you feel after the game?"

"Good," I said flatly.

"And now? How do you feel about it now?"

"Good."

Mr. Davis smiled. "You have a lot of anger inside of you, Youngster. And that much anger pinned up inside is not good. Not good at all."

"I used it on the football field, instead of grabbing a baseball bat and beating the shit out of someone," I told him.

Again he smiled and nodded. "There are worse ways for anger to manifest itself, I'll give you that. But then, there are also better. That kind of anger is like acid, C. B. It's poison, it'll kill you slowly from the inside."

"That's why I'm getting it out of me on the field," I told him.

"Let it go, son. Just let it go. Hurting someone else, is not going to bring your friend back."

"Quick. His name is Quick."

"Who the hell you think you're talking too?" Mr. Davis asked. "I know who the hell Quick is. How are you gonna come at me like that?"

I lifted my hand to my face and I rubbed my tired eyes.

"Let it go," Mr. Davis repeated. "You have so much in front of you. So much! Let it go."

"How can you just let someone go?" I asked growing upset. "*How?* He was my friend? *I can't just let his life go!* I can't just let his *memory* go! I can't just forget about him, walk away, and go off to college like he never existed, or like none of this ever happened! *My life isn't just a bad fucking dream!*"

"Hey, watch your mouth!"

I nodded. "I'm sorry."

"I'm not asking you to forget about him or his memory. I'm

226

saying don't let the anger you have inside burn you up. You can let what happened go, without letting go of his memory. Quick was a great football player. You're going to have the opportunity that he wanted so desperately to have. Carry him with you. Go and make a future for both of you, that's how you honor his memory."

Again, I rubbed my eyes. "I'm tired."

Mr. Davis recoiled. A half smile came to his face. "You're seventeen."

"And I'm so tired," I said, shaking my head.

"Being a young Black male in America can *be* exhausting."

"How did you do it?" I asked. "How? How did you make it, how did you even know what right decisions to make?"

"I didn't" Mr. Davis said, shaking his head. "I made plenty of wrong ones. It was all about trial and error. But at the end of the day, through it all, I just kept moving forward. That's what you have to do, C.B. You keep moving forward. Times get tough, you just have to keep going."

"Faith," I said lowering my head and laughing. I thought about what Adanna said.

Mr. Davis nodded. "Faith. And I guess I had a little bit of luck on my side as well. I didn't have to pay for the mistakes I made with a prison sentence, or with my life. You just have to be careful, think things through, try to not make mistakes or put yourself at risk. You're so close."

"I keep hearing that," I told him. "But I don't *feel* like I'm close. I feel like I'm about to start something I never could even began to imagine. It feels like I'm about to step into a giant pile of dog shit. But it's a pile a dog shit that everyone is expecting me to step in."

Mr. Davis looked confused. "What are you talking about?"

"College, and then the NFL."

"Oh, so you're already in the NFL are you?" Mr. Davis said laughing. "Don't count your chickens before they hatch. You know how many college football players there are in this country? Do you know how many NFL teams there are in this country? It's simple mathematics, son. The chances of making it into the NFL are slim. I'm not saying you can't or you won't, I would never piss on your dreams like that. But have a back up plan, C.B. Go to college, find something that you love to do, major in it. If the NFL happens for you, then wonderful, if not, then you'll be able to earn a living in a career that you love."

I nodded toward the football field. "Not what they're saying. They pretty much think it's a foregone conclusion. College football on Saturdays, and then an early exit to the draft, and then NFL football on Sundays. They have it all mapped out for me."

"*They?* Who is they?"

"All of those recruiters in there and out here and all over the damn country!"

"Is that what you have mapped out for yourself?" Mr. Davis asked.

I shrugged my shoulders. "I thought I did."

"You're not sure now?"

I nodded. "I always wanted this. I've wanted it for as far back as I could remember. I have a talent, and I want to use that talent to get my grandmother out the hood."

"Do you enjoy playing the game?"

"Does it matter?"

Mr. Davis nodded. "Yes, it matters. There are plenty of other ways to get your grandmother out of the hood. A college education will accomplish the same things. Maybe not as lavish at first, but it'll have the same results."

I peered off into the distance. I could see the emptying school parking lot, and the ramshackle houses of my neighborhood. I wanted out of this place, that was for sure.

"I still love the game," I said softly.

"Then what is it?" Mr. Davis asked. "What am I missing? What are you not telling me?"

"Feels like a dirty game," I answered bluntly.

Mr. Davis lifted his hand to his chin, and rubbed the lower

half of his face. I could hear his rough hands rubbing up against the stubble that had grown on his unshaven face.

"I saw them from across the field," he said softly. "What were they doing, measuring you?"

I nodded. "And checking out my muscles. Squeezing my calves, measuring my height. I felt like an animal."

"A show horse?" Mr. Davis said shaking his head.

"A work horse," I said correcting him. "I felt like a slave."

Mr. Davis nodded. "Fuck them."

Silence interrupted our conversation for several moments, with neither of us knowing what to say.

"That's the game they play, C.B." Mr. Davis continued. "They use you. A lot of times, they use you up, and then put you out to pasture. They get rich off of your talent and your skills, off of your hard work, your dedication, your persistence. But it's up to you to reverse the game and to use them back. They want you to give them piles of money from TV revenue, then that's what you have to do in order to get a free education from them. You do it. And you use their alumni network, and you use the fame and the contacts and the connections that you'll get, and you do something with those things. You use them, like they're going to use you. Two can play at that game."

"I have to sell my soul..."

*"You're not selling your soul to the devil!"* Mr. Davis said forcefully. "Don't even think of it like that. "You're getting a free education, doing something you love to do. And you *get* that degree. And then you take that money from that contract, and you get your grandmother out the hood, and then you use that money to help others who are going through what you went through, what your mother went through, what you father is going through, what your grandmother has gone through. You use that money to help others. You hear me, St. Claire?"

I nodded slowly. And I would. I would use them, like they were going to use me. I knew what I had to do. I didn't feel good about what had happened to me today, or about what was going to happen, but I knew that I had to keep my eyes on the prize.

# **Chapter Twenty One**

I walked home that evening with much on my mind. I had Quick weighing heavily on my thoughts, my SAT's, my conversation with Mr. Davis, my experience with the recruiters, my father, and even thoughts of my mother. My head felt heavy, like I had the weight of the world resting on top on it, and all of the world's problems dancing between my ears. My head was spinning, and lately, I had even began to get migraines from all of the stress and pressure that I was under. I had so much to work through, and the two cats who understood what I was going through better than anyone else, were dead. I walked up on the homies at the hood store.

I don't know why I stopped, or what brought me to the hood store. It wasn't the same; the atmosphere wasn't the same. Quick had meant so much, to so many, it was as if the entire hood was in mourning. The color, the sunshine, the life, and the laughter had somehow left the hood. All of the homies gathered at the hood store had long faces. Even their hustling seemed lifeless, like they were all just going through the motions. Dirty walked up on the side of me and wrapped his arm around my neck.

"How you doing?" Dirty asked. He lifted his forty and took a swig from it.

I nodded. "I'm okay. And you?"

"Fucked up," Dirty confessed. "It ain't the same. Shit just ain't been the same. I ain't been able to sleep since my nigga got hit."

I nodded. I knew what he meant and how he felt.

"You know that nigga loved you like a brother, right?" Dirty asked.

I paused, and then nodded. I knew that he did. I knew that he thought of me as a little brother. I knew that he wanted me to make it out of the hood, to go on and do the things that life had denied him.

"He would want you to keep on doing good and shit," Dirty continued.

I could smell not just beer on his breath, but something much stronger. And when I peered into his eyes I saw the redness that covered them. He was drunk.

"I know."

"We got to keep moving, my nigga," Dirty told me. "We got to take care of each other."

I had never thought about Dirty in terms of someone who made much sense, or who thought rationally, or as someone who even thought about tomorrow. He was tatted up, and ten toes into the game, and so I always thought of this as being his entire world. The hood, the game, this life, this was his world. He as a product of the hood, and the hood wasn't a place of tomorrows, it wasn't a place of plans, or dreams, or any such thing. It was a holding place, a place where we milled around until prison or the graveyard. That's what it was for ninety-nine percent of us, while a fortunate few escaped. I always thought of Dirty as being one of the ninety-nine percent. What did 'keep moving' mean? What did it mean to him?

"I got love for you too, my nigga," Dirty said, slurring. "I'm here for you if you need anything. If you need anything at all. Any bread, if anybody is fucking with you, anything! You hear that, my nigga?"

I nodded.

"We fam," Dirty proclaimed. "And we gone stay fam."

Lil Roc and Deuce walked up.

"For my nigga Quick," Deuce said, pouring some beer out

onto the concrete.

"For my nigga," Lil Roc said, joining him in his salute. He poured out some beer, and then took a long swig from his bottle.

"We gonna handle all them niggaz," Deuce proclaimed.

"I shot one of them bitches yesterday," Half Dead said, walking up and joining in the conversation. "Caught that punk ass nigga slipping at Greenspoint Mall. I put three hot ones in him."

"Word, my nigga!" Dirty said, with he and Half Dead exchanging handshakes.

"This little old chicken head I fuck with, say them niggaz be up in Rays Rib Shack on the weekends," Deuce said.

"Word?" Dirty asked.

Deuce nodded. "Word, my nigga. We can catch them hoes up in that bitch and let the choppers holler."

"It's on then," Dirty said, again exchanging handshakes. "We gone get with they ass."

"Hell yeah," Lil Roc said, nodding.

The scene at the hood store was almost surreal. The fact that some of us had gathered at the cuts, made others stop and stay. Within the blink of an eye, the hood store was packed with young, angry, armed niggaz from the hood. They all had Quick on their mind, and they were all looking for payback.

"What you been up to, nigga?" Lil Roc said, slapping me on

the back of my head.

Lil Roc was another NOLA transplant. He and I grew up in the hood together, and he and I both played football together while growing up. He was good. But like so many others, he quit playing after his freshman year, and then dropped out of high school altogether after his sophomore year. He started getting his hustle on, and slowly we stopped seeing each other and grew apart. Our activities were different, and so was our paths. We did, however, still count one another as close friends.

"Check this out," Lil Roc said, nodding for me to follow.

I followed him out of the store parking lot and across the street, where he pulled a key fob out of his pocket and hit a button. The alarm chirped on his new whip. It was a candy orange colored Camaro sitting on some chrome and candy orange colored thirty inch rims. It screamed ghetto, it screamed dope boy, but still, it was clean as hell.

I stuck out my hand, and we slapped hands. "I see you riding donk, my nigga!"

"And you know this!" Lil Roc said with pride.

The paint on the Camaro was custom. Not only was it metallic, but it was candy coated, with a technique that made it look like it was still wet. On top of that, it was also chameleon. It looked yellow, and even changed to a dark orange or almost black, depending on how you looked at it, where you stood, and how the sun was reflecting off of it. It was a ten thousand dollar paint job at least. Lil Roc had definitely came up.

He hit another button, and the doors popped open, and lifted up slightly. They took me by surprise, because the last thing I was expecting was that they were Lamborghini doors and tilted up in a scissor type motion. I lifted open the door and peered inside. The interior had been completely redone. Custom candy orange and black leather covered every surface of the interior, while the center stack played host to an expensive looking stereo and navigation touch screen.

"Get in, nigga!" Lil Roc told me.

We both climbed inside. The car reeked of weed smoke.

"Close the door," he told me.

I closed the Lamborghini door, and watched as he pulled a large blunt from his sun visor. He lifted a lighter from the car's center console and lit up his cigar.

"You smoke?"

I shook my head and waved him off.

"More for me, nigga!" he said with a smile. He inhaled deeply, and then blew smoke rings into the air. "Fucked up about Quick."

I nodded. "For real."

"I know that nigga cutted for you.

Again, I nodded.

"We gone get them niggaz," Lil Roc declared. "Believe that. You can bet your ass on that, my nigga."

I leaned back and exhaled. I knew Quick, I knew how he was, how he thought, and what he would do. He would be the first to hop in the car and ride for a nigga from the hood. That's just who he was. I couldn't say that Quick wouldn't want this, because he would. He would want every nigga from the hood to mount up, and go out and take out every son of a bitch that had something to do with his death, and then take out they momma's for having them. He would want blood running through the street.

"And what happens then, my nigga?" I asked, turning toward Lil Roc. "What happens after they are dead?"

Lil Roc shrugged. "Shit, then they dead. That's good enough for me."

"And then they homeboys have to come back for revenge. And then we have to go back for vengeance again, and then it never stops. This shit has been going on since before we got here, since before we were born. Some fools got into it at Jamaica Jamaica, or Club Northside, or at some fucking mall back in the day, and both the hoods have been paying for it in blood ever since. When the fuck does it stop?"

Lil Roc took a long pull off his blunt and peered at me sideways. "Not now. Maybe another time, maybe when they want to call it quits, but not right now. You know the homie would want us to ride for him."

I nodded. "I know. I also know that the homie wanted to get the fuck outta the hood. He wanted to go to college on a football scholarship, and after that wasn't a possibility, he wanted to raise up outta the hood by coming up in the game. But at the end of the day, he wanted out of this bullshit. He wanted out of this cycle."

"Ain't nobody asking you to ride," Lil Roc said, staring at me. "We all know that Quick wouldn't have wanted that."

"I don't want it!" I said forcefully. "Quick shouldn't want it! You shouldn't want it! Nobody should want it!"

"What's up, man?" Lil Roc said, leaning back and staring at me. "Talk to me, homie."

I turned and stared out the window. The crowd had grown even larger. Someone had cranked up their car stereo system, and what seemed to be the entire hood was gathered paying tribute to Quick. Everyone had a forty in their hand, and I could see a few of them pouring beer out onto the concrete in Quick's memory.

"I'm tired," I said, shaking my head. "I'm just tired."

Lil Roc offered me the blunt once again. "We all get tired."

I waved him off, declining the Dodi.

"I get tired," Lil Roc continued. "Tired of the police, tired of these niggaz trying to jack, tired of these shady ass bitches trying to set a nigga up, or get in a nigga's pocket. I get tired of the hustle. The deals, the pistols, walking into warehouses with dozens of fucking Colombians, not knowing if they going to blow my fucking head off."

"So why do you do it?" I asked.

"What else am I gonna do?" Lil Roc asked with a half smile. "Quit? Not eat? So, what is it that's got you so tired?"

"Everything. I got SAT scores that got to be high, or I don't get into college. I got football games I got to play, I'm worried about getting Big Momma out the hood, I got Adanna on my back, and her brothers fucking with me. I got Quick on my mind. I got Pop's in the streets. Man, I got so much shit on my mind it ain't funny."

"Big Momma is strong, and ain't nobody in the hood gonna let nothing happen to her," Lil Roc declared. "You got to study for them SAT joints, can't nobody help you with that. As for football, you know you got that shit. Don't worry about ya girl, she gone be there. And as for her busted ass brothers, I got something that'll get them off of ya."

He reached beneath his seat and pulled out a forty caliber

Smith and Wesson semi-automatic pistol. He ejected the clip to make sure that it was full, and then handed me the weapon.

"What's this?" I asked.

"What the fuck it look like, nigga?" Lil Roc asked with a smile. "It's a muthafuckin tool to make niggaz act right. It'll make them niggaz raise up off you."

I tried to hand the gun back, but he pushed my hand back. "Naw, homie, hang on to that. At least for the time being. Shit is about to get crazy around here. This shit is full blown, and you be walking home and jogging around the hood and shit. You need that."

"They ain't gonna come through here no time soon," I told him.

"Yeah, they are," he insisted. "They are gonna want some get back, once we get with them this weekend. Just keep it. Make me feel safe, homie."

"You don't need it?" I asked.

"Nigga, I got fifty more where that one came from!" he said laughing. Lil Roc rubbed his stomach. This weed got me hungry as a muthafucka. You want to get something to eat?"

I shrugged.

"What you feel like eating?" he asked. "I got you."

"Shit, don't matter to me."

"I want some soul fool," he declared. "We can roll over to the hood and hit up Just Oxtails and get some soul food."

I nodded, and he started up his whip, and we boned out.

---

I made it home sometime around two o'clock that morning. The trip to the soul food restaurant was followed by a trip to the liquor store, and then back to the cuts to kick it with the homies. We drank, and we celebrated my nigga Quick's life. We celebrated until it was time to move around. Dirty dropped me off at home, and I stumbled inside the house and into my bedroom. Big Momma hand long ago gone to sleep. I found myself sitting in a dark room, staring at a picture of my mother that was being illuminated by the moonlight filtering into the room. I missed her with every fiber of my being.

The alcohol didn't *make* my tears come, but simply made it *easier* for them to come. They would have flowed anyway. I lifted my mother's picture and stared at it.

"I miss you," I whispered.

She had been taken away from me too early, she had been taken away from me too suddenly. There was no warning, no sickness, no moments to steel myself for the upcoming departure.

One morning she was there, we left for Houston while she stayed to help out at the hospital, the winds came, and then she was gone. I missed her more than words could say.

"I wasn't ready for you to leave me," I said, staring at her picture. "I wasn't ready to let you go."

I had so many things I wanted to say to her, so many questions to ask, so many moments to have. I wanted her to see me graduate from high school, I wanted her to see me graduate from college, I wanted her to meet Adanna, I wanted her to see me walk down the aisle, and I wanted her to see her grand kids. I wanted my family back.

I sat down on the edge of my bed, only to realize that I had a nine millimeter handgun still tucked into my waistband. It jabbed uncomfortably into my gut, so I leaned to the side slightly and pulled the gun from my belt. I held it up to the light so that I could examine it. It was beautiful, as far as guns go. Not that I had seen many, or even held one in my hand before. But it was something about this one, that radiated power. I wondered how many times it had been fired, how many of the bullets that left it's barrel had actually struck someone, and how many people had it killed.

I laid back onto my bed, and for some unknown reason, placed the barrel of the gun against my temple. It could all be over in an instant, I thought. No need to worry about the SAT, about carrying my entire community's hopes on my shoulders, or about my father being on the streets. I wouldn't have to worry about Adanna's asshole brothers, or about Quick, or Augustine, or about anything else. No more worries, no more problems, just me and my Mother and Quick and Augustine reunited once again.

"Reunited," I whispered.

At my Mother's funeral, there was a poem on her program about a broken chain. About God calling each of us home, and about the chain linking up again. It was beautiful, poetic, it made death seem like the answer.

I could hear Big Momma's footsteps falling in the hallway. I quickly hide the gun beneath me, and pretended to be sleep, as she opened the door to my bedroom. I could hear her as she tried to tip toed into my room quietly, and then I felt her place her hand on my forehead, and she began to mumble. I knew what she was doing. She was doing what she had done so many times in the past. She was laying hands on me, and praying for me. I could feel the power of her prayers radiating through the warmth of her fingers. She prayed for me, she prayed for my safety, she was thanking the Lord for bringing me home safely one more night.

As Big Momma crept out of my bedroom, I knew that there was one thing that I would not do. I would not destroy the one thing in her life that had kept her going, that had made her strong, that had allowed her to weather many storms, I would not destroy her faith in God. I placed the gun beneath my pillow, and I rolled over and went to sleep.

# Chapter Twenty Two

Friday night football came quick that week. The roaring crowds, the bright lights, the smell of the freshly mowed grass of the football field; all these things combined to make me feel at home. The sights, sounds, and smells had made the stadium sort of a second home to me, as it was the only other place on Earth where I felt safe. On the field, I couldn't be touched, on the field I couldn't be harmed, on the field I was the master, and everyone else was subservient to my skills. Here, I was the predator, and everyone else was the prey.

The other team kicked off the football, and I got started early. I caught the ball at our twenty yard line, and ran it back to the forty. I jumped up angry at the fact that I had been tackled.

"Whew!" one of them shouted in my face. "Whew! You gonna get that all night boy!"

"Fuck you, White boy!" I shouted.

"What did you call me?" he asked, walking toward me.

"You heard me, you inbred muthafucka!" I said, walking up to him.

Players from both our teams scrambled to get in between us. The refs quickly intervened.

"You want to get tossed out the game?" one of the refs asked.

My teammates pulled me back to our side, and I walked to the huddle. I peered up, and saw that he was staying on the field. That was a good thing. I was going to see where he lined up, and I was going to go at him. I wanted to embarrass that fool; I wanted to shake his ass out of his shoes and make him trip and fall down.

"Just give me the ball, nigga!" I told the quarterback.

"Okay," our quarterback said nodding. "You want the ball, nigga. Thirty-eight pistol. On three. On three."

We all nodded, clapped our hands, and broke the huddle. I walked back to the line slowly, so that I could see where the big ass, country ass, White boy was lining up. Turns out, he was their middle linebacker. It was good in a way, because he would be too slow to get to the outside and help out his corners. But it was bad because I was about to hit the corner and he would be no where around, and I wanted that fool.

"Down!" The QB shouted. "Set!" And then he clapped once, then twice, and then finally a third time, signaling for the center to hike the football. Once the ball touched his hands, my line sprung into action. I got the ball instantly, and instantly, I headed right.

I made it only ten steps before I got blindsided and hammered from the left. I hit the ground hard, but managed to hold on to the football. I peered up from the ground to see Big Country standing over me with a big, wide grin, beating his chest.

"Whew!" he shouted. "Whew! All night, boy! All night! I own your ass! I own you, you hear me?"

I hopped up off the ground and dusted myself off. The only thing I could do is smile and nod.

"You got that one!" I said nodding. "You got that!" The big White boy was fast. Really fast. That's why they had stuck his ass in the middle. In addition to being fast, the muthafucka hit hard and could blow through our line. He was obviously the reason why they had the top defense in the area. I had to teach him a lesson about speed, and how to use it. He wanted to be aggressive and blow through the line, then we'd let him. We'd taught plenty of fools this year, and last year, about speed. There was individual speed, and there was team speed. Our whole fucking team was fast. And then there was White boy speed, and nigga speed, and then nigga-from-the-hood speed. We had nigga-from-the-hood speed. He was about to see the difference.

We huddled up.

"Hook and ladder his bitch ass," told them in the huddle.

They all knew who I was talking about.

"I don't know, their corners are pretty fast too," the QB declared.

"Fuck them," I declared. "Add the bootleg to it. I'm a show this fool."

"Don't get caught up in a personal battle with this fool." the QB told me.

"I got this, nigga!"

"Alright, on two," the QB declared.

We clapped our hands, broke the huddle, and jogged back to our positions.

The Quarterback clapped once, and then twice, setting everything in motion.

He handed the ball off to our fullback, he ran left. I was way off to the left, like we were in a triple set, with a running back. It looked like we were all going to take off and block for the full back. And just like clockwork, big boy blew through the line, and was about to blindside our full back. I went in motion, and he pitched it to me just before Big Country pummeled him.

The play called for me to get to the right hand side of the field, and either throw it to our Quarterback, who was down the field, or one of the receivers who had lined up in trips on the left. I could also keep it. The field was open on the right, and I could have hit it. I was angry, and I wanted to punish someone, but my anger somehow, someway, didn't get the best of me. I still did the level headed thing; I lobbed the ball down field to the Quarterback, who caught it in stride, and raced into the end zone. It had been a beautiful play.

I jogged over to Big Country who was getting up off of the ground from leveling our fullback, and began clapping my hands in his face.

"That's how it's done, Beeyotch!" I told him. I laughed and walked off the field.

\*\*\*\*\*

Our usual lopsided games had us expecting to win each and every game by a significant margin. Someone had forgotten to tell the other team. They had pride, and they knew that they were good, and they felt as though they could play with anyone, including the defending state champs. At the end of the game, the score was 56 – 42 in our favor. We had been in a dog fight most of the game, and hadn't been able to break away until the fourth quarter. They finally ran out of gas.

I stood on the sidelines, and peered up into the dispersing crowd. I knew that he was there. He never left a game early, and I knew that he wouldn't have left this one. In fact, no one had. Usually our blowouts are so significant, the crowd begins thinning at half-time, and by the end of the third, the opponents side is usually empty save for a couple of hundred parents and die-hard fans. Since this had been a dog fight, both sides of the stadium were still full up until the clock ticked down to zero. It had made him harder to spot, but finally, I caught a glimpse of my father.

I tossed my helmet down, climbed onto a table, and from there, climbed up over a rail and into the stands of the stadium. I had to catch him. I had to catch up to him. I parted the crowd forcefully, and made my way to where I saw him. The density of the crowd had slowed everyone's egress enough to where I was able to catch up to him.

"Dad!" I shouted, standing only a few feet behind him. "Dad!"

My father stopped, paused, and then slowly turned to face me. I could see fatigue in his eyes. Where it came from, I didn't know. It could have been from the streets, it could have been from grief, it could have just been from living life. Whatever it was from, I saw less resistance in them. Maybe he was just tired of running away from me, from our past, from the memories of my mother.

"I need you," I said softly.

My Dad lowered his head as if admitting something that he had tried so hard for so long not to acknowledge.

"I know it's hard, I know what you're going through," I told him. "I loved her too. I lost her *too*. And everyday it hurts. It hurts like it just happened. Sometimes, I think about her, and I cry."

My Dad eyes shifted rapidly from some unremarkable spot on the ground and locked into mine. It was if my admission had taken him by surprise. As if he had been unaware of the pain that I too had been experiencing.

"She would want us to be together," I continued. "She would want us to stay together, to get through this together, to keep our family together. She was strong, Dad. Stronger than both of us. She was a fighter. And she would've wanted us to fight. She would have wanted *you* to fight. She wouldn't have wanted neither one of us to quit. She wouldn't recognize you today, Dad. She wouldn't. She wouldn't recognize the person you are right now."

My father shifted his gaze toward the night sky and began to blink rapidly, as tears fell from his eyes.

"Please, Dad, come back to Big Momma's," I pleaded. "Get

off the streets. And if you don't want to do that, at least go to the shelter, go and get some help. You can go back to The Salvation Army, we can do this together. We just need to be a family again. *I need you!*"

My father looked at me, and for the first time in a long time, I saw something there. For the longest, whenever I peered into his eyes they had been lifeless, as if I were peering into the dark, soulless eyes of a dead deer.

"I..." he stammered trying to find the right words to say, and get them out. "I don't..."

"*You can!*"

He exhaled forcibly, as he relenting. "I can try."

"That's all I can ask," I said softly. "That's all it takes. Just trying. We don't have to take giant leaps. Baby steps will do. I just need you to get off the streets, I need you to talk to somebody."

My father shook his head. "What would talking to somebody do? They can't change nothing. They can't bring her back. They can't take Katrina back. It happened, son."

"*It did, Dad!*" I told him. "It happened. And now we have to keep going. We have to pick up the pieces, and we have to keep going."

"Pieces..." My father said, hold out his hands and showing me the shards of his broken life. "That's all that was left was pieces."

I reached out and closed his hands and held my hands on top of his. "No Dad, *I'm* left. I was left, and *you* were left. *We're still here. And we still have each other.* And we can help each other."

I watched my father's mouth fall open, like he was letting out a long silent scream. Tears poured from his eyes. I know that he had cried many nights, so it wasn't as if the flood gates we finally opening. If anything, it was the acknowledgment that we had to move forward that had him bawling. I guess that acknowledgment made the finality of her death finally hit home. Having to move forward, made him face the reality that she wasn't coming back, and that he had to live in a tomorrow without the woman that he was supposed to spend the rest of his life with.

"I need help too," I said, leaning in and wrapping my arms around him. "I need to talk to somebody. And I need to talk to you too. I need somebody who remembers. Somebody who remembers everything about her. Somebody who remembers everything we did, all the good times we had, all of the birthdays and Christmas mornings."

As I hugged my father, I felt movement with his arms. It was slow, paced, hesitant, but finally, he wrapped his arms around me. I don't know why, but him wrapping his arms around me made me burst into tears and cry uncontrollably. Maybe because for the first time in a long time, I genuinely felt like I wasn't alone. For the first time in a long time, it felt like I had my family back. For the first time in a long time, I had real hope for the future. Not just a football future, but a future where I felt whole, where I felt complete. I had half of my parents left, but like any child from a single parent home could attest, half of your parents could feel like having two parents. Half of your parents could make the whole world feel all right. Having half was better than having none at all. I felt good.

# Chapter Twenty Three

Monday afternoon I found myself in the library with Adanna. She was making sure that I had all of my shit together. She was like a study Nazi, and she was ruthless. She drilled Math, Science, Chemistry, English, and History into my head. And she also drilled into me African History, because she hated the history books that we were forced to study here in the U.S. She said that our history books were full of lies and propaganda. She would also quote this African proverb about how until lions got there own historians, the tales of the hunt, would always glorify the hunter. I got what she was saying. She was always throwing African proverbs my way, and teaching me about world history and African history. She was forceful in her assertions that African culture was the greatest culture on the planet, and how all other cultures were misguided copies. And I hated to get her started on the Ancient

Egyptians. She argued with our world civilizations teacher for weeks about how the Ancient Egyptians were Black Africans, and how Egypt had been a colony of Ethiopia, and how the racist Western powers and Arab conquerors conspired to hide this truth from the world. My baby was fierce when it came to Black history, Black people, and Black culture. She was smarter than any woman I knew, and *way* smarter than me. I knew that I was lucky to have her as my woman.

"You have to focus on this report!" she insisted, removing my hands from her behind. "Focus! You're not going to be able to write this history report with you hands on my arse."

I loved her British accent. It drove me crazy.

"Okay, what's the difference again?" I asked, lifting my pen.

Adanna exhaled forcibly, demonstrating her impatience at having to explain things to me again.

"Okay, listen up," she said, in her thick British accent. "The major difference between Sunnis and Shites is the order of succession after the death of the Prophet Muhammad. Sunnis believed that all leaders could be elected by a majority vote of the people, and so they elected Abu Bakr to serve as leader of the first Caliphate. The Shia believed that the Prophet himself chose his successor before his death, and that he chose his cousin/son-in-law

Ali to succeed him. The Shia felt like The Prophet's wishes were not respected and that Ali was betrayed because after Ali, the people elected two other people to serve as Caliphs before finally giving him the job. The Shia also believe that only the descendants of The Prophet can serve as religious leaders, and that because these people have the blood of The Prophet coursing through their veins, that they too are ordained by God. That's the biggest difference."

I closed my eyes and acted like I was snoring. Adanna punched me in the arm.

"Stop acting silly!" she said. She tapped at the paper sitting on the table just in front of me. "Are you getting all of this. Write it down before you forget it."

I wrote down as much as I could remember. I asked questions, she answered, and quickly I managed to compose the framework for my world civilizations report. We wrapped up our studying after about two hours, gathered our belongings, and headed out of the library. I usually walked her to her bus stop and waited with her whenever I didn't have football practice, or whenever I had football practice and she stayed late after school. I loved being able to spend this extra time with her. Lately, the only time we got to see each other was either at school, or on Sundays when we managed to sneak away and meet up at the hill overlooking the rail yard.

"What's on your mind?" I asked. I knew that something was bothering her, because if it was one thing Adanna was not, it was quiet. Her silence told me that something was on her mind.

"Weird things happening lately," she said.

"Weird things? Like what?"

"Like weird phone calls, like people sitting outside of my house," she said exhaling. "My house is being watched, of that I have little doubt."

"Watched?" I asked, lifting an eyebrow. "By who?"

"I don't know. The police maybe? Maybe others. Things are just getting weirder and weirder. Nelson, Wilson, Edward, who knows what my brothers are into at this point. All I know, is that they've seem to have gotten their hands on a significant amount of money."

What she was saying was bothering the fuck outta me. Lots of cash, somebody watching her, it all sounded like a bad situation about to get worse. I knew the Feds wouldn't hesitate to arrest everyone in the house, including her. And that was *if* it was the Feds. If it wasn't the police, then that was even worse. That meant it was jackers, and they wouldn't hesitate to kill everyone in the house. Home invaders in H-Town didn't leave witnesses, it was that simple. She needed to get out of there.

I knew that I couldn't ask Big Momma if she could stay with

us, because Big Momma would never go for anything like that. She was old fashioned and bible toting, and would slap the taste buds outta my mouth for even thinking such a thing. But Adanna needed to be safe. She needed to get away from those asshole brothers of hers before they got her indicted or killed. There had to be a solution.

Adanna peered at her cellphone checking the time.

"I'm running late," she said, exhaling forcibly. "They've been going crazy if I arrive home five minutes later than normal. Something is not right."

"C'mon," I said rising and gathering my belongings. "I'll walk you home."

"You know you can't do that," she said, tilting her head to one side. "Besides, I'm taking the bus. I don't have time to be leisurely today."

"I know," I smiled. Those asshole brothers of hers would have my head on a stick. "I'll walk you to the bus stop and wait with you until the bus arrive."

Adanna and I tossed our backpacks over our shoulders, headed out of the library and down the street. The bus stop was just down the street from the campus. We never made it to the stop.

Wilson pulled up beside of us, and he and Nelson quickly jumped out of his vehicle.

"Is this why you're late?" Wilson thundered. "This fucking cockroach?"

"I told you to stay away from my sister, cockroach!" Nelson shouted. He stormed toward me. Before I could react, he punched me in the face, sending me to the ground.

"Nelson! No!" Adanna screamed. She tried to rush him, but was grabbed by her brother Edward.

"You're hard of hearing, huh, Cockroach?" Nelson shouted. He kicked me in my ribs, and then leaned down and punched me again.

He was cock strong, and could hit as hard as a bulldozer. I felt each and every blow, and reeled from the force of them. Still, my pride forced me to try to fight back. I kicked Nelson on the side of his knee, causing him to buckle slightly. It allowed me time to roll away from him and stand.

"Leave him alone!" Adanna shouted. She struggled desperately to free herself.

"I told you to stay away from her!" Nelson shouted, coming after me again. "I don't want your filthy roach hands on my sister!"

"I love him!" Adanna shouted.

"Oh, you love him?" Wilson asked, with a cynical laugh. "You would dishonor your family with a peace of Haitian driftwood?"

Wilson shouted something to Adanna in Igbo, and whatever it was, it must have been pretty insulting. Rarely had I heard Adanna speak in Igbo. Maybe a word here or there, but never in full sentences, and never this rapidly, and never in anger. She sounded like a completely different person. I knew that she knew some Igbo words, but it never occurred to me that she was fully fluent in the language.

Nelson came after me again, and I raced around the car to avoid him. Adanna elbowed Edward in his stomach, causing him to let go, and she raced toward me. Wilson grabbed her. I rushed to her defense, and Wilson clocked me with a nice right haymaker. I stumbled back.

"Stay away from my sister!" Wilson shouted.

"Run!" Adanna shouted. "St. Claire, just run away!"

I hurried down the sidewalk away from them, while keeping a wary eye on Nelson, who stood brooding in the street. I watched as they forced her into the car, climbed inside, and then drove away. I stood silently in the middle of the street seething with anger. I felt a little ashamed, embarrassed even, that I had not been able to do more to keep her away from them. Sure, it was three against one, and sure, they were big ass, muscle bound, grown ass men. Still, I felt a tinge a humiliation, coupled with tons of anger. It would be the last time they would put their fucking African hands on me. I had an ass whipping limit, and they had passed it a long time ago.

I needed to keep some protection with me. I knew that I was close to finishing school, and I knew the story of how so many who were so close, fucked it all up so badly. I didn't want to join that statistic, but I wasn't going to allow them to beat me again.

# **Chapter Twenty Four**

Again my bruises heeled.  Time was that great soothing balm that eventually lessened the pain, if not taking it away all together.  I had been able to hide my bruises from everyone, including my coaches, my teachers, my teammates, and most importantly, my grandmother.  The last thing I wanted to do, was cause her to worry about me.  She had enough on her plate, and she deserved peace at this age.  She didn't need to stay up worrying about me getting into trouble.  I loved her so much, and I owed her so much, the last thing I wanted to be was trouble.

"That old mailman done finally brought his behind around," Big Momma said, peering out the window.

I sat up on the couch.  "I'll get it."

"Nonsense!"  Big Momma said, waving her hand.  "Sit your behind down and finish watching that game!"

"Naw, Big Momma, I can get it!" I told her.

"St. Claire, sit your ass down," she said through clenched teeth. "I ain't dead yet. I can walk to the mailbox. I need to get a little exercise anyway. I ain't been on my walk in two days."

"Yes, ma'am," I said, sitting back down. When Big Momma said something through clenched teeth, it meant she was serious, and you didn't argue with her. She wanted to get it, so she was going to get it. She usually walked up and down the street about twenty times a day, and she hadn't done it in a couple of days, so she must have been feeling guilty about not exercising. "Everything okay, Momma?"

She tilted her head to one side, rolled her eyes at me, and was out the door headed for the mailbox. It made me laugh. I loved her more than life itself. She was my old school, feisty, Bible toting, Bible quoting sweetheart. To see her happy, and feisty and energetic brought a joy to my heart that was indescribable. I turned my attention back to the game.

On the television, TCU was whipping Baylor's ass in what was basically the Big Twelve Championship game. I was a Baylor fan, but I was an even *bigger* TCU fan. It was my future school. And seeing them get the recognition they deserved felt good. It also meant that they would get more national attention, which meant that I would get more national exposure when I got on the field. It was all gravy.

Big Momma walked back inside with a handful of mail. She also had a smile on her face that was wider than the Mississippi. She couldn't hide joy for anything in the world.

"What?" I asked.

She stood in front of me. "I got something for you."

"What?" I asked, rising from the couch. I knew it couldn't be another college offer, because I had offers from every college in the country already.

Big Momma held the envelope out in front of her. "SAT scores."

My heart jumped out of my chest. My nervousness went from zero to one hundred in a matter of seconds. Big Momma tried to hand me the envelope.

"You open it," I said, eying the letter like it contained Kryptonite, or Racin, or Ebola.

"It's not for me," Big Momma said, shaking her head.

"I can't." I said nervously.

Big Momma reached down, clasped my hand, and closed her eyes. "Close your eyes C.B."

I did as instructed.

*"Lord, we come to you today, asking You to bless us, and to make us Your humble servants. We beseech You, and ask that Your*

*will be done, and that it be a part of Your plan to bless St. Claire so*
*that he can go on and do Your works, Dear Lord. We ask that*
*everything we do, be pleasing to You, and that You please touch us,*
*and touch everything and everyone that we touch, and let us let the*
*world know that it is Your glory that moves us forward and brings*
*us bounty. Let us glorify You, Dear Master, and all that You do, and*
*all that You have done. We don't want these scores to be high so*
*that we can do bad things, but so that he can go on and do good*
*things! Work through him, Dear Lord. Please bless him from the*
*crown of his head to the soles of his feet. Let every step he takes be*
*in Your direction, let every word he says be pleasing to Your ears!*
*Father God, let each and every one of his works, be Your works!*
*We ask You this in the name of Your beloved son, Jesus. Amen!"*

"Amen," I uttered.

"Open it," Big Momma said, handing me the envelope.

My hands shook slightly as I took the envelope from her.

"Peace be still!" Big Momma said, tapping my hand. "We
done prayed over this here, Baby. You ain't got nothing to be
worried about."

I smiled. Big Momma had her faith. It brought her peace
and comfort. I wish that I had it, but I wasn't there yet. God still
hadn't squared His decision to take my Momma, to take away my
Father, my home, my entire fucking city. He still hadn't saw fit to

explain why Augustine had to die, or even why Quick had to die. Again, my faith and belief in the Man Upstairs wasn't too strong right now.

I slowly began to open the envelope. Inside, was my future. Most of the schools that I needed to get in, required a heck of a score. TCU wasn't a slouch academically, and neither was Baylor, or Texas. You needed serious grades, serious test scores, and a serious GPA. Thanks to Adanna helping me study, and to Big Momma staying on my ass, I had the GPA. Now, I just needed the test scores. According to the way my life had always played out, I doubted that they would be there. God always seemed to be taking away the people and the things in my life that I wanted. I was certain that this time would be no different.

I pulled the test scores out of the envelope, and read them I had a 740 in Reading, a 690 in Math, and a 700 in Writing. I dropped down to my knees in tears. Big Momma snatched the scores from my hands.

"St. Claire!" she said, covering her mouth. I could hear her voice trembling. Soon, she joined me on the floor. Big Momma wrapped her arms around me as I balled like a baby. "I'm so proud of you, Baby."

I hadn't thought that I had done this well on the test. In fact, I had been second guessing myself since the moment I walked out

of the testing center. I knew who I owed the scores to. The one
person who stayed at school and studied with me. The one person
who met me at the library on the weekends and forced me to study
and concentrate. I owed my scores to Adanna. I loved her more
than words could say. Not just for the help that she gave, but
because of *everything*. I loved her because of who she was, I loved
her because she gave up her weekends for me, I loved her because
she encouraged me, and because she never stopped believing in me.
No one, was going to keep her from me. I was going to marry her.

Big Momma clasped my chin and turned my face toward
her.

"Thank, God, St. Claire," she told me. "God is good! He's
so good! Your Mother would be so proud of you! She is looking
down on you right now, smiling her heart out."

I wanted to say that if God really cared, my Mother would
be sitting next to me, telling me how proud she was of me. But I
would never say that to Big Momma. Instead, I just nodded.

"I know."

"Never doubt how proud she was of you, how much she
loved you, how she would give anything to be here with you," Big
Momma said. "You are all that she has left, to carry on her
memory, to let people know that she was here. What you do,
reflects on her. What you do, tells the world what kind of mother

she was. You make her proud, and you make sure that everyone knows how special she was. You go on, and you be somebody. That gives glory to God, *and* to your parents."

I leaned over and kissed Big Momma on her cheek. "And to you."

She smiled.

"I owe you so much," I told her.

She waved her hand dismissing the thought instantly. "You don't owe me nothing!"

"Yeas I do," I said, nodding. "I owe you everything."

On the television, TCU scored another touchdown, and the crowd was going crazy. I peered over at the TV.

"I'm going to make it, Big Momma," I said softly.

"I know you are, Baby."

"I'm going to make it for you," I told her. "I'm going to run and run and run, and play harder than anyone has ever played before. And I'm going to go high in the draft, and I'm going to get a guaranteed contract, and I'm going to buy you a house."

Big Momma waved her hand, dismissing me again. "Boy, I don't need no house. I'm fine just where I am, and with what I got. The Lord has *always* taken care of me!"

"And I'm going to help Him," I told her. "I'm buying you a big, pretty house, over where the White folks live."

Big Momma laughed. "I don't want no house way out in the middle of no where. Beside, I'm happy where I'm at. Me and your Grandpa bought this house a long time ago."

"And he would want you to have the best," I told her. "You deserve nothing but the best."

"You just worry about you!" Big Momma said, pinching my cheek. "You make me happy by doing good."

Gunfire erupted somewhere in the neighborhood, causing both of us to jump. It had been close.

"I'm getting you out of here!" I told her.

"The Lord will protect me," she said with a smile. "He always has, and He always will."

"You just start thinking about what kind of car you want, and where you want to live," I told her.

And I meant it. I was going to move heaven and earth, and do whatever I could, to get my Big Momma out of the hood. I was going to buy her a new house. I was determined to make good on that promise.

# Chapter Twenty Five

The State Championship game came. It would be the last football game of my high school career. I had long memories, some were good, some were bittersweet, some were complete nightmares. I sat on the bench thinking about how long I had waited for this day to come. How I would feel, how I would react, how I would take it. For many, they would never play the game of football again for the rest of their lives. For many others, they had only four years left, if they didn't make it into the NFL. For others, after college would come a pro career, and how long that lasted depended on the individual and what position he played. Some guys got used up in as little as three or four years. Running backs usually were amongst those whose careers were short lived. The knees, the constant pounding, the constant bruising; it all took its toll on a body. For running backs, it was get your money quick, while the getting was good. And after about four years, you'd better had invested your money well. That was the nature of the NFL beast.

I sat staring at my locker, as thoughts of my future gave way to thoughts of my past. It seemed like forever since I first walked onto a football field at the age of four. I started off playing flag football, and then moved up to Midget level football at the age of five. That was fourteen years ago. Fourteen long years. Fourteen years of running, training, working out, learning plays, perfecting my skills, honing my craft. You do anything for fourteen years, you can't help but master it. And I had mastered it.

I was about to head out of the locker room, and I was about to lead my team to another state championship. I was about to earn scholarships for teammates, and destroy the hopes and dreams of my opponents. I was about to bring pride to my community, and tears to someone else's. There was no doubt in my mind as to what was about to happen. It wasn't going to be pretty.

"C.B."

It was said in a distinctly British accent. Not Adanna's, but another. It was a voice that I hadn't heard in ages. It instantly broke my concentration and caused me to peer up from the locker room floor. It was Victoria, Augustine's girlfriend.

I hadn't seen, nor spoken to Victoria in ages. In fact, it had probably been since just after Augustine's funeral when we had last spoken. She had been the love of his life. She had been to him, what Adanna was to me. She was his soul mate. We lost touch, because each of us had to grieve in our own way.

"Victoria!" I said, rising from the bench. I hurriedly embraced her, as if I hadn't, she would turn out to be little more than an ephemeral illusion. "What... what are you doing here?"

"I came to see you." she said with a smile. It was a smile tinged with sadness and irony. The last time we had been in this place together, was before last year's state championship game. She had been there to wish Augustine good luck. It hadn't dawned on me, that today was the one year anniversary of Augustine's death.

"Are you okay?" I asked.

She nodded. "I'm fine."

Victoria's accent was pure British, unlike Adanna's which was tinged with just a touch of Igbo. Victoria's parents were of West African descent, but they were British citizen, born in Britain, raised in Britain, and completely of British culture. So too was she. She had only found her way to Houston because of her Dad's job as a petroleum engineer with British Petroleum. She met Augustine soon after arriving, and convinced her parents to let her attend public school under the guise of experiencing the "real America." Like Adanna, she too lived in a wealthy neighborhood that by the unfortunate luck of the draw, was redistricted and zoned to our fabulous super ghetto high school. She didn't mind attending, as long as she had a reason to, and that reason died on this night, exactly one year ago. Victoria changed schools the day after Augustine's funeral. Being there without him, was too much for her. That, I completely understood.

"I just wanted to see you," she said softly.

I clasped her hands. "Are you sure you're okay?"

Again she nodded.

"How have you been getting along?"

A fake smile spread across her face. "As well as can be expected."

"You can call me, you know?" I told her. "You should have been calling me."

"I know," she said softly. "You know... With everything... It was difficult."

"That's why we should have stayed in touch," I told her. "We *both* lost him. We both loved him. We needed to help each other get through it."

Victoria pursed her lips and nodded. "I miss him so much."

I pulled her close and hugged her. "I do too."

"I miss him like it was yesterday," she confided. "I still see him. I dream about him. I see his smile. I see us strolling along the boardwalk. I see us hanging out above the rail yard. I see us just hanging out and having fun."

"It's going to hurt for a long time."

"I know," she nodded. "I want it to. I'm not ready for the pain to go away. I don't want to let him go."

"Me neither," I said softly.

She sniffled, and then pulled away. "That's not why I came here. This is not the conversation that I wanted to have."

"What did you need to talk about?"

"You!" She said. "I came here to talk to you about you. And about Augustine. We're both not ready to let him go, and maybe we'll never let him go, nor should we. In a way, he'll always be a part of us. He touched our lives, and we can't help that. But what we can help, is the way we choose to carry him. That *is* our choice."

"What are you saying?"

"I've watched you play, C.B. I've watched just about all of your games. I see the way you play, I see the way you run, I see so much anger on the field."

Her truth hit me hard. I felt like I had been slapped in the face, and then had the covers yanked off of me. I felt exposed.

"Why are you so angry?"

"You aren't?"

"I can't be," she said turning away from me. "If I allowed

myself to be angry, I would burn myself up from the inside. I can't live like that. I can go through life seeing red, red, red!"

She lifted her hands as if she were clawing at her face. "I wouldn't survive. And you're not going to last very long if you keep allowing your anger to burn uncontrollably."

Victoria turned back toward me. "We don't get to choose that, C.B. We don't get to choose life and death, or who will live and who will die."

"I can't chalk it up to that!" I said angrily. "I can't just let it ride like that!"

"What can you do about it, St. Claire? Think! You can't go to war with God! And because you can't lash out at Him, you want to take it out on everyone else around you? You're going to burn out."

"So what am I supposed to do? Let it go?"

"Live, St. Claire! You're supposed to live!" Victoria clasped my shoulders and peered into my eyes. "You have to live for you, and for Augustine. You have to carry him with you, and continue the dream that you both shared. He's gone. And now, you're trying hard to sabotage your life. Don't you know they're watching you? Each and every single game, all of those fantastic scholarships that you've been offered, are being put at risk. No one wants a hot head on their football team, C.B. No one. You can go on without Augustine. You have to. He would *want* you to. Don't secretly sabotage your life in order to protest God. It doesn't work that way."

I was angry at her telling me this, and even angrier because I knew that she was speaking the truth. I wanted to be angry. I was comfortable in my anger. I needed someone to take my anger out on, and God appeared to be indifferent to my passions. Had I been subconsciously trying to sabotage myself? Augustine's death hurt. It felt as though my soul had been ripped from me. We had become one after the death of my mother and his siblings during Katrina. We became closer than brothers in our pain. And then, he was gone. Taken. Ripped away. I had been left alone. I felt as though I had a right to be angry. And now, the one person who I just knew would understand my anger, was telling me not to be angry. It was too much to digest at once. I sat back down on the bench, and tried to gather my thoughts.

"He's not coming back," Victoria said softly. "It took me almost an entire year to be able to say it, and even longer to accept it. "I love him, and I would give anything to bring him back. But he's not coming back. We have to go on."

"I know," I said nodding.

Victoria stepped closer, and wrapped her arms around me. It was this hug that opened the floodgates. Today being the anniversary of his death, and me seeing Victoria again, brought out too many emotions. I couldn't control myself.

In the middle of my bawling, Victoria produced a small locket.

I wiped away my tears and tried to regain my composure.

"What is that?" I asked.

Victoria flipped open the locket. Inside, was a tiny picture of me, her, Augustine, and Adanna. I instantly recognized the picture. We had taken it at Kema on the boardwalk, only months before he died. That had been one of the best summers of my life. We were state champs, we had scholarship offers from all over the country, our junior year was coming up, and we were kicking it with our girls on the boardwalk.

"I had this made for you," she said, placing it around my neck.

"I can't..." I told her.

"I have another," she insisted. "This one is yours."

I lifted it, and angled it toward me so that I could examine the photo once again. "Thank you."

"Remember him like this," she told me. "Remember his smile. Remember how much he loved you. Remember how much you both loved football. I can't remember a single game you two ever played in anger. Football was always something that brought joy to your life. Look at his smile. Remember what this game was about, remember what it meant to him, and remember what it meant to you."


I played football that night. And for the first time in a year, I played in a game where I wasn't angry. With every carry I thought about Augustine, or something silly he would say, or something crazy he had done. And every carry I had a smile on my face. I don't know if playing with the charm on my neck, made me feel as though he were on the field with me, or whether it was because Victoria had pulled all of the anger out of me. What I do know, is that I played the game and it felt like it used to feel. I played a football game with joy in my heart. And I joyfully broke the high school record for the most touchdowns scored in a state championship football game. And I joyfully beat the shit out of the other team, and led my team to a third state championship.

# **Chapter Twenty Six**

I met Adanna on the hill overlooking the rail yard at our usual meeting place. Christmas was upon us, and naturally we couldn't sit around the fireplace at her house and exchange Christmas gifts.

"Hey, Bae," Adanna said, leaning forward and kissing me.

"Oh, that's all I get?" I asked, wrapping my arms around her and pulling her close. She laughed. "The 2014 Texas High School State Champ, and I can't get nothing but a peck on the lips?"

I kissed Adanna passionately for what seemed like an eternity.

"You keep that up, I'm going to have to do something to you," she said, once I let her go. Adanna reached into her pocket and pulled out an envelope and handed it to me. "I have a surprise for you."

I took the envelope, turned it over and saw the sender's address. It was from SMU. Judging by the look on her face, I knew that she had gotten in. I opened the envelope and pulled out the letter inside. She had been accepted.

"That's awesome, Babe!" I said, hugging her.

"It's in effect!" she told me. "Everything is falling into place."

"Just like we always knew it would," I told her.

"I talked to my aunt," she said. "She's already got the building for her new location, so she's definitely opening up a second restaurant. She asked if we were definitely coming up. I told her we were."

"Well, we'll have jobs," I said with a smile. We were both going to be on full scholarship at our respective schools, and that was without any educational grants or student loans. Our education was covered, and we would even have money left to live on. The jobs would allow us to began saving even more money for our future. Maybe even buy a car while we were up there.

"Are you happy?" she asked, peering into my eyes.

I nodded. And it was the truth, I was happy. I was happier than I had been in a long time. I could see the end. The end of the nightmare I had been living in, and I could also see the beginning. The beginning of a new life with the girl that I loved. I was so close that I could taste it.

"She said that I could start off as a hostess," Adanna said with a devilish grin. "I guess she'll put you either busing tables or washing dishes. How's that superstar?"

I laughed. "Hey, if she's smart, she'll have me standing out front smiling at all the women that are walking by and bringing in tons of customers."

"Silly Billy!" Adanna said, while laughing and punching me in my shoulder. "No one wants you, with the exception of myself of course. And why I want you, remains a mystery."

I made a muscle. "Everyone wants some of this. Two hundred pounds of sexy, rippling abs and muscles. You can't even resist these battleships."

"Battleships?"

"Eighteen inch guns, baby!" I said, flexing my biceps. "Battleships!"

Adanna laughed, clasped my arm and pulled it down. "Nobody but me better see those abs or those so called battleships!"

"Only you, Bae," I told her. "These are only for you. But you know, I ain't trying to be around no hog."

She tilted her head to one side. "Since when, St. Claire!"

"Since never!"

"I've seen you eat a double bacon cheeseburger!" she said

laughing. "What are you talking about?"

"I can't mess with no hog, woman!" I told her with a smile.

"Whatever!" she said dismissing me. I guess you're a Hausa now?"

"I don't have to be a Hausa or any kinda Muslim to not mess with the hog," I replied. "That stuff is bad for you. It'll clog your arteries."

"Says the boy who eats a ton of meat everyday and calls it protein," she said lifting a chastising eyebrow toward me.

"I'm going vegetarian," I told her.

"I'll believe it when I see it," she replied. "Here."

Adanna turned and reached into her small purse, and pulled out a small gift. She handed it to me. I took the gift and pulled the wrapping off of the box. It revealed a small white box. I pulled the top off of the box and examined the contents. Inside, where two necklaces. The charms hanging from the necklace formed a single piece when paired together.

"It's a Mizpah necklace," Adanna told me. "It's for when you're at home, and I'm at home, and for when you're at TCU and I'm at SMU."

The inscription on the necklaces read; *The Lord watch between me and thee while we are absent from one another.*

Adanna lifted my chain from the box and place it around my

neck. She then took the box from my hand. I lifted her chain from the box, and place it around her neck. It was a powerful and greatly symbolic moment. I felt as though we had just made a lifetime commitment to one another. And I wasn't nervous, or hesitant, or second guessing what had just transpired. In fact, it felt just the opposite, it felt right.

Adanna was not the girl I always envisioned I would eventually marry. But once she came into my life, it felt like I had been waiting for her. I could feel my heart asking, "What took you so long to get here?" It was said that in Heaven, every boy is shown the girl that he is to marry. And when I met Adanna, it felt as if some deep memory had been stirred. I knew her. I had saw her before. I knew I loved her, before I even met her.

"Okay?" Adanna said, motioning with her fingers. "Gimme, gimme, gimme."

"Christmas is about giving, not receiving," I said, teasing her.

"Don't play with me," she said in her thick British accent. "You will get killed on this hilltop."

I laughed. I pulled from my pocket a small jewelry box as well. I wasn't wrapped, as I wouldn't know how to wrap a piece of foil around a plate of barbecue. It was in a nice, blue, felt box. I handed it to her.

Adanna opened the box and peered inside. Inside there was a Juicy Couture charm bracelet. It held only three charms. One, was the Juicy Couture heart charm, the second was a tiny locket, and the third caught her completely by surprise.

"Is this?" Adanna asked.

I produced the tiny key that fit into the locket and held it up. "Yes, I have the key to your heart."

Adanna waved her hand dismissing me. "You know what I'm talking about!" She examined the third charm carefully. "It is! Where on Earth did you find this?"

Adanna wrapped her arms around me and hugged me tight.

"It wasn't easy, I can tell you that," I told her.

The third charm was a tiny flag from her ancestral home, the Benin Kingdom. And it had been a bitch finding it.

"It's beautiful!" she exclaimed, while trying to place it on her wrist. "How did you..."

"I was listening," I said with a smile. "Everything you say doesn't go in one ear and out the other. All of those history lessons. And all of that talk about the Igbo, The Hausa, The Fulani, The Yoruba, I was listening."

Again, she hugged me.

Adanna held her bracelet up toward the sun and examined it.

"We're going to add more charms to it, as we get older," I

told her.

She turned and kissed me. "I wish that it could be like this all of the time. Just me and you, together. Not having to go home or be apart, or worry about my brothers or anything. Just me and you, in our own place."

"It's going to happen," I told her. I pulled her close and wrapped my arms around her. "I do have a question for you though."

"What?"

"Did you call me Bae?" I asked.

Adanna laughed.

"Are you serious?" I said laughing. "You been hanging with them chicks from the hood too long."

"And it's just registering with you?" she asked with a smile.

"No, I mean... yeah. It took me some time to process," I said laughing. "You're turning hood one me."

"I may be," she said with a smile. "I may be turning a little bit hood."

Hearing her say that with her proper British accent was hilarious. She lifted her cell phone and peered at the time.

"I have to get going."

I nodded. "I know. C'mon, I'll walk you to the bus stop."

We started down the hill.

"I don't want you to walk me too far," she cautioned. "My brothers may be circling and searching for me already."

"You're not even late."

"I know, but they've been really paranoid lately. I mean *really* paranoid. Always checking the windows. They have guns all over the place. They added more locks an cameras. They've turned the house into a fortress. And it feels like a prison."

"What's going on?" I asked.

"I don't know," she said. "They don't really talk around me, but they are worried. *I* am worried. I saw them counting a lot of money, C.B. A *lot* of money."

"What's a lot of money?" I asked. "Heck, to me, a thousand bucks is a lot of money."

"Millions," she said flatly. "It had to be millions."

"Are you serious?" I asked, stopping and clasping her arm. "Millions?"

She nodded. "Undoubtedly."

"Two, three, five?"

"Millions!" she repeated. "I don't know exactly how much, but it was a ridiculous sum."

I could tell she was scared just talking about it. "Hey, don't worry about it. You'll be out of there soon. Just hang in there for five more months. That's all we need, just five more months. We walk the stage in June, and we can leave that night."

Adanna nodded. I pulled her close and held her. I knew that we had to get away, and soon. Grandma was always praying for me. And despite the fact that me and the Man Upstairs weren't exactly on speaking terms, I found myself staring up at the heavens asking Him to keep my baby safe.

Caleb Alexander

# Chapter Twenty Seven

The closer we got to the end of the school year, the closer my school became like animal house. The seniors could smell graduation, the juniors could smell their senior year coming up, the sophomores were hyped because they knew that they would be moving up to play varsity ball next year, the freshman were relieved that their first year of high school was almost over, and everyone was happy because they could taste summer vacation coming up.

"Hootie Hoo!"

I turned in the direction that the shouts were coming from. It was Savawn's retarded ass. And then came the barking. Big Matt, and Lil Dice sounded just like Pit Bulls and American Bullys when they barked.

"Running Back Baby!" Savawn shouted down the hall.

"What's up, my nigga!"

"What's up, baby boy!" I shouted back, lifted my arms.

"TCU, baby!"

Who?" I asked pointing. "You!"

"You mthafucking right!" he said approaching. I could see him grinning from ear to ear, and he held several letters in hand. We shook hands and snapped our fingers once he got close.

"I see your work!" I told him.

"I'mma be up there with you now, my nigga!" he said. "You didn't think you was going to get all the Dallas pussy and I wasn't gone get none!"

We laughed.

"I'm just fucking with you!" he said, snapping the letter in my face. It was an offer from Notre Dame.

"Get the fuck outta here!" I shouted, hugging him. It had been his dream for the longest.

"Notre Dame, baby!" Savawn shouted.

"What's up with you?" I asked Big Matt.

"Shit, 'Bama, nigga!" he said, grinning from ear to ear as well.

"Get the fuck outta here!" I said, shaking his hand again.

"Crimson Tide on mine!" Big Matt said.

"Too bad I'mma have to bust your ass for a national

championship!" I told him.

"In your dreams," Big Matt said slapping my back.

"I'mma bust both of your asses!" Savawn told us.

The school bell rang, dismissing school for the day. I already had my back pack, and so did the others. We headed for the door together.

"You waiting on your girl, or you catching the bus?" Big Matt asked.

"Naw, I'm catching the metro," I told them. "Her brothers are picking her up from school today."

We walked outside, and headed for the waiting school bus.

"Alright, my nigga!" Savawn said, slapping hands with me.

"Alright." I said, returning the handshake.

"Alright, my dude!" Big Matt said, clasping hands with me. We gave each other a quick chest bump style hug.

I turned, and headed down the street toward the bus stop. I turned the corner, just in time to run into a Harris County Police Department patrol car. The officers saw me, and instantly hit their lights.

"Whoop, whoop!" the sirens blared twice.

The officers climbed out of their patrol car, and quickly rushed to where I was walking.

"C'mere!" the driver told me.

I exhaled, turned toward the officers, and allowed my backpack to slide off my shoulders.

"Where are you coming from?" the second officer asked.

"School."

"What's in the backpack?" the driver asked.

"Books," I said, in the most sarcastic way possible. I wanted him to feel like an idiot, for asking such an idiotic question. Books are carried in book bags, especially when people are walking from school.

"Let me see your backpack?" the second officer asked.

I extended my backpack toward them. The driver took it. He opened it and began rambling through it. I watched him, to make sure that he didn't place anything inside that wasn't already there. If he did, I was going to do my best impression of Usain Bolt and jet. I wasn't about to be hit with a bullshit charge.

The officer handed the back pack to me. "Where do you go to school?"

"Booker T," I told him.

"Hmmph," the driver said. "You don't look like one of them Booker T. thugs."

"I'm in disguise," I told him.

"Oh, we have us a smart ass here," the driver told his partner. "Okay, smart ass. Put your hands on the hood of my car and spread 'em!"

I walked to the police car and placed my hands on the warm hood. The officer kicked my legs apart. He started at my neck, made his way down my side, stuck his hand into my waistband, made his way down my manhood where he clasped it.

"What's this?" he asked.

"My dick," I told him.

"Your what?"

"My dick!" I shouted.

"Oh," he said, quickly releasing my private and working his way down my legs. Embarrassed, he tossed me my backpack. "Get the fuck outta here, smart ass!"

I put my arms through my backpack, eyeballed him for a few moments, and then turned and headed down the street. They had made me miss my bus.

I crossed the street, and headed down the block and out of sight of those assholes, only to run smack dab into a second set of assholes. Adanna's brothers were turning the corner to go and pick her up from school.

"Shit!" I said, shaking my head. Sure enough, they spotted me.

Her brother Wilson rolled down the window of his car, and stuck a gun out of it, pointing it at me. He squeezed the trigger and the gun clicked. My heart felt as if it had skipped several beats.

"Fucking cockroach!" Wilson shouted out the window.

"Oh, you don't think we'll shoot your black ass?" Nelson asked from the passenger side. He lifted a second weapon and cocked it.

I hurried away.

"You better run!" I heard Nelson shouting. I could hear them laughing.

I was beyond pissed, beyond frustrated. I was tired of all of the bullshit, I was tired of getting picked on, tired of running away. This is the last time I would run, I told myself. The last time.

I jogged to my neighborhood, and came across the neighborhood store. And like clockwork, it was full of guys hanging on the corner. I spotted Dirty.

"D!" I shouted. "Let me holler at you."

Dirty finished serving a customer, wrapped up the plastic baggy that held his crack rocks, and walked to where I was standing. "What's up, Homie?"

"Hey man, you gotta extra strap?" I asked.

"A strap?" Dirty recoiled. He smiled, and his gold and diamond grill sparkled in the sun nearly blinding me. Dirty was all in. He was tatted from head to toe, and his tatooes showed clearly on his high yellow skin. He wore his hair in long dreads, and still rocked Dickey pants and Chuck Taylor tennis shoes. "What you need a strap for?"

"Man, I tired of the bullshit," I said, shaking my head.

"What bullshit?" he asked, eying me condescendingly. It was if my problems weren't real.

"Man, I tired of Adanna's fucking brothers!" I said forcefully. "Those muthafuckas just pulled a strap on me!"

Dirty laughed. "Man, look here. If they was gonna do something, they would have done it. They cowards. You don't pull no strap on nobody and don't use it, ya heard me? And you don't need no strap, cause if you pull it, you gotta use it."

"I'll use it," I said nodding.

"No you won't," Dirty said eying me. "What you gone do, is you gone take your ass to college, ya heard me? You ain't finta fuck that off. Nigga, Quick would come outta his grave on you if you fuck yo shit off, and he'll come outta his grave on me if I gave you a strap. Them coward ass muthafuckas ain't trying to do nothing."

"Man, I'm tired..."

"Nigga, *we all* muthafucking tired!" Dirty shouted, interrupting me. "You think you the only one whose tired of the bullshit? But you got a solution, nigga. You got a way out. And now, you wanna throw that shit away? Are fucking kidding me?

C.B. You gotta be stronger than that, you gotta be better than that. Your mind is stronger than that. Leave this hood shit behind, and get the fuck on."

Dirty held up his hand with his index finger and thumb just centimeters apart. "You is dis close, my nigga. Dis close. Quick wanted nothing more than for you to do what he couldn't do. He wanted you to make it. Don't let the homie down. Don't let the hood down, don't let your Big Momma down, don't let yourself down, and don't let your T Lady down. You know your ma dukes is looking down on you right now, my nigga."

Dirty pulled out a nine-millimeter handgun, cocked it, and handed it to me.

I took the gun, examined it for a few seconds, and then handed it back to him.

"Good decision," he said smiling. "Now stick to it. Just like you made that decision, keep on making the right ones. Don't let nothing side track you from doing what you supposed to do."

I nodded.

Dirty was the last person on Earth that I expected to get good advice from. He had more bodies that Quick. He was a killer, a drug dealer, a gang banger, and a drop out. He was the poster boy for everything that White folks thought was wrong with young Black men in the hood. And yet...

Dirty would be one more person added to the long list of people that I owed. He could have simply given me a gun and sent me on my way. He could have said "Let's ride," hopped inside of his whip, and took me to gun down those assholes. The situation could have gone a multitude of ways, most of them ending bad. But he talked me through my anger and allowed me to make a choice. He helped me to keep my eyes on the prize, and now, like so many others, I owed him.

# Chapter Twenty Eight

Spring Break came before we knew it. And so did our now annual trip to Kemah, Texas. Kemah was about thirty miles outside of Houston on the beach. It was a boardwalk, with restaurants, an amusement park, boat rides, retail stores, motels, and plenty of other shit. It was like Venice Beach, and Coney Island combined, but on steroids.

Me and a lot of the guys from the football team started going going to Kemah a few years ago during Spring Break. It had become kinda a varsity tradition at our school after Freaknik in Atlanta was shut down, and after the Galveston Beach party died out. We shifted our wild out parties to Kemah, and they were glad to have us, and all of the revenue that the high school and college students brought to the town.

Our motel was right on the beach off of the boardwalk, which put us in the middle of all the action. It also made our spot one of the prime party spots in the town. Our beach parties were the stuff of legend.

"It's time to get fucked up!" Savawn shouted. He tossed me a beer, and began stripping in the middle of the room.

"Man, don't nobody want to see your naked ass!" Bear said, twisting a towel, and then snapping it against Savawn's bare ass. "Put some clothes on, nigga!"

Savawn twirled, showcasing his privates. "You gone see naked ass in the air all night, once I get a hold of one of these hoes running around here!"

Laughter went around the room. Savawn, Big Bear, Big Matt, Dirty Curt, along with a few others, including myself, had rented the room. It was football players only, no girlfriends, and no freshmen or sophomores. The only sophomores that had ever been allowed in the past, had been Quick during his day, myself, and Augustine, and that's only because we were starters on varsity. Other than those instances, it was junior and seniors only, varsity players only, and no squares. Kemah was about staying drunk and high, and having sex with as many girls as possible for an entire week. The rules were simple; What happens in Kemah, stays in Kemah.

Adanna, like all other girls knew what Kemah was about. She knew the tradition, and she viewed it as a right of passage. It was my senior year, and football was over, and college was looming. This was going to be one of the last times I would party with these guys, and so she didn't protest too much. Her instructions had been simple; don't fuck up. Don't bring back nothing I hadn't left with, and don't disrespect her. She didn't want any bitch on Facebook, or any bitch coming up to her telling her what she did with her man. She didn't want to run across any pictures on Instagram, or any other site either. She didn't want to know.

"This is for you," Big Bear said, sticking a hand full on condoms in my hand. "This is for you," he told Savawn. "These are for you," he said, passing out Trojans to everyone in the room.

"Nigga, can't nobody use this tight ass shit!" Savawn told him.

"Nigga, I use Maxims!" Dirty Curt said, chiming in.

Everyone laughed.

Savawn tossed on some loose fitting gym shorts, pulled some lotion out of his gym bag, and began lotioning his body.

"Nigga, what the fuck you doing?" Big Matt asked him

Savawn smiled his usual Cheshire smile. "I got to get all oily and sexy for the bitches!"

"I already seen some bitches that I wanna smash!" Dupriest declared.

They were all hyped to the fullest. We were state high school football champs, all of us had big time scholarships to some major division one universities, and we away from home and completely free to wild out for an entire week. And the boardwalk, well, it was crawling with college and high school girls who only wanted to get drunk, have a week full of uncommitted sex, and then go on about their lives without ever talking about it again. It was high school heaven, or close to it.

Big Matt cracked open a giant bottle of Grey Goose that we had sitting on the motel table. The 1800 was already open, as was the Belvedere, the Hennessey, and the Tanquerey. A bottle of Don Julio, a bottle of Grand Marnier, and a bottle of Crown Royal XO sat unopened on the kitchen counter. We had come to party, and party hard, and the partying had already began in earnest. I could hear bass thumping just on the other side of the thin motel walls, on each side. Both of the adjacent rooms had already swung into action, and music poured through the front door from the beach area as well.

"Baptiste!" Brandon said, calling from the front door. "I got somebody that want to meet you!"

Brandon stood in the doorway with two beautiful females,

one of each arm, and he was surrounded by five others who were equally gorgeous.

"They from TCU, my nigga!" Brandon said with a smile. "They want to meet the schools future star running back."

Before I could react or say anything, Savawn, Big Matt, and Dirty Curt were pushing my ass out the door.

"You ain't fixing to fuck our night up, nigga! " Big Matt said. "Get your ass out there and holler."

I quickly found myself out the door, staring face to face with a drop dead gorgeous female. She was more beautiful than Rihanna, with the same emerald green eyes, combined with an ass like Nicky Minaj *after* her implant surgery. She extended her hand.

"Tyaishia," she said, with a distinctive Caribbean accent.

"C.B." I said, shaking her hand. "Your accent, where are you from."

"Jamaica," she answered with a perfect smile.

I was a sucker for women with accents. Tyaishia. The name rolled around in my head. It was as unique as she was.

"My father is Swedish, my mother is West Indian and Chinese," she said, anticipating my next question. It was a question those fools in Dallas must asked her a lot.

"I wasn't going to ask that," I said, shaking my head.

"Why?" she smiled. "Don't you want to know more about

me?"

Suddenly, I was slapped across my shoulder. I turned to find Savawn standing next to me, ogling Tyaishia's body.

"Got Dam, Running Back Baby!" Savawn shouted. "It 's your lucky night, Baby Boy! You one lucky ass muthafucka!"

Everyone within earshot laughed.

"So, you are going to be the next big time football star on campus?" Tyaishia asked.

"No, that would be me," Big Matt said, cutting in between us.

"Oh," Tyaishia said. "Well, let me introduce you to my friend Chrystyna. Chrys, this is?"

"Big Matt," he said, sounding disheartened.

"Homies!" Brandon said. "This here is Maisie, this is Stephonjia, this is Yanika, this is Vontrice, that there is Teona, and this lovely lady on my arm right here is Mylandra. Ladies, that's Dirty Curty, Big Bear, Big Matt, Savawn, and big head ass Baptiste!"

"Baptiste?" Tyaishia asked. "So, the 'B' in C.B. Stands for Baptiste? That's a very island name."

"My father was Haitian," I told her. "*Is*, I mean. My father *is* Haitian."

"Oh, an *island* boy!" Mylandra said with a smile. The rest

of the girls giggled.

"What you know about dem island boys?" I asked.

"Me know 'bout dem Island bwoys," Maisie replied with a smile. She was gorgeous as well.

"Who else from the islands?" Stephonjia asked. "I need me an island boy as well."

"I be from de islands tonight!" Savawn shouted. Everyone laughed.

"Naw, you can't fake being from the islands," Stephonjia said giggling.

"Let me tell you something," Savawn said stepping to her. "I am *Legend!*"

Again, everyone laughed.

"King Kong ain't got nothing on me!" Savawn continued. Again, the group broke into laughter. I knew that Savawn was about to get his clown on.

Tyaishia clasped my hand. "Want to go for a walk?"

"Why not?" I shrugged.

Tyaishia and I walked away from the others, heading toward the beach.

"The boardwalk is gorgeous at night." she said. A slight breeze blew, sending her long, chestnut hair blowing gently. "So tell me, what made you choose TCU."

I shrugged. "I don't know. I guess we chose each other. I always wanted to go there. It was a dream of mine for a long time. Me and my friend."

"Your friend?" she asked, lifting an eyebrow. "Is he going too?"

"No," I said, shaking my head gently. "He won't be going. I'll be going for the both of us. He past away."

"Oh," she said, peering down at the planks off the boardwalk. "I'm sorry to hear that."

"His parents were from the islands too," I told her. "He was my best friend. I guess in a way, he will be going there as well. I'll always carry him with me."

"That's sweet." she said.

We stepped off of the boardwalk, and she pulled off her sandals and held them in her hand. I took them from her.

"I'll carry them for you."

"You're such a gentleman," she said with a smile. "Good Caribbean manners. Those girls in the Metroplex are going to be all over you."

I laughed and shook my head.

"Why are you laughing?" she asked.

"Because, they'll have to deal with the wrath of Adanna."

"Adanna?" she asked, lifting an inquisitive eyebrow.

"Who's Adanna?"

"Adanna is the love of my life," I told her.

"Oh, so you have a *girlfriend?*" she asked with a smile.

"Yep," I said nodding.

"Hmmmm," she said interlacing her arm with mine. "I thought I was getting the jump on everyone."

"Sorry," I said, staring into her gorgeous face. "Adanna beat you to it."

"And where's she going to school?"

"SMU," I answered.

"Oh, so she'll be across town?" she asked, lifting an eyebrow.

"Yeah."

"And you'll be all alone and defenseless on campus with *me.*"

Again I laughed.

"She could be a million miles away, and it wouldn't make a difference," I told her.

"Oh really," she said, pausing. She turned and faced me. "And where is she at *now?*"

"At home."

"In Houston?"

I nodded.

"And you're here with me?"

"Adanna could be across an ocean," I told her. "She could be on another planet. It wouldn't make a difference."

"Damn," she said softly, turning away. She faced me again. "And you've never cheated on her? Keep it real."

I shook my head. "Not in a million years."

"*You're serious?*"

Again, I nodded. "Never have, never will."

"Wow!" She paused, and blinked several times as if she were taking in the full measure of my statement. She released my arm. "Wow. Must be nice."

"What?"

"To have a man like that," she said softly. "She's one lucky lady."

I shook my head. "Naw, I'm the lucky one. She's the most beautiful woman in the world to me. I love every inch of her. I love her from the top of her head, to the bottom of her feet. I love the way her mouth twist when she's angry, the way her accent changes from British to Nigerian when she's cursing me out. I love the way her skin glows in the moon, and glimmers in the sunlight."

Tyaishia raked her hand through her hair sending it back over her shoulders. Her words now came out stammered and uncertain. "I... I would give anything for a man to talk about me like that."

"You're beautiful," I told her. "I know that you have a line of guys following you around on campus."

"Yeah, but I *know* what they want, and they are easy to get."

"So, you want a challenge?"

"No, not that. I want what Adanna has."

"Adanna is a queen. My queen. And she always carries herself like one. You attract the kind of guys that your vibe gives off."

"So what are you saying?" she asked, leaning away. "I'm coming off whore-ish."

"No," I said with a smile. "I know that you *know* you're gorgeous, and that you just like to flirt. You know that you can have any guy you want, any time you want him. And that's the vibe you put out."

"Confident?"

"Yeah," I said nodding. "We'll call it that."

"I couldn't have *you*," she said matter of fact.

I shook my head. "No one can. Nothing to do with you. I just know what I have at home, and how much she means to me."

"So you're telling me, that if one of these girls out here said c'mon, let's get busy and no one has to know, and there are no strings attached, just a one night deal, you wouldn't go for it?"

I laughed. "Is that an offer?"

"No," she said shaking her head. "But I'm just asking, since we're keeping it real."

"Keeping it real?"

"Keeping it one hundred percent real," she said eying me closely. No B.S."

"Between me and you?" I asked.

"Between me and you," she said, crossing her heart.

"This doesn't go nowhere, not to your girls, not to the fellas, nobody."

"Between us, I swear," she said.

I paused and examined her closely. "I wouldn't want to, and keeping it one hundred, I don't even think I could."

"What?" she asked surprised. "What do you mean?"

"Seriously. I don't want nobody else. I saw you, and I thought to myself, damn, she's beautiful. I see a chick, and I'm like, damn, she's fine. But that's it, I keep it moving. I see beautiful girls, but I don't trip. I really, honestly, truly, *don't want nobody else*."

"Why? Is she from Louisiana? Did she put something in you're spaghetti?"

We both laughed.

"I loved Adanna when I first saw her at the park," I

admitted. "And I haven't been able to love anybody else. Sex is sex. But the way I feel when I'm with her, is something else."

Tyaishia leaned forward and kissed me on my cheek.

"That's for being the coolest, realest guy I ever met," she said. "If I can't have you as a boyfriend, I want you in my life as a friend. You *and* Adanna. I have to meet this lucky woman. Make sure when you get to campus, you look me up. I need cool ass people in my life."

I nodded.

# Chapter Twenty Nine

The last days of high school were fast approaching. Everyone was gearing up for graduation. Caps and gowns had been ordered, class rings had came, state championship rings had came, my last varsity letters in football, basketball, and track had came. We were all on autopilot, trying to make it to the big day. It seemed as though everything was moving in a way that almost seemed surreal. As fucked up as Booker T High School was, I would miss it. I would miss the ghetto ass hallways, the hoochies popping gum and being extra wretched, and hood cats cursing and talking loud, the smell of weed smoke wafting from the restrooms. I would miss it all, the good and the bad.

"Look at what this nigga found last night," Wiz said, tapping my arm and breaking me out of my thoughts.

I peered over at Dupriest's desk, where he had a photo of our kindergarten class. Instantly I laughed.

"Let me see that shit," I said, holding out my hand.

Dupriest handed me the photo, and others gathered around my desk to take it in as well. There were faces on the photo that I hadn't seen in quite some time. Some were long gone, while others were just *gone*. Some had been lost to prison, some to the streets, and others to the cemetery. Out of thirty-eight kids in our kindergarten class, roughly have of them were boys. And out of that twenty, only five were about to graduate and walk the stage. We had lost fifteen.

"There's your big head ass right there!" Flip said laughing and pointing.

The picture was from when we lived here before my parents moved to New Orleans. There were three kindergarten classes in total at that elementary. About a hundred of us in total. We all knew each other of course, because we were pretty much from the same neighborhoods, and we all are lunch and took recess together. Out of all three kindergarten classes, there were a total of about fifty two boys. Out of fifty two young Black faces, less than twenty would be walking the stage come June. The numbers were staggering.

"You remember that fool?" Flip asked, pointing at a face in the picture. "What was that nigga's name?"

I examined the photo carefully, trying to recall his name, as well as some of the others. "Lil D."

"That's right!" Dupriest said excitedly. "That was that fool whose momma's boyfriend killed them ain't it?"

I nodded slowly. I remembered the incident. I was young, maybe in third grade when it happened. It had been big news back them. A major story, and now we were left trying to remember his name. It felt wrong.

People's live meant more than this. More than just an old photo, that would be soon put away again, not to come out for perhaps another ten, fifteen, or twenty years. Perhaps to be discarded accidentally on day while cleaning out the house. People's lives were worth more.

"There go Wiz!" Dupriest shouted, staring at the photo. "And Duck's ugly ass."

"There go the homie T-Dog," Flip said pointing. "And Flash's black ass!"

I took in all of the faces, one by one, row by row. There was Ant Man, Flash, Tee, Bone, and Q-Dog. Bawz, Quick, Skibo, Duck, Wiz, Killa, and Dirty. There was Low Life, Skeeter, Flip, Dice, Mouse, Dupriest, Lil Man, and Foots. Capone, myself, C-Low, T-Dog, Lil O, Money, Studd, Gangsta, and Slim on the front row. A lot of them were dead, too many of them in prison, and the rest of them were just gone. The hustle game and the streets had

took a lot of them.  What the fuck happened to us, I wondered?
What happened?

Thinking about my graduating class, it was clear that it
wasn't just our elementary school that held these horrible statistics,
but all of the elementary schools that fed into Booker T.  The boys
had a survival rate of less the fifty percent, while the girls were
running at eighty-eight percent.  The few of them that did drop out,
was because they got pregnant, and went to an alternative program
so that they could get their GED quickly and be done with high
school.  It was crazy.

"Could you sit down in your seats?" Mr. Stock asked,
peering up from his laptop.  "What are you doing now?"

We pretty much ignored him, like he had ignored us the
entire year.  He rose from his desk and walked to where we were
gathered.

"Group mug shot?" he sneered, as he peered at the old
photo.

"You would say some old racist shit like that," I said,
peering up from my desk at him.

"What?" he asked, seeming stunned that it came from me.
"Truth hurts sometimes."

"The truth is, you sit in that fucking desk all year, stalking
young ass bitches on Facebook and Instagram, collecting a check

while not teaching us shit, and treating us like we're fucking criminals."

"What?" he asked, turning up his palms. "You want to learn something, is that it? What good is Shakespeare going to do any of you in Huntsville Prison?"

"Fuck you!" I said, rising from my desk. I was so tired of his shit.

"Get the hell out of my class!" Mr. Stock shouted, pointing toward the door.

"I'm going to TCU, Muthafucka!" I shouted. "And after that, I'll be living up in River Oaks with the rich muthafuckas, while you'll still be here pulling down your bullshit salary, and driving your bullshit ass Volvo."

"Get out of my class!" he shouted again.

"I don't need this bullshit ass class!" I shouted. "I ain't learn shit in this bitch anyway! Old punk ass racist muthafucka!"

Mr. Stock lifted his phone and dialed the front office. "Can I get security."

I flipped over my desk. "I'm outta this bitch!"

I wasn't alone. The entire class rose, flipped over their desks, and followed me out the door.

"That's right, get out!" Mr. Stock shouted. "All of you! Trying to teach you proper English is a waste of time anyway! Get

out!  Go to the Food Stamp Office, to the Welfare Office, to the
County Jail.  You may as well get your lives started today!"

"Let's go set this muthafucka's Volvo on fire," Dice told Flip
and Wiz.  The three of them nodded and headed toward the school
exit.

"What's going on?"  Mr. Davis said, racing down the hall
with his walkie-talkie in hand.  He and the other male teachers were
all racing to Mr. Stock's classroom because of his call for security.

"We just tired of that prejudice ass cracker," I said, shaking
my head.

"What happened?"  Mr. Davis asked.

"We were looking at an old class picture from elementary
school, and that fool gonna say its a group picture from prison."

Mr. Davis shook his head.  "Baptiste, you are always going
to run into idiots like Stock.  Your whole life, you are going to run
into people who don't like you, simply because of the color of your
skin.  *They* have a problem, not you.  And the trick is, to not *make it*
your problem.  Let them carry all of that baggage around.  It's hard
to hate.  It's hard to carry all of that anger around inside.  It's even
harder to live with yourself knowing that you're wrong.  It eats
people up inside."

"How do you fight that?"  I asked, nodding my head in the
direction of Stock's classroom.  "How do you work with someone

you know is like that?"

"I don't," Mr. Davis said. "I don't no where near that asshole, and he knows better than to come anywhere near me."

"And if he did?" I asked with a smile. "If he came to you with all of that racist ass crap he's always spouting. You would lay him out. Keep it real. You wouldn't pray for that fool, you would put hands on him."

Mr. Davis smiled. He knew that I was trying to formulate a gotcha moment, and point out some hypocrisy on his part.

"I would tell his as to get the fuck out of my face," Mr. Davis admitted. "But even before that, I wouldn't even be around that fool."

"I can't always run away from it," I told him.

"You don't have to run away from the individual, you just have to steer clear of the trouble," Mr. Davis explained. "People are going to try to push your buttons. They are going to try to get a rise out of you. They want you to react, they want you to behave violently, to act irrationally, that way they can say, 'Look, see, I told you how *they* act.' That's what they want, to prove themselves right, to justify *their* prejudices."

Mr. Davis wrapped his massive, muscular arm around my neck and started down the hallway. "Let me tell you something, boy. These folks are prejudice, because of their fear. They don't

want to compete with us or anyone else. The more of us that
succeed, the greater the competition will be for them and for their
children over resources and power. It's chess, son, not checkers.
It's long term. You stay focused, and you keep your eyes on the
prize. Stock, and the people in this school just like him, know what
kind of future you have. And they would love nothing more than to
ruin it. It would bring them incalculable amounts of joy. The best
way to get back at people like him, is to succeed. And then you
come back to this school, to this community, and you encourage and
help other young men succeed. You roll up here in one of those
fancy cars, with a college degree, and a great career, and that son of
a bitch will die inside. You stay focused, you hear me, son?"

I nodded. "Yes, sir."

"All right, then." Mr. Davis released me, and started to walk
away.

"Mr. Davis!" I shouted.

""What *now*, big head?" he asked, turning back toward me.

I walked up to him, wrapped my arms around him and
embraced him. He was surprised at first, and then I felt him
wrapped his arms around me and embrace me in return.

"I just wanted to say thank you," I told him, after our
embrace.

"Thank me by..."

"No!" I said cutting him off. "I don't want to hear that shit. Thank me by doing well, thank me by succeeding, thank me by blah, blah, blah. *No*, I'm thanking you, man. I wouldn't have made it without you. A lot of us here wouldn't have made it without you. I want you to know that. I want you to know that *we* know that. You're like a Dad to a lot of us."

I could see his eyes growing watery. But he wasn't going to allow a tear to drop in front of me.

"Baptiste, get your big ass head out of here and get to your next class," he said gruffly, before turning and walking away. I watched as his hand made his way to his eyes as he stormed down the hall. There are many kinds of heroes in this world, Mr. Davis was on of them. In fact, he was at the top of the hero heap. He saved young peoples lives, and he did it day in, day out, year after year, without any recognition or fanfare. He did it without getting paid to do it, he did it because he cared. He was a true believer, and because of that, he made many of us true believers. The best way to become a good Black man, is to see a good Black man and emulate his actions and beliefs. I wanted to make Mr. Davis proud of me.

# Chapter Thirty

I woke to the smell of pan fried sausage, cheese eggs, and homemade buttermilk biscuits   Grandma was up doing her thing in the kitchen again.  I climbed out of bed, walked into the bathroom where I drained the main vein, and then proceeded to wash my hands, and face.  I stared at myself in the mirror for a while, taking in a face that appeared to be exhausted.  I was eighteen, and I felt like I was eighty eight.  If the world had been this rough on me the first eighteen years of my life, I could only imagine what it held for me the next seventy or eighty years.  If I made it that long.

I pulled my toothbrush from its holder, applied some paste, and commenced to brushing my teeth.  It was going to be a long day at school.  Mr. Stock's entire class was now assigned to the library, where we would have a substitute.  Mr. Stock himself, had been reassigned to an alternative campus for the time being.  Once the news of the walkout that our class had staged went around campus, all of the other classes follow suit. We weren't going to take it anymore.

I wrapped up my morning grooming, and walked into the kitchen to get my grub on before I got dressed for school. Grandma was at the stove putting the cheese in the pot of grits that she had made.

"Something smells delicious, sexy lady!" I said, kissing Big Momma on the back of her neck.

"Boy!" She shouted, shoving me away. "That tickles. Go wash your hands and get ready to eat."

I held up my hands to show her that they were clean. "Already took care of that."

Big Momma pulled a plate out of the cabinet, and started shoveling food on it.

"This almost looks as good as Waffle House," I told her.

"Waffle House is right down the street," Big Momma said pointing. "You can go and catch their early bird special right now."

"I'm just playing!" I said, slapping Big Momma on her romp.

"St. Claire, don't play with me!" she said, giving me her signature stare.

I laughed, and seated myself at the table. Big Momma

placed a heaping plate of food in front of me.

"How are things going at school?" she asked.

"Same," I told her. "It's picked up a little bit. Was going slow after football season. It felt weird not being in spring ball, and watching the team practice without me was even crazier. Seeing someone else carry the rock wasn't right."

"How they looking?"

"They looking all right," I told her. "I mean, they don't look as good as they did with the big dog running the ball, but they look all right."

"St. Claire, stop!" Big Momma said. She sat down at the table with her plate. "Why are you eating all ready? Did you bless your food?"

"I already did!" I told her.

"We'll say grace together," she said, clasping my hand. "Family that prays together, stays together."

Big Momma closed her eyes. Silence engulfed the room.

"Waiting on you, St. Claire," Big Momma said after a while.

"Oh, I thought you was gonna say it," I told her. "Lord, thank You for this food we are about to receive. In Jesus name we pray, Amen!"

Big Momma looked at me and tilted her head. "You want to

give the Lord that old quickie prayer, after He done gave us abundant blessings? Lord, help my grand baby."

A knock came to the door.

Big Momma and I both nearly jumped in our seat. No one knocked on the door this early. Not since Augustine died. We could count on him showing up every morning for breakfast, and after that, it was just me and Big Momma.

"Lord, who could this be at *this* time of the morning!" Big Momma huffed, as she rose and headed for the door. She opened the door, and to her surprise, stood a person that neither of us had seen in over a year. "Caridad!"

Caridad Fortier was Augustine's mother. She was a gorgeous Caribbean woman whose deep, dark chocolate brown skin appeared as though it had been made by the finest chocolatiers in Switzerland. She had long natural hair, that she kept in fine braids that were intricately twisted to form a crown upon her head. Her tall, slim figure accentuated her regal nature, while her natural beauty provided the incentive for and untold number of "Your momma so fine," jokes while we were growing up. I rose from the table and walked into the living room when I heard Big Momma call out her name.

Caridad stood in our living room as beautiful and graceful as ever, with one exception, she appeared as though she had aged ten years in the past year. Her eyes now showed a wrinkle or two where previously there were none, no doubt burrowed into her face by the tears that had constantly streamed from her eyes after a year of dealing with the loss of her son. Her always gorgeous and well kept black hair, was now interspersed every so ofter with a few strands of silver.

"Momma!" I said, rushing to her with open arms. We embraced tightly. I called her that, because she had always treated me like her son, and because I had spent nearly as much time at her house with Augustine as I had at my own house with Big Momma. She had taken me in, and given me the advice that I knew that my mother would have given. She was my mother's age, younger than Big Momma, and so she understood the ways of the modern world in ways that Big Momma didn't. We could relate in ways that Big Momma and I couldn't. She was in her forties, whereas Big Momma was in her sixties. She was rap and hip hop, whereas Big Momma was jazz and gospel.

"It's so good to see you baby!" she said excitedly.

Big Momma and Caridad hugged as well.

"C'mon in here!" Big Momma told her. "Girl, c'mon in here and get some breakfast."

"Well, you know I can't resist your cooking, Madear!" Caridad said with a smile.

The three of us walked back into the kitchen. It was then that I noticed that Caridad was carrying a large bag. We sat down at the kitchen table, while Big Momma fixed her a plate of breakfast.

"How have things been C.B.?" Caridad asked.

"Just trying to wrap things up," I told her.

"Where are you going?" she asked.

"TCU," I told her. I felt awkward talking about my future to her, when I knew that Augustine had been deprived of his, and because Augustine and I had shared the same dream.

"So, it's TCU!" she said excitedly. She rose and hugged me. "Congratulations, baby! I'm so proud of you!"

"Thank you," I said, swallowing hard.

Big Momma placed her plate on the table. "I told him that we were all so proud of him. He worked hard for it, and the Lord did the rest."

"Big Momma," I said, trying to stop her. I was sure that Caridad didn't want to hear what the Lord had done. It had been that *same* Lord that had taken away her son. She sensed something. Call it motherly intuition, but she knew how I was feeling.

Caridad exhaled forcefully, tilted her head to one side and stared into my eyes. "St. Claire, I don't have any problems with the Lord. I'm at peace, baby. And I hoped that you would be at peace too. What happened to Augustine was an *accident*. It wasn't the

Lord's fault, or the coaches fault, or the other player's fault, or anyone else's fault. It was an *accident*. And at the end of the day, it was simply his time, baby. The Lord blessed me with seventeen wonderful years with Augustine. Seventeen years that I will always cherish and thank Him dearly for. I would have rather had him for seventeen years, than for none."

I shook my head and swallowed hard. I didn't understand how she could take it all in stride like that. An accident? His death needed to be chalked up to being more than just an accident. If his death didn't mean anything, then his life didn't mean anything. And I refused to believe that. Life and Death *meant* something. *It had to mean something.* If it didn't then what the fuck were we here for? We were all just wasting our time. If none of it meant anything, then why the hell was I bothering? Why were any of us bothering. Why suffer?

Caridad placed her hand on top of mine and leaned in. "C.B., I'm sorry. I know how much Augustine loved you, and how much you loved Augustine. You two were brothers. I'm sorry that I couldn't be here for you this last year. I was lost. I was a shell of a person, just trying to find my way through life. I was getting up, I was eating, I was working, I was going through all the motions, but it was all just muscle memory. I was doing things out of habit. I would still going into his room everyday and look for dirty clothes.

I would still fix his plate, I would still get up in the morning, walk into his room to wake him up for school, I would go into his room at night to check on him and make sure that he was safe asleep. I did this for months! And one day it finally hit me. It finally hit me that my baby was gone. I was sitting on the edge of his bed, and I was clutching his shirt, sniffing it, trying to catch a scent of my baby, but it was gone. My baby's scent had faded away."

Caridad rose from the table, and started pacing around our tiny kitchen and breakfast area, nervously fidgeting with her hands. "I used to lay in his bed, so that I could *smell* his scent. And slowly, that faded as well. I realized that it was my baby telling me that it was time. It was time to wake up, time to keep moving, time to start living again. I felt as though my heart had been pulled from my chest. When they rushed my baby to that hospital, and they worked and worked and worked on him, and they gave us hope, and then they took it away, and then gave us hope, and then they took it away. And then finally, the surgeon walked out of that operating room, the look on his face!"

Caridad placed her hand in claw like form in front of her face. "His face! I could see it on his face, that my baby was gone!"

She broke down into tears. Big Momma wrapped her arms around her and held her. The two of them rocked gently from side of side, embracing tightly, until Caridad was able to compose herself once again.

"I'm sorry," she said to me softly.

"No," I said, shaking my head. "That's okay. I understand."

She nodded, letting out a half smile. "I know you do. If anybody in this world knows what I was going through, it was you." She caressed the side of my face. "He loved you so much."

"He was my brother," I said nodding.

Caridad turned and reach for the large bag that she had brought. She placed the bag on the table, and reached inside, pulling out Augustine's old necklace. It was a crucifix that he had worn since we were kids, and it never left his neck. He said that it had been a gift to him from his grandfather, who promised him that it would always protect and watch over him. I wondered if he had been wearing it during the football game, would things have gone differently that night. Caridad handed me the necklace.

"I wore this for a long time after it was returned to me by the school after they cleaned out his locker," she said softly. "I wore it, caressed it, prayed with it. And then I came to realize that it was not mine, it was yours."

I recoiled slightly, not understanding what she meant. We all knew that it was Augustine's necklace.

"This necklace belonged to Augustine, and there is no one

on this earth that he would rather have it, than you. Not me, not Victoria, not his sister, *you.* It is not mine to keep, nor mine to give, and so I know who my son would have wanted to have this necklace."

I lifted the necklace, examined it, and closed my eyes for a brief moment. I could picture it around his neck. I could see him in the locker room talking trash before a football game, with the crucifix dangling across his chest. I could see his smile. Not just the smile he would have before the game, but his smile now. I could feel him, I could feel his presence. I knew that he would want me to have it.

"I'll wear it proudly," I told her. "I'll always keep it with me." I placed the necklace over my head and around my neck. "Thank you."

Caridad smiled and nodded. "It fits you. It was time for me to give it up."

She reached down into the bag and pulled out several pictures of me and Augustine, some dating back to our days playing Pop Warner football in New Orleans.

"We were six on this picture!" I said smiling and tapping one of the pictures.

"I know that he would want you to have these as well," Caridad said.

"Are you sure?" I asked, lifting an eyebrow.

"I have plenty of pictures of Augustine," she said, reassuring me. "*And* of you two together." Caridad closed her eyes, nodded, and let out a half smile. "It's time. It's time."

I knew what she meant. I took the pictures from her hand.

"I have slept in Augustine's room, I have cried on his pillows, I have sniffed every remaining scent of him from his clothes, but I haven't gone through his belongings. I know that it's time, and I know that I'm ready, but..."

Big Momma wrapped her arms around Caridad's shoulders. "Take your time, baby."

Caridad nodded, and peered up at me. "I want you to do it. If you can, that is. I want you to come over, and I want you to go up to his room, and I want you to take whatever you want. And I mean *whatever* you want. If you want it all, then take it all. It's yours. And I want you to search his room real good for me, and whatever you think that I shouldn't find as a mother, or what you think I don't want to see, you take that as well!"

We all laughed.

"What ever is left, I'll box up and stick in the attic for right now," she continued. "But I need to change his room a little. I can't keep walking past it, staring into it, and seeing it like it is, seeing it just like he left it. I can't do it. When I see it, my mind keeps on playing with me, making me think that my baby is going to walk through that door any minute and jump onto his bed. And I can't do it anymore. I need to change it, if even just a little bit."

"I understand," I said nodding.

Again she nodded. This time, it was a less certain nod. It seemed to be the type of nod that one does to pump themselves up, to convince themselves that they can actually do something. "I'm ready."

Caridad peered up at me after a few moments of nodding to herself. "Are you?"

"What?"

"Are you ready?"

"To go in his room?" I asked.

"Are you ready to move forward?"

I peered over at Big Momma, knowing that she knew that answer. I wanted to say *yes*, but I didn't want Big Momma's *'you know you lying'* glare to melt me into my seat and have me slinking down and feeling two feet tall.

"I *think* I'm ready," I said, thinking that was close enough to not earn myself a stare from Big Momma.

"If you don't think you're ready, don't do it," Caridad told me.

"No, I'm good," I answered.

"We will always carry Augustine inside of us," Caridad said, tapping my chest with her finger. "We're not putting him away, or trying to forget about him, or leaving him behind. He'll always be a part of us. We are just moving forward, and we are going to carrying his memory with us."

I nodded. "I understand."

"Augustine would want nothing more, than for you to keep going, to follow y'all's plan, and to do good," she said. "He would want and expect, nothing but the best from you. The best effort, the best future, the best life. You live a life that is going to make Augustine happy, and proud of you, do you hear me?"

"Yes, ma'am," I said nodding.

Caridad stood, and opened her arms. I rose, walked around the tiny breakfast table and embraced her. She kissed my forehead.

"I'm proud of you for graduating, and for getting into TCU," she told me. "You keep it up now, you hear?"

"Yes, ma'am."

"And if you need anything, I mean *anything*, you don't hesitate to call me, understand?"

"Yes, ma'am."

"You're still my baby, St. Claire. You and Augustine will *always* be my two boys. And I will always love you, and be proud of you. You just continue to make me and Madear proud."

"I will," I said nodding. "I promise you, I will."

And I meant it. I loved Caridad like a mother. She had been like a mother to me while my mother was alive, and even more so after I lost my mother. I would make her proud. I would make Augustine proud. I was determined to make my mother proud, and Big Momma proud, and Adanna proud, and most of all, I wanted to be proud of myself. I was going to carrying Augustine's legacy, and I was going to forge one for myself. *I knew what I had to do.*

# **Chapter Thirty One**

I went to meet Adanna at the hill overlooking the tracks. Our time in Houston was winding down, and our days in high school were numbered. We were close to getting out, close to getting away, close to starting our new life away from this place. If there were any days in my life that could be called happy, these were the days.

I spread our old tattered blanket out on top of the hill, and plopped down on my behind. Usually she would get here about the same time, if not first. I guess that today would be my turn to wait. And I didn't mind waiting. She was worth waiting for.

A Union Pacific engine blared it's massive set of horns, sending an ear splitting blasts across the rail yard and into the surrounding hills. It was leaving. And it wanted everyone around to know that it was leaving. The locomotive slowly began to pull forward, tugging it's massive cargo along with it. I wondered where it was going, and the places that it would see. I thought of the places that it *had* gone. I knew that the world was big, and I wanted to see some of it for myself. One day, I thought. One day.

Adanna and I often thought about the places we would go if we had the chance. I wanted to see Jamaica, she wanted to see Trinidad and Tobago. I wanted to see Africa. I wanted to see the Door Of No Return. She wanted to see Paris, and the Eiffel Tower. We both wanted to visit London. Her parents lived there. I wanted to see the castles, the towers, the palaces, the history. We both had The Pyramids on our list. I added the Great Wall, she wanted to visit Bali. I said Tahiti, she said Japan. I wanted to see Greece, and all of the ancient temples and ruins. She agreed, but only if we also did the Italian peninsula. Rome, Venice, Tuscany, Vatican City. We wanted to take it all in.

And then there was America. The Grand Canyon, Niagra Falls, The Great Lakes, the Hover Dam, Mount Rushmore, and all of the other beautiful places spread throughout the country. And more than the big tourist attractions, there existed the little things. I wanted to make snowmen in Minnesota. I wanted to watch the leaves change in Vermont. I wanted to see whales off the coast of Washington and Oregon. Strawberry festivals in Texas, Pumpkin festivals in Nebraska, paddle boat rides down the Mississippi. I wanted to live life, and I wanted to live it with her. And I would. *We would.*

I pulled out my old band-less wristwatch and checked the time. Adanna was late. *Big late.* She had never been *this* late. This wasn't like her at all.

I rose, gathered the blanket, and headed off in the direction of her house. I was thinking that I would run into her along the way. Going to her house, was a risk that I really wasn't up for taking. Another ass whipping at the hands of her brothers was not something I was looking forward to.

I made my way to Adanna's house. Sure enough, her brother's 7 Series BMW was in the driveway, while her other brother's Lexus LS was parked behind it. The third brother's Range Rover was gone. I knew for sure that I would potentially have to deal with two muscle bound assholes if I were caught. There was a third care parked on the street. It was a brand new Cadillac Escalade.

"Good, maybe they have company," I said to myself. "Here goes nothing."

I exhaled forcibly, and made my way into the yard, and around to Adanna's bedroom window on the side of the house. I peered through the blinds, and instantly, my heart started beating like I was getting rammed from the inside by a pro football player. Adanna was lying on her bedroom floor, bound and gagged, with her hands tied behind her back. Instantly, I bit down on my knuckles. Seeing her like this, made me want to hurt somebody.

I placed my hands flat against her bedroom window, and pushed up. To my amazement, the window slid open. I opened the window all the way, grabbed the string that controlled her mini-blinds, and pulled it down, causing the blind to slide up. I was going to get her out of there, and I was going to kill her brothers.

I quietly climbed inside of Adanna's bedroom, dropped down to my knees, and pulled the duct tape from around her mouth. I kissed her.

"Quiet!" She said, in a hushed voice.

"What the hell is going on?" I asked, untying her hands.

She quickly tossed her bonds to the side, and immediately freed her legs. We rose, and I grabbed her hand and started for the window.

"You can stay with me," I told her.

"No," she said, pulling away. *"They have my brothers!"*

"Who?" I asked, truly confused. "What are you talking about?"

*"Men, with guns,"* she said. "They came, and they are holding us hostage. They took my brother Wilson to the bank to

withdraw the money he owes them. Two of them are in the salon watching Nelson and Edward. We have to *do* something!"

"We can get out of here and call the cops!" I whispered, clasping her hand and pulling her toward the window.

Again, she pulled her hand away.

"*I'm not leaving my brothers!*" she whispered emphatically.

I was frustrated, as well as scared out of my wits. Leaving her was not an option, and it was understandable that she would not leave her brothers while they were in danger. Leaving and calling the cops would be the best solution in my mind.

"If I leave, and they discover that I've escaped, my brothers are dead," Adanna explained. "They will kill them and hurry up and escape. And they will call their other associate who is with Wilson, and have him do the same. And even if we can get the police to come, what will they do? Surround the house? How long will that take? First police car they see, these thugs will kill my brothers and escape through the back door, and Wilson is dead. *We must do something!*"

She was right. Putting my life on the line for these assholes was not something I was looking forward to doing. But in a way, I wasn't doing it for them, I was doing it for Adanna, and that brought me some comfort. I had to think quickly. She walked to her closet, opened the door, reached inside and pulled out two cricket bats.

She handed me one.

"You're kidding right?" I asked.

"It's all that I have," she replied. The look on her face told me that she was serious.

I shrugged. It was what we had to work with, and playing with the shitty cards I had been dealt, was my life story.

"You stay in here!" I told her.

I pulled open the door slowly and quietly. I had a clear view down the hallway, all the way into the kitchen. They were in the living room, or the *'salon'* as she referred to it. I crept down the hall, and once I arrived at the kitchen, I peered around the wall into the living room. I could see her brothers sitting on the couch, and I could see two men standing in front of them. The gunmen had their backs toward me, and their hands were empty, which means they had tucked their weapons away. I felt a presence behind me, and turned. It was Adanna's hard headed ass.

I wanted to tell her to go back, but I couldn't, as the gunmen would hear me. She knew this as well. I wanted to kill her myself for putting herself in danger. I couldn't do what I had to do, worrying about her. My mind was telling me to go back into the bedroom, and try to convince her to go and call the police. She took that option away.

Adanna raced into the living room, and swung her cricket

bat as hard as she could, whacking one of the assailants across the back of his head. I followed suit. I raced into the room, and cracked the other guy across the back of his head, dropping him to the floor. The strength in my swing was a lot greater than the strength in hers. The guy she cracked across the head, reeled backwards for a few moments, before regaining his composure and reached for his weapon. I through my cricket bat at him, striking him in his chest, and then raced toward him. I dove over a chaise and tackled him onto the ground.

Adanna raced to her brothers and began to untie Nelson. On the ground, I grabbed this assholes hands, and wrestled with him for control of his gun. He was strong. A lot stronger than I had anticipated. I was a football player, an athlete, but I was still in high school. This was a man I was tangling with, and he was bigger and stronger physically. He had muscles. Big ass prison muscles. And the longer we struggled, the more his consciousness began to return, and the more I came to realize that I was in a struggle for my life.

Adanna untied Nelson's arms. The guy I had cracked with my cricket bat began to stir and moan. Adanna lifted her cricket bat from the ground, and struck him across his head again. After her first whack, he covered his head. Nelson, removed the tape from over his lips, and then began to untie his legs.

Adanna raced to her brother Edward, and began to untie him. The guy she had just struck began to stir even more. He rubbed his head and sat up. The man that I was struggling with, began to slowly get the advantage. I didn't know how much longer I had, but I knew that eventually he would be able to maneuver the weapon to a place that would not be good for me.

Adanna untied Edward's hands, and began to untie his legs. He helped. Nelson finally removed the restraints from his legs. He freed himself just in time. The assailant on the ground pulled out his weapon, and although his head was still throbbing and his was a little groggy, he was able to get an aim. He pointed his weapon toward me and fired.

Nelson kicked the gun out of his hand, and lifted the cricket bat, and split the guys head open. He raced toward a piano bench, lifted the seat, pulled out a gun, and turned toward me. The guy I had been tangling with, tossed me off of him, and rose. He pointed his weapon at me, and Nelson fired, putting two holes into his chest. Nelson fired a third time, sending a bullet into the asshole's forehead, putting him down for good. Adanna raced toward me.

"Are you okay?" she asked, dropping to her knees next to me.

"Yeah," I said, rising.

Edward finished untying his leg, pulled the tape from his

mouth and rose from the sofa.

"Cockroach!"

I peered over toward him. He nodded at me.

"Thank you," he said softly.

Nelson walked up to me, wrapped his massive arm around my head, and then rubbed my head with his other hand.

"Maybe we were wrong about you, Cockroach," Nelson told me. "You *can* take care of my sister?"

"He wouldn't leave me," Adanna told them.

Nelson nodded. "You two have to go."

"Go where?" Adanna asked.

"Leave tonight," Nelson told her. "Go. Go to Dallas."

"And don't come back!" Edward told her. He shifted his eyes to me. "You take care of her, Haiti. Do you hear me? You take good care of her."

Adanna wrapped her arms around me. "He always has."

Nelson pulled some keys off of a wall mounted key holder, and tossed them to her. "Take the car, and get out of here."

"It 's going to be bad, really bad," Edward told us. "Don't come back for any reason."

"What about Wilson?" Adanna asked.

"We are going to go and get him," Nelson told her. He began pulling weapons out of cabinets and laying them on the table.

"He's going to be fine."

"Are you sure?" Adanna asked. Tears began to fall.

Edward rested his hands on her shoulders and peered into her eyes. "I promise you. We will rescue him, and he will be fine. You have my word. Now go."

"I have to get my things," Adanna told them.

Nelson produced a bag of money. He handed it to Adanna. "Take this. Buy whatever you need. We will send the rest of your belongings to Dallas. But right now, you must go, Adanna!"

Edward hugged his sister, and then he embraced me.

"I love you," Nelson said, as he hugged his sister.

"I love you too!" she replied.

"I'm sorry for beating you up, Cockroach," Nelson said, embracing me. "Take care of her. Love my sister. Start your life together. Go!"

Adanna and I glanced at one another, and then headed for the front door. We hurried to her brother's big, white, 7 series BMW and climbed inside. Adanna behind the driver's wheel, and I on the passenger side. She started up the big sedan, pulled out of the driveway, and headed down the road.

I wanted to go and say good-bye to Big Momma, to lay my eyes on her one more time, but didn't know if that would be safe to do. It was about to go down in a major way, and I'm sure the authorities would probably be looking for her brother's car if things went bad. The further away from Houston we were, the better.

And then, my breathing changed.

"Adanna, I want to tell you something."

"What?" she asked, peering at me nervously.

"I don't want you to get scared, and I don't want you to panic."

"What?" she asked, peering in the rear view mirror, thinking that we were being followed.

I lifted up the shirt I was wearing over my compression shirt, and showed her my wound. She screamed.

"You've been shot!"

"I *do* want to see Big Momma one more time," I told her.

My adrenaline was slowing down, and the pain was growing by the second. Fatigue from blood loss was also creeping in.

"We've got to get you to a hospital!" Adanna screamed.

"I want to see... Momma..."

I don't know what happened. I just remember feeling light headed, and then relaxed. I felt a relaxation and a peace that I had never felt before. I felt as if I were free. I felt as if all of my problems, all of my struggles, every burden that I had even borne, had been lifted.

"St. Claire! St. Claire! St. Claire!" Adanna screamed.

Her voice was that last thing I heard, before I closed my eyes..

# Chapter Thirty Two

"And with the third pick, in the two thousand and nineteen draft, the Chicago Bears selects... TCU's St. Claire Baptiste!"

I rose to wild applause, hugged Big Momma, I hugged my father, and then I rushed onto the stage, where I was given a baseball cap with the Chicago Bears moniker on it. I placed the cap on my head, smiled for the cameras, and then walked back into the audience and grabbed my girl. I thought that she had walked to the podium with me.

I couldn't stand at the podium and bask in one of the greatest moments of my life, without having by my side, the woman who made it possible. Adanna had been by my side from day one, tutoring me, encouraging me, helping to make me a better man, a better son, and better person. She was my life, my love; she was the air that I breathed. And without her, there would be no me. I stood on that stage, because she helped to make it happen, so there was no way that I was going to stand up there without her.

"No, you go!" she said, bashfully. "It's your moment in the sun. Go, you deserve it."

She tried to clap, but I clasped her hand and pulled her along. This was *our* moment. I walked back to the stage, wrapped my arms around her, and kissed her in front of all the cameras. I wanted the nation to see us, I wanted the world to see us. This was my woman, and there was no air between us. We had *both* been drafted by the Chicago Bears.

My Father stood clapping. I could see tears streaming down his cheeks. They were tears of pride, and also tears of regret. I knew that he wanted my mother to be there. This was as much *their* moment, as it was mine. It was my parents who put the love of sports in me. And despite all that had happened, even during his time on the streets, my father had never missed a single one of my games.

The conversation that I had with my father the night of the football game had been the beginning of our new relationship. It sparked something inside of him, a flame that we both thought had been extinguished. But it had been there. It took me reminding him of my grief as well, to bring it back. No parent, no matter what they are going through, wants to see their child hurting. And once he realized how bad I was hurting too, he slowly began to get himself together.

My father had checked himself into St. Dominick's Rehabilitation Center not long after our conversation. It wasn't that he needed rehabilitation from drugs, but he needed it from life. It provided him the opportunity to rest his mind, to get off the streets, to rest his body. He had time to think, to process, to grieve. He would never truly finish grieving, as he had lost his soul mate, but he could process it, and learn to push through it. I needed him, and he came to me. He came *with* me.

My father stayed by my side in the hospital during my recovery. And when I left for college after my hospital stay, he went with me. He got a job coaching middle school football, and then high school football as an assistant. It provided him with enough money to live, to eat, to be near me. And together, we made it through my college years. And together, we healed and bonded over those four years. We became a family again.

I know you want to know what came next right?

Well, first, I flew back to Houston, and I went house shopping. I bought Big Momma a big ass crib in Riverstone on a lake in Sugarland. Of course she objected, saying she was happy

with what the Lord gave her, but I made her take it. If the Lord
didn't want her to have it, then I wouldn't have made it, I told her. I
also got Big Momma a Jag. Seeing her face when she walked out of
the house and saw it sitting in the driveway was something I'll never
forget. It felt good. Better than good. A son's greatest joy, is
putting a smile on his Momma's face.

Down the street from Big Momma's house, I bought another
house. Not for me, but for Augustine's mom. She didn't believe it,
and didn't want to accept it, but in the end she did. The house
wasn't from me, it was from Augustine. He was my brother, and if
one of us made it, then *both* of us made it. He would have done no
less from me. I fulfilled my brother's promise to get his mother out
of the hood, and it felt good doing it. It felt right. I also wrote
Quick's mother a check big enough to get herself a house in Sienna
Plantation, a community just down the street from where Big
Momma's new house was. That felt good as well. It left me with
only one other promise to fill.


"Do you, Jean Claude Henri St. Claire Baptiste, take Adanna
Adeyemo Omene, to be your your lawfully wedded wife?" The
minister asked. "To have and to hold, from this day forward, for
better or for worse, for richer, for poorer, in sickness and in health,

to love and to cherish, until parted by death?"

I peered into Adanna's eyes, and in those eyes I saw my life. And for reasons unbeknownst to me, tears began to flow from my eyes. She was beautiful beyond words, beautiful beyond measure. I remember a song that I heard on the radio a long time ago. I don't even listen to that kind of music, but for some reason, the song stayed with me. It was a song by a group called Savage Garden. And the song described how I felt about her to a tee. I knew I loved her, before I even met her. I believed that I did dream her into life.

"I do" I answered, with my voice cracking.

"And do you, Adanna Adeyemo Omene, take Jean Claude Henri St. Claire Baptiste to be your lawfully wedded husband? To have and to hold, from this day forward, for better or for worse, for richer, for poorer, in sickness and in health, to love and to cherish, until parted by death?"

Adanna stared at me and smiled the smile of an angel.

"I do," she said softly.

She looked gorgeous in her elegant, white, wedding gown. It was a simple design, nothing special, as she wouldn't allow me to splurge on something she said was a waste of money, since it would only be worn once. Instead, Adanna chose a white, cotton, knee length Vera Wang dress, that ended just below her knees. A beautiful white orchid sat perched on the side of her large afro. The sun glistened off her flawless Nubian skin. She radiated a beauty and a spirit that was effervescent. Adanna chose for me a white Vera Wang button down, some white knee length shorts, and that was it. Our wedding guest wore white as well, and all of us went shoe less. She wanted the sand to be felt between our toes, and she wanted to walk to the water and toss her bouquet into the ocean and make a wish once the ceremony was done. Getting married on the beach, had always been her dream. And I wanted nothing more, than to give it to her.

We turned back toward the minister, who was also clothed in white. He smiled at us, and in his thick Nigerian accent, pronounced us man and wife.

I didn't wait for his command, I kissed my beautiful bride, and then lifted her into the air. All of our guest rose from their white beach chairs, threw rice, and began to applaud. I carried my wife to the ocean, sat her down next to waters, and watched as she tossed her flowers into the ocean. Again, she turned to me and we kissed. And then, she was surrounded by her bridesmaids.

I knew we had a first dance to conduct, as well as a reception to attend in the nearby beachfront clubhouse, but for the moment, I wanted to take some time to myself, and reflect on all that had happened, all that I had been through, on all that I had yet to face.

I peered out into the ocean, and watched as the waves came rolling in and crashing gently onto the beach. It was blue today, and the smell of salt and of sea life wafted heavily in the air. Adanna wanted a beachfront wedding, and the truth be told, I did too. I wanted it, because I thought that it would bring me closer to my mother, the one person in my life who I would give anything to have here that day. I wanted to have my wedding at the beach so that I could peer out over the ocean, and allow it to bear witness to my life, to my triumph. I wanted it to see, that it didn't beat me. The monster that it sent to my home, the monster that it sent to take my mother away and nearly destroyed my father's mind, didn't beat me. We survived. And we rebuilt. Like my city rebuilt after Katrina, so did we. Putting back together the shattered pieces of our lives took longer than expected, and was more difficult than I ever imagined, but we did.

My father walked up behind me, and placed his arm around my shoulder. "You okay, son?"

I wiped away the tear that was slowly making it's way down my cheek.

"I am now," I said, peering out at the ocean.

He understood. He understood completely what I was saying.

"Ocean's powerful, son," he said softly, peering out into the sea. "Mother nature, is nothing to play with. We ain't nothing, compared to that out there. Nothing, compared to the power of God."

My father patted me on my back, and then strolled away to join the rest of the wedding party, which was slowly making its way toward the reception area. He was right. He was *absolutely* right.

I spent my life running the football. Running, running, running as fast as I could. I always thought that I was running toward something, but now I realized that I had actually running away from something. I was running away from Katrina. I thought that I had been able to face my fears, to get over what she had done to my family, and to so many others. But the truth is, I was running from her, running from facing up to her, and in a way, running from God Himself. I wondered and questioned how could He have let this happen? How could He have done this to me? And in running from that question, and running from Katrina, I was running from the answer. Sometimes people make it out of the hood with a microphone, sometimes they make it out of the hood with a football or a basketball, and sometimes, they leave in a hearse. But then there are those times when people leave the hood, because God runs their asses away from there. They leave, because He has a mission for them. They leave, because it is their *destiny*. They may not see it, and they may not understand it, but they make it out, because

God has a plan.

I wondered why I made it out of New Orleans alive. I wondered why I didn't go in on that play instead of Augustine. I wondered why Quick took the bullet that was meant for me. I wondered how I made it out of Adanna's house alive that day. And then I wondered why I was drafted by the Chicago Bears of all teams. And it wasn't until I stopped running, and listened, *really listened*, that I really understood. My money, my mission, my ministry, is in Chi-raq. I was *drafted* by the Bears, but I was *being sent* there, by the Man Upstairs, and I knew what he wanted me to do.

I started my foundation in Chicago to help at risk teens. It was a center geared toward inner city conflict resolution, non-violence, and job training. I'm teaching young Black men how to program, and how to code, and giving them the skills to make it in tomorrow's job market. I'm also giving them a safe place to come and chill, and relax, and have fun. My center has an indoor basketball court, and indoor swimming pool, an arcade, a daycare, and a learning center. And it's run by my father.

I get all of the professional athletes from around the city to come by, and talk to the kids, and to mentor as well. We also have a guns out of the hood program that the mayor has rated an unbelievable success. I'm here in Chicago, making a difference. Not by playing football, not because I'm a professional athlete, but I'm making a difference just by my virtue of being here, and giving a damn. Black boys respond positively to Black men, who show that they give a damn. It was a lesson that I learned from Mr. Davis. I made it out of the hood, and I'm showing them that they can too. It takes a little bit of work, a willingness to listen and to learn, and most of all, a willingness to listen and believe, that God has a plan and a destiny for each and every one of us. He saved me. And now He is helping me to save many many others. God is Great, I want to bear witness. *GOD IS GREAT!*

Made in the USA
Columbia, SC
11 June 2017